The Ambleside Alibi

A Lake District Mystery

REBECCA TOPE

WITNESS
IMPULSE

An Imprint of HarperCollinsPublishers

First published in 2013 by Allison & Busby Limited in the UK.

Excerpt from *The Windermere Witness* copyright © 2012 by Rebecca Tope.

EPub Edition March 2015 ISBN: 9780062397263

Print Edition ISBN: 9780062397270

10 9 8 7 6 5 4 3 2 1

Another one for Paula,
the best of friends

Author's Note

THE TOWNS AND villages featured in this story are all real. However, the actual homes and shops, as well as the characters, are all products of my imagination.

Chapter One

THE FLOWERS FELL short of Simmy's usual standards by some distance. 'I can only afford the cheapest,' said the husky-voiced young woman who ordered them. 'It's the message that matters.'

The message said *Happy Birthday from a granddaughter you never knew you had.*

The recipient of the flowers lived in a little row of dwellings that was approached through the low-roofed 'ginnel' that led up to the steep Peggy Hill on the northern fringe of Ambleside. It was an unusual little passageway, white-painted and crooked, more a tunnel than an alley. Knowing there was unlikely to be anywhere to park, Simmy had left her van some distance away. When she arrived panting and self-conscious at the small but perfectly maintained cottage, she saw that she'd been right. There were cars everywhere, including a small red one close to the cottage in question and a big black Range Rover at an angle a few yards further along. She rang the bell and waited. The door was a long time opening and when it did, it came outwards towards Simmy, accompanied by an odd warbling chuckle that sounded scarcely human.

An elderly woman came into view, smiling apologetically. The door, Simmy realised, was a perennial cause of embarrassment. If a visitor stood too close, it would hit them when it opened.

She tightened her grip on the flowers, waiting for the woman to realise what she was there for. It was a moment she generally enjoyed – the surprised delight on the faces, the automatic questing for scent. But this time there was a long moment of sheer bewilderment. 'Flowers? Surely not for me?'

'Mrs Joseph?' Simmy read confidently from the label. 'I believe that's you?'

'Yes, that's right. But who are they from?'

'See for yourself. It's on the card.' The intriguing message ensured that Simmy hovered longer than usual, telling herself that the likely shock on reading it could result in the need for a steadying arm at the very least.

There was a false start, when the woman read, 'Persimmon Petals? Is that you, dear? What a lovely name!'

'Yes, it's me. But look at the other side.'

Simmy need not have worried: the unwitting grandmother turned out to be made of sterner stuff than she'd feared. 'Oh!' she said on an intake of breath that contained less excitement than a sort of fury. Her eyes glittered and she clutched the flowers to her chest as if violently hugging the granddaughter herself. 'I always knew this might happen,' she explained. 'I told Davy it would one day. And on my birthday, too!'

'Davy?'

'My daughter. Davida. This must be her baby; the one she gave up for adoption all those years ago.'

Simmy tried to calculate the chronology. Mrs Joseph looked about eighty. Her daughter was therefore likely to be over fifty and the rejected baby at least in her twenties and probably more. Or not. It was impossible to guess, when a woman could become a mother at any point from fourteen to forty-eight. 'But ...' she began. 'It says she's a granddaughter you never knew you had. And you *do* know about the adoption. Do you have a son? Isn't it more likely that this is a child of his?'

The old woman eyed her as if only then aware of her as an independent being capable of unwelcome thoughts. 'No,' she said. 'No son. Just the two daughters, Davy and Nicola. They're taking me for lunch today, so I mustn't dilly-dally. Now, thank you for bringing the flowers. I don't expect I owe you anything, do I?'

It was a sharp dismissal from a woman who didn't look capable of sharpness. 'No, nothing to pay,' Simmy said, before heading down the hill again. She had been forced to leave her van some distance away, since the car park she preferred was out of commission on a Wednesday. There had been a plan to wish Mrs Joseph a happy birthday, but Simmy quickly lost the urge to do so. Had she been intrusive, she wondered? Had she asked too many questions? She very much feared that she had.

It was a quiet day and she was in no hurry to get back to her shop in Windermere. The van was good for a while yet, with traffic wardens hardly bothering to check when the allotted hour had expired at this time of year. There would be little activity back at the shop. In the winter months, custom dropped off to a trickle. Melanie would be there until lunchtime, and could easily manage any passing trade. A cup of strong coffee would warm Simmy, both physically and emotionally, after the abruptness of her customer, and give her time to pause and reflect.

There were few establishments to choose from, but one offered itself irresistibly. The Giggling Goose café was in a former mill, with the great wheel still standing on the edge of the beck. It had a fine reputation locally and Simmy had intended to try it for some months. It occupied a position on a sort of ledge above the beck, with an open air area that was closed off in winter. The approach to it was through a small arcade, past one or two other businesses designed to appeal to tourists. Simmy found her way quite easily, and once inside, the café was warm and full of enticing smells. A cheerful woman was waiting for orders. 'Find a seat and I'll bring it to you,' she told Simmy.

'It's a shame we can't sit outside,' she said.

'It's much too chilly for that.'

'I suppose it is,' she agreed regretfully, looking out onto the attractive setting. 'But it does look lovely out there.'

'Sit by the window. It's almost as good.'

She followed the advice, and stared ruminatively at the rushing water. Patchy cloud covered the sky, leaving encouraging stretches of blue here and there.

There was another person at the next table, doing the same thing. She half recognised him, but spent only a few seconds trying to remember where she'd seen him before. Then she went back to idle musings about nothing very much. The beck was called Stock Ghyll, she recalled, and it flowed over the famous Stock Force, a short distance out of town. It cried out for painters, poets, photographers to capture its elemental qualities, the hypnotic pace of its flow. The buildings scattered around it had all adapted to it in different ways – employing the power of the water, positioning their windows for the best possible views of it, and erecting bridges and walls to keep it in place. Making the most of these quiet moments, Simmy congratulated herself on coming here to live, where such beauty was so readily available.

It was nearly a year since she had moved to the Lake District, following her parents after her marriage broke down. The florist business had become a passion, much to her own surprise. She had never anticipated the scope it offered, the sidelines and specialities that presented themselves. She had impulsively bought a cottage in Troutbeck as a mark of her commitment to the area, and was doing her best to put down firm roots. The time had passed in a whirl of paperwork, flowers, business worries and learning from mistakes. She promised herself to get a better balance in the year to come, with a spring and summer of extensive explorations of the surrounding fells and forests, walking them all in turn and becoming an expert on every path and tucked-away settlement. 'That's all very well,' said Melanie, 'but you need to get to know more people first.'

Her house had been chosen quickly, in a scramble to beat off competing buyers. The allure of the landscape, with a great fell taking up the whole of the view from her front windows, dwarfed every other consideration. Only later did she pause to absorb the implications of the steep, narrow lanes in a bad winter. Reassurances abounded: everyone pulled together, they told her. The farmers, many of them living right there in Troutbeck, would forge a trail through the snow, or go for provisions and distribute them to anyone too timid to risk a slippery ice track. Besides, in a land where walking remained a means of transport as valid as any other, there was always going to be a way out to the civilised benefits of Ambleside and Windermere. Simmy had never seen so many walkers. They mainly operated in pairs, and they swarmed in all directions, with their backpacks and sticks and stout leather boots. They were like a distinct species of human, and she found them cheerful and appealing and rather enviable.

The local people were mainly friendly, but she had yet to establish any real intimacies. There was Julie, a hairdresser much her own age, who had caught her up in the first weeks and made a concerted effort to draw her into the Windermere social life. There were regular customers who asked after her health and her parents and her plans for the weekends. But by Melanie's standards, there really weren't any people in her life. Melanie believed in couplehood and romance and living life to the full. In her eyes, Simmy was a persistent failure.

The man sharing the waterside view with her was about her own age – a little short of forty, she judged. He was probably a fellow shopkeeper, glimpsed in one of the sporadic meetings called by the Chamber of Commerce. He had mid-brown hair and heavy-framed spectacles. He looked as if he had a great deal on his mind. When Simmy's coffee was delivered, along with a wedge of home-made ginger cake, he glanced up as if only then aware of another person. 'Oh!' he said. 'It's the Persimmon Petals lady, isn't it? You probably don't remember me.'

'I know your face,' she prevaricated. 'Aren't you from one of the Windermere shops as well?'

'Actually, no. I came to you for the flowers for my mother's funeral, a month ago now. You were very kind.'

'Oh, yes. I should have known. Mr ... don't tell me ... Mr Kitchener! It was a burial in that lovely little churchyard the other side of the lake. I drove up there the next day, and saw all the flowers on the grave.'

'You did a great job,' he assured her. 'And I'm amazed you remember my name.'

She smiled self-deprecatingly. The name had stuck no more firmly than many others. The necessity of avoiding any mistakes when it came to funerals made sure the customers were all firmly logged in her mind.

The man went on, 'It's been very hard, you know – coming to terms with it all. I can't seem to convince myself that she really has gone for good. I used to tell her everything, you see. She was such a good listener, always keeping up with my work and all the family's doings. And it was all so terribly sudden ...' He trailed away, his gaze once again on the waters of Stock Ghyll.

'I can imagine,' said Simmy, not entirely honestly. The prospect of losing her own mother had not yet occurred to her as imminent, or even credible. Angie Straw was clearly set fair for at least another twenty years.

'Well, I mustn't bother you. You've probably come for a bit of peace.' He looked at his watch. 'I'll stay a while longer, but I won't interrupt your thoughts.'

'That's all right,' she laughed. 'My thoughts can very easily bear interruption.'

But he stuck to his word and turned away from her, saying nothing more. He sighed heavily at one point, but was clearly in no mood for further conversation. It wasn't Simmy's thoughts he had any concern for, she realised, but his own. He probably resented her coming to sit near to him in the first place. The more she tried to ignore him, the more acutely she became aware of his presence. She drank her coffee quickly, and demolished the cake in three bites. Then she noticed a small scratch on her left thumb, caused by a staple she had used in a bouquet she'd made up that morning. The bouquet for the old lady in Ambleside, in fact. The staple that had attached the message card to the outer wrapping had not fully closed, and had snatched at her thumb when she gathered up the sheaf. She had not properly looked at it until now.

Her train of thought led quickly back to the message itself, from the unknown granddaughter. Again she went through the woman's reaction, and her insistence that it was a baby she had known about all along. And again she found it nigglingly unconvincing. The husky voice on the telephone had suggested otherwise, the significance of the approach so great as to render her almost speechless. Or was that Simmy's own unwarranted interpretation? She had personal reasons for overreacting to stories concerning lost babies, which were likely to cast doubt on her judgement.

Peals of girlish laughter diverted her attention. A group of three young women had arrived and were seating themselves at a table in the middle of the café, where she could not possibly ignore them. They all had long hair and inadequate clothing for December. Students, probably, she assumed, thinking they were slightly too old to be sixth-formers. Her acquaintance with people of this age group had become close in recent months, with Melanie who helped her in the shop, and Ben who had simply attached himself to her because he liked her. Since their involvement with a murder investigation, they had become firm friends.

The girls could easily be at the same college as Melanie. Term would be finishing in a few days' time, and the imminence of Christmas was a likely source of their exuberance. Parties, free time – all the usual excitement would explain the flushed faces and high voices. They made Simmy feel middle-aged and jaded, with more in common with the depressed man at the next table than with giggling youngsters.

She tried to ignore them, only to find herself face to face with another girl, very much the same age as the others, but at a table on her own. She must have been there when Simmy first came in, quietly occupying a shadowy corner. Simmy wondered about it, in an idle sort of way. She was dark-haired and had a habit of fingering her mouth that suggested a desire to smoke. She had no book or magazine to distract her, but simply sat there, apparently in deep thought – very much like Mr Kitchener, in fact. Was this a place where people came to think, then? Wasn't Simmy doing it herself? Was there some sort of magical aura that facilitated a relaxed introspection? If so, the group of three hadn't noticed it – their chatter filling the whole place, their laughter irritating. The solitary girl had barely glanced at Simmy, or at anybody else. Something internal was absorbing all her attention.

It was time to go. Business called, as always, even if it was a quiet time of year. Christmas had little impact on flower shops, other than sporadic sales of poinsettias and wreaths, neither of which were especially popular in this area of the country. Even so, there was always work to do, and Melanie would not be there that afternoon.

In an odd piece of synchronicity, the man at the next table stood up at the precise moment that she did. They both headed for the exit from the café, on a course for collision. Simmy stood back, letting him go first, noting without rancour that he showed no inclination to allow her to precede him. He walked with a long stride that highlighted the fact of a limp, or a stiffness to his right knee. The leg did not bend normally, forcing him to throw it forward from the hip as if about to kick something. And then he really did kick the chair on which the dark girl was sitting. A glancing blow knocked it enough for her to spin round to see what had happened. 'Sorry,' he muttered.

She looked at his face, eyebrows raised, and nodded at him. Simmy still hung back, the way between the tables too narrow to do anything else. She was not absorbed in any gripping thoughts, not distracted by haste or anxiety. She saw both faces – the man and the girl, as they looked at each other. There was no small start of recognition. No lurking emotions dating back to past encounters. The man carried on to the street door and left without looking back. The girl threw a look at him that caused a ripple of giggles from the threesome. It was a moment so ordinary that it was highly unlikely to leave any trace on the memory of anybody present.

Except for Simmy. She had recognised him, recalled his name, winced at his evident unhappiness and observed his limp with real concern. She had assessed his character as he kicked the chair and imagined his next movements. He would go home, she surmised, and deal with some more minor paperwork concerning the death of his mother, before grabbing a minimal lunch and opening a bottle of beer. It was all quite vivid in her mind.

Chapter Two

MELANIE LOOKED BORED, tinkering with the rack of ribbons that they sold to people wanting to create their own floral displays. 'Any customers?' Simmy asked, as she always did.

'One. Wanted to know if we sold snowdrops. I told her they didn't work as cut flowers and she should try a garden centre. And a bloke who makes vases. Thinks you should sell them for him.'

'Right,' Simmy nodded resignedly. 'Not a profitable morning, then.'

'Nope. How did you get on? You've been a long time.'

'It was a bit weird. I stopped for some coffee in that Giggling Goose place, above the river.'

'Weird? How?'

'You know the message on the card? "From a granddaughter you never knew you had." Well, the old lady said she did know she had her, but she was adopted as a baby. I don't think she got it right. I don't think it's the same granddaughter.'

Melanie blinked in confusion. 'I couldn't follow that – what you just said. It was gibberish, in fact.'

'Never mind. We're never going to know, are we? And I saw Mr Kitchener. Remember him? He's terribly sad, poor man.'

'Who?'

'We did his mother's funeral flowers, four or five weeks ago. That little church – Grizedale, was it?'

'Rusland, to be exact. It's in the Grizedale Forest. I remember you said how lovely it was. Didn't you go there for a look, specially, after the funeral?'

'I did. It was an excuse to do a bit of exploring. It really is amazingly beautiful. You should go and have a look sometime.'

Melanie huffed a syllable of scorn. 'Not my thing,' she protested. 'You want Ben for that sort of stuff.'

'Arthur Ransome is buried there,' Simmy went on, unable to stop herself. More than once, Melanie had accused her of being a teacher in disguise, her true vocation somehow missed.

'I don't *care*,' she cried.

'Even though you did remember its name,' Simmy teased. 'You know better than I do how much interesting history there is all around here. Stop pretending to be so cool.'

'Yeah, yeah,' Melanie muttered. 'So can I go now? It's gone twelve.'

'Did you say *snowdrops*? It's far too early for them, anyway.'

'That's what I told her. Some people are awful fools. Can I *go*?'

'Yes, yes. Be off with you. I'll see you tomorrow. The Christmas rush might be getting going by then.'

'Not in Windermere. They all go to Keswick or buy everything online.'

Simmy nodded absently. She still had a mental picture of Mrs Kitchener's hilltop grave in the serene setting between the two lakes, close to a large forest. It was a fairy-tale position in which to spend eternity. She thought she might go there again before too long, and perhaps take a few photos.

Wednesday afternoons tended not to be very busy, and this one was no exception. Still two weeks before Christmas, with the schools not yet broken up, there was very little festive atmosphere in evidence. Her parents were closing their B&B for ten days over the holiday, opening again on New Year's Eve. As Angie said, anyone who was driven to stay at such an establishment during Christmas had to be too depressing to contemplate. Simmy thought that very unfair and said so. 'There might be all kinds of interesting single women – writers, for example. They might just have terrible families they need to escape from.'

'More likely sad divorced men who never get a turn with the kids when they're at their most enjoyable. And widows with no idea what to do with themselves.' The outrageous stereotypes flew to and fro until Simmy's father pleaded for reason.

'We just like a bit of a rest and time to ourselves,' he summarised. 'It can get pretty exhausting, changing all those beds and being pleasant at breakfast time.'

The shop window had been transformed the previous month with a model of a local landmark made largely by Ben Harkness. It had been his own idea, inspired by a visit to some botanical gardens in New York. It represented the Baddeley clock tower that stood on a junction slightly to the south of Windermere's centre, and had been made of lengths of twig, embellished with beech mast, dry leaves, acorns and other natural materials gathered in the local woods. The project had taken a month or more to construct, Ben impatiently gathering as many small twigs and dry leaves as he could find in mid-November with more than one total collapse necessitating starting again from scratch. But Ben and

Simmy had persevered, until the whole thing was finished. The tower itself was miniature – perhaps ten or twelve feet tall. The model was barely two feet high, which fitted perfectly into Simmy's shop window. Countless people had been in and expressed admiration for it, and Melanie said it was fantastically good for business. She freely acknowledged Ben's abilities in constructing it, despite a lingering reluctance to accept him as a friend. Ben's brother Wilf had gone out with Melanie earlier that year, and there were awkwardnesses to navigate.

Half an hour after her assistant had left, a man came into the shop. He had hair tied in a ponytail and wore a baggy sweatshirt that was far from clean. His eyes were blue and he was at least six feet tall. 'Mrs Brown?' he asked. It was hard to discern from two small words, but she thought his accent was northern, but not local.

'That's me.'

'I came in earlier today, and your colleague said you'd be back soon. My name is Ninian Tripp. I'm a potter. I do vases, among other things, and thought we might come to some arrangement.'

'You want me to sell your pots?'

'It makes sense. You can't lose anything by it.' His tone was in no way supplicatory, nor did he have the irritating brashness of many salesmen. He was confident and friendly, with a subtle expectation that other people would be the same.

'Space. Paperwork. Liability if they get broken.' She sounded pusillanimous in her own ear.

He waved each word away. 'No need to get formal about it. I'm used to breakages, but they're a lot less common than you might think. You can stand them right here, look.' He sketched with his foot an area on the floor that was already full of other things. 'You put your flowers in them, you see. That way you don't need any more space. I promise you, the vases will make the flowers more appealing, so we'll both gain.'

'You make it sound ludicrously easy.'

'It is. I had the idea last week, when I was walking past. I only just started making vases the past few weeks, and it's working out well. They're a great combination of decorative and functional – do you see? Nobody *has* to have displays of flowers in their house, but when they do, it makes a massive difference.'

Simmy felt she was being outmanoeuvred in some way. The man was using lines that rightfully belonged to her. 'Of course I know that,' she said.

'Of course you do.' He smiled easily, as if a joke had been made by one of them. 'So that's agreed then, is it?'

'What are they like – your pots?'

'Big. Bold. Expensive. I'll bring you a few to see, shall I?'

'All right, then,' she said. 'So long as they're not so big they take the place over.'

He gave a mock salute, meeting her eyes with a long blue scrutiny that she couldn't ignore. Only the arrival of one of her regular customers forced her to break the connection. In another moment he was gone.

Mrs Weaver had developed the habit of calling in shortly before closing time on a Saturday and haggling over the price of flowers on the verge of drooping. 'You'll only throw them away,' she insisted. 'Let me have them half price, and we're both happy.' Simmy accepted that she had little grounds on which to argue, while at the same time feeling mild resentment. The woman did appear to be far from affluent, and the custom went back two centuries or more, she supposed – waiting for the stale and broken loaves, the meat on the edge of turning rancid, the overripe fruit and wilting vegetables, and then buying them for a pittance. But with flowers it felt different. If Mrs Weaver's friends saw the tired blooms and knew they'd come from her shop, it would reflect badly on her. Either that, or they'd all be queuing for Saturday afternoon bargains when they should be buying them fresh and full-priced earlier in the week.

But all she said was, 'You're early this week, aren't you? It's only Wednesday.'

The woman was in her late fifties, with well-dyed fair hair and a deeply grooved frown line between her eyes. 'I came to say I'd be in as usual at the weekend, and would really love a few over-the-top gerberas, if you've got any. I can take them off your hands for you.'

'You know it doesn't work like that,' Simmy said crossly. 'If you want gerberas, you should buy them now, at the proper price.' It pained her to speak harshly to anybody, feeling quite fluttery as she did it.

'Oh, no – I can't have them now. I'm not going home yet – I can't carry flowers around with me, can I? I'm going up to Ambleside in a minute,' she said, slightly breathlessly. 'Something's happened. They've found an old lady, apparently. Haven't you heard? It was on the local radio just now. She might be somebody I know.'

Simmy shook her head. After almost a year in Windermere, she still had to come to terms with the bush telegraph system for passing on news. The permanent residents of the little towns numbered sufficiently few for there to be a web of family connections and old schoolfellows who contacted each other constantly. 'I haven't heard anything.'

'Well, I don't know for sure, but it sounds as if somebody's died – *in suspicious circumstances.*' She hissed the last words like an excited child.

Simmy's reaction came as a surprise. A tight hand squeezed her guts. 'Do you know which road it's in?' she asked softly.

'Compston Road, I think. The one near the church, opposite that row of shops. Don't look so worried, love. After all, a funeral's good for florists, you know.' She laughed unfeelingly, and Simmy's fragile liking for her took a final terminal knock. The phrase 'ambulance-chaser' came to mind, tainted with disagreeable associations. But the main thing was that the road mentioned was nowhere near that of Mrs Joseph, which brought considerable relief.

'Mmnng,' she said vaguely, hoping to convey distaste and disinterest, while she analysed her own undue sensitivity to any mention of violent death. It had been barely two months since she and Ben had been much too closely involved in a double murder, and any suggestion of a repeat experience made her shudder. The extremity of ill-doing had shaken her world view almost off its foundations. Her own moral compass needle had swung erratically off course at times. A major element in her settling down again afterwards had been the certainty that nothing so vile could ever happen to her again.

'Anyway,' she went on firmly, 'I've decided not to let anything go at a discount again, even at the weekend. It's not good for business.'

'O-o-oh,' sang Mrs Weaver sarcastically. 'Like that, is it? Just you be careful, Miss. It doesn't go down well in these parts to get all snotty. Keep on the right side of people, is my advice. You never know when you'll need them.'

That was probably true, thought Simmy disconsolately. When the winter weather descended and the fells were deep in snow, it would be a big reassurance to know that everyone was prepared to help you out. The road down from Troutbeck that she had to traverse every day would be lethal if it iced over. The network of gossip would surely turn into something more benign and constructive when people had to huddle together in a blizzard. Simmy's mother only laughed when she voiced these concerns. 'It's never as bad as you're imagining,' she said. 'It's not Iceland, you know. Here on the west coast we can sometimes get through a whole winter with no snow at all.' But she'd been forced to admit that the past five or six winters had in fact seen weeks of disruption thanks to the weather.

'Sorry,' she said. Then a new customer came to the rescue and Mrs Weaver went off to investigate the death of an old lady in Ambleside.

THE REMAINING HOUR or so of Wednesday afternoon drifted past without further event. Simmy sold three bowls of hyacinths, a week away from flowering; two Christmas wreaths that she had made herself; and a single, long-stemmed lily to a small boy who wanted something for his teacher. There were also two new Interflora orders on the computer, for the coming week.

Outside, the final flourish of December sunshine before twilight took over had long passed. It was almost dark by half past three. The shortest day was a little over a week away. There were no tourists in Windermere or Bowness this weekend, and would be very few for the next three months. Simmy's shop felt like a fragrant little cave where she could pass the short days in peace, assessing the year gone by and making resolutions for the one to come. Her divorce from Tony was at last absolute, after a lengthy hiatus in which he had made a succession of tedious objections, or simply failed to sign the paperwork. Tony had become an unpredictable stranger whose motives and values suddenly made no sense to her. The final months of their marriage still carried a haze of bewilderment with them, a host of unanswered questions as to exactly what had been going on. Nothing so banal as adultery, nor so stark as domestic violence – although he had once hit her when she'd badgered him to justify himself. The easy explanation, given to friends and family, was that they had failed to coordinate their grief over their lost baby, and somehow that failure had eaten away at the seams of their couplehood, so they simply came apart. It had felt as if they were floating in space, the connecting umbilicus accidentally severed so they could no longer communicate. Tony had blamed her for little Edith's death, wordlessly, almost secretly, but nonetheless implacably. He had wanted the baby so fiercely that the disappointment had changed him into a man Simmy no longer recognised. His eyes had filmed over with accusation and a terrifying rage. He tried passing the blame onto the hospital staff, in the traditional manner, but logic was against him. Edith had died before labour even started, the placenta failing to sustain her, for no good reason. All the tests had shown normality, until that thirty-ninth week when it suddenly went wrong. 'It just happens sometimes,' said the doctor helplessly. 'There were no indications that it was going to.' When Tony tried to insist that the small size of the baby should have warned them, he was shown charts to prove that Edith had been well within the parameters of normality.

Simmy did at first understand the male frustration of having to entrust the safety of the child to a capricious female body. But it was a core fact of nature, and to kick against it was foolish. She herself, holding the little blue body, seeing her own father's features on the inert clay-like face, wanted something to blame, as well. She wanted reason and logic to hold onto. As the days and weeks crawled by, she realised that Tony, her husband, had become irrelevant. They ought to be rapidly working on creating a new baby, forging hopefully onwards, but they lacked the courage because they no longer trusted each other.

None of which quite explained why Tony had been so hesitant about the divorce. In Simmy's case, the very word came redolent of failure and humiliation. Nobody in her family had been divorced – not that there *were* many people in her family, anyway. Tony's sister, Cat, had been appalled at his behaviour. Simmy's parents, proprietors of a bed and breakfast establishment in Lake Road, had held their breath and left her to work through it with relatively detached support. When she announced an intention to start a new life close to them in the Lake District, they had been uncertain as to the wisdom of that move.

So far it was working out nicely. Always treated with fondness by her father and a somewhat careless approval by her mother, she was finally getting to know them as individuals in their own right. Angie's insistence on following her own principles in everything she did was both inspiring and embarrassing. It also served to highlight the prevalence of brainless rules across every aspect of life, which Simmy might otherwise have overlooked, despite the discomfort they could give rise to. Her mother would not let anything pass. She had no personal objections to tobacco, muddy dogs, junk food or minor household dangers, and could see no reason why petty officials should try to force her to change. These officials all regarded such things with horror, especially those who took it upon themselves to regulate B&B establishments. 'I don't expect we can get away with it for ever,' admitted her father, 'but it's going pretty well up to now.' Indeed, there was a growing crowd of enthusiasts for the home-from-home atmosphere of Beck View in Windermere.

The matter of Simmy's divorce was seldom discussed. It had been assumed that it would come through eventually, and since neither party wished to remarry, there was no suggestion of urgency. Her father pointed out that there were unresolved financial details that might work against Simmy's interests, if her business began to make appreciable profits. She shrugged it off. 'Tony's not interested in money,' she said. But now, at last, the whole thing was settled.

She closed the shop ten minutes early, convinced there would be no more customers on this dark afternoon. As she carried the display rack in from the pavement, she thought again of Ninian Tripp, the potter. It would make a nice change, she supposed, to have some attractive vases carefully placed around the shop door, enticing people in. They would have to be stable, and relatively chunky – well weighted to prevent them from falling over. Nothing slender or too small. She stepped away to get a better impression of how they might look.

'Careful!' came a female voice behind her. It was Julie, one of the few people in Windermere she regarded as a genuine friend. Not because the general population was stand-offish, but because she was still new and busy with the business and had not quite grasped the social systems of the place.

'Hi!' she said, with a smile. 'How's things?'

'Have you heard what's happened in Ambleside?' Julie seemed breathless, her eyes flashing with a sense of drama.

'Not really.' She had swept the story aside the moment she'd heard it from Mrs Weaver, anxious not to know anything about it. It had nothing whatever to do with her, and she lacked any wish to behave like a ghoul.

'What does *that* mean? Either you have or you haven't.'

'Simply that a customer said something, but I took no notice.'

'An old lady was done to death in her own house, in broad day-light. Everybody's talking about it. It'll be on the news. It's a ter-rible thing to happen, Sim. You can't just ignore it.'

'No,' said Simmy slowly. 'I don't expect I can. But I'm not going to dwell on it, either. It has nothing to do with me,' she said loudly.

'No man is an island,' Julie reproached her. 'It has to do with all of us – especially women living on their own in isolated little villages,' she added. 'Doesn't it scare you?'

'Only if people like you do their best to spread panic. And Troutbeck isn't an "isolated little village". It's really quite big and I'm right in the middle of it, with houses on all sides.'

'People like me?' Julie frowned. 'What does that mean?'

'Nothing. Sorry.' She could hear her mother inside her head, groaning at yet another taboo phrase that was sure to give offence. Julie subscribed wholeheartedly to such thinking, while at the same time laughing in genuine amusement and admiration at many of Simmy's turns of phrase. It was as if she would have liked to share her attitude, but was afraid to. It made their friendship lopsided at times, but such was Simmy's gratitude for Julie's gen-erosity with her time and attention that it was never seriously in jeopardy.

'Anyway, I didn't mean we ought to care because it scares us. I meant – nobody should have a thing like that happen to them. You agree with that, don't you? It's so *wrong*. It's uncivilised.'

'It's barbaric,' Simmy confirmed. 'Utterly awful. I hope they catch him quickly, Whoever he is that did it.'

'Yes. So do I. Although it might be a her, of course. Girls do wicked things these days, as well as boys. They break into houses carrying crowbars and baseball bats and think nothing of bashing people. On drugs usually.' Julie shuddered. Simmy suppressed a smile at the world weariness of a divorced forty-year-old hairdresser. No doubt she heard some gruesome stories as she snipped and styled her customers.

'I can't really stop,' she apologised. 'I need to get on with the Christmas cards.'

'Blimey! I don't do mine for *ages* yet. I don't even want to think about it – I send them to all my regulars, you know.'

'How do you know their addresses?' Simmy couldn't recall ever giving such information to a hairdresser. 'There must be hundreds of them.'

'I'm very organised,' boasted Julie. 'I send them reminders about their appointments and special offers and so forth. I'm doing depilation from next year as well – and nails. I'll be needing another girl.'

'Great,' Simmy approved absently. 'Well …'

'Yes, all right. Go and do your cards. And mind you lock your door properly. I'm serious. You just can't trust people these days.'

Simmy's urge to argue was weak enough to resist quite easily. Trusting people remained her default position despite Tony's lapses and the shocking double murder a couple of months earlier. 'Oh – one thing I wanted to ask you. Do you know a man called Ninian Tripp? He's a potter.'

Julie's eyes widened. 'Oh, yes, I've met him once or twice. He lives in a tumbledown cottage up on Brantfell. Doesn't he make tiles mostly?'

'I don't know. He wants me to sell vases for him.'

'He's from Yorkshire or somewhere. Had a breakdown or something. He's very good-looking.' She gave Simmy a searching look – like Melanie, she was always on the lookout for a new love interest for her friend, having vowed she was herself sworn off men for ever.

'Breakdown? Poor man.' She supposed she'd come close to a breakdown of her own, when Edith had died, and a flash of fellow feeling went through her. 'He seems okay now, though.'

'What did you tell him?'

'That I'd look at his stuff if he brings me some. I suppose it's worth a go, if they're any good.'

'His tiles are gorgeous, apparently. Terribly expensive.'

'Hmm,' said Simmy. 'Thanks for the information. I'm off now.' She checked her bag for keys and headed for her car, parked in a nearby side street, while Julie disappeared in the other direction.

'Mrs Brown?' A man's voice was calling to her from somewhere across the street. 'Just a moment.'

She looked around in confusion, over the roofs of passing cars. An arm was waving at her, she realised. Then the man attached to it trotted over to her, through a gap in the traffic. 'Hello, again,' he said, before grimacing. 'I'm sorry about this, but I'm afraid I'm going to have to ask you to come with me to the police station to answer a few questions.'

Chapter Three

It was Detective Inspector Moxon, who had been centrally involved in the investigations into the local murders Simmy had witnessed two months earlier. His face was startlingly familiar to her, as if it had only been a few days ago that they had sat facing each other across a small table in a Windermere hotel. 'What?' she said. 'Is it something to do with Bridget?' – the young woman who had been at the heart of the previous trouble she had shared with Moxon.

His blank expression was almost comical. 'No, she's called Nancy. Miss Nancy Clark.'

'Who is? What are you talking about?'

He threw a careful glance up and down the pavement. 'Not here,' he said, like a guilty lover. 'We can't talk here.'

'I don't understand,' she protested. 'What am I supposed to have done? Are you arresting me?'

'No, of course not. Don't be silly. I should have sent a constable for you, by rights, but I thought ... after last time ... When your name came up again, I just thought it should be me. We could talk in the car, if you'd rather, but I do need it to be official, you see.'

'I'm not being silly,' she corrected him. 'I can't imagine what you want. I don't even know where the police station *is*.' This was true – all her previous encounters with him had taken place in hotels or houses or her shop.

'You must do,' he said incredulously. 'On Lake Road, going down into Bowness. You can't miss it.'

'It's not the kind of thing I notice,' she apologised.

'So, will you come? It's important.'

'Taken in for questioning,' she mused. 'Is that what's happening? I wish I knew what I'd done.' Her mother's broad rebellious streak had a habit of surfacing at such times, creating a lack of deference that DI Moxon had already commented on. Apparently most people went weak at the knees when addressed by a senior detective, and did everything they could to placate him. Simmy had been brought up to regard the police as public servants, deplorably inclined to exceed their powers at every opportunity. Somehow she failed to be afraid of them, despite an awareness that almost everybody else was.

'You haven't done anything,' he snapped irritably. 'You've been named as a witness by somebody we have reason to suspect of committing a crime. He claims you can vouch for him being in a certain place at a certain time.'

'Me?' she said daftly. 'So who is he? Why can't you just ask me now and get it over with?'

'Because it has to be properly recorded, your statement signed, his identity established. Paperwork. I can't just ask you here in the street and use that as evidence.'

'Can't you?' Not for the first time, she wished she watched more police dramas on TV, or read more whodunnits. She had no idea what was usual procedure, or what some of the jargon actually meant. It seemed to her quite reasonable that a simple question could be posed and answered almost anywhere, with perfect validity.

'No.' He folded his arms and stared her down. He was two inches taller than her and about five years older. He had behaved politely with her every time she had met him, eliciting disclosure of the loss of baby Edith during their first interview. He had even suggested, in a light moment, that she consider joining the police force herself. When she laughed in his face, he had been dignified. He had no discernible personal vanity: his hair always needed a wash and his shirts were badly ironed. He did not strike her as especially intelligent or angry or frustrated. A man doing a job of work that often made him tired, and which engaged the whole of his attention, was her instinctive summary.

'Okay, then,' she said. 'Let's get on with it.'

'You don't change, do you?'

'Should I?'

'Some of my colleagues might think so. They might find you a bit … insolent.'

'And some of my relatives might find you rather irritating. I thought this – whatever it is – was urgent? We've wasted a good five minutes already.'

He made an ushering motion with his right arm, and she walked ahead of him to a plain black car parked down the street. A young man was in the driving seat, and Moxon followed her into the back. 'Right, Preston – let's get going,' he barked, in a tone quite different from that used with Simmy.

She waited in vain for any further elucidation as to what was required of her. Curiosity vied with impatience and a mild amusement as they drove the half mile to the police station in Lake Road. 'Oh, now I recognise it,' she exclaimed. 'How silly of me. I never made the connection, somehow.' It even had the traditional blue lamp outside, she noticed, for the first time. She could just hear Ben Harkness mocking her for her outrageous lack of observation.

He took her into a small room with a bright light and summoned Preston to join them. Then he asked her if she had been in Ambleside that morning.

'Yes – I delivered some flowers. Why?' Only then, again to her dismay at her dim-wittedness, did she connect his sudden appearance to the killing of an old lady somewhere in Ambleside. 'Mrs Joseph isn't hurt, is she?'

He glanced down at a page of notes on the table. 'Joseph? Not that I know of. No – the person in question is a Mr Malcolm Kitchener. He says you saw him; that you spoke to him.'

'Mr Kitchener? Yes – he was in that café above Stock Ghyll. The Giggling Goose.' Her brain was slowly turning over the implications of the question. 'We didn't say much. His mother died.'

'What time was it?'

'Oh – eleven-ish. A bit before, possibly.'

'How long did you stay?'

'Twenty minutes,' she hazarded. 'Or half an hour. How long does it take to drink a cup of coffee? I wasn't in a rush. Melanie was in the shop.'

'How well do you know him?'

'Not at all, really. Just to put a face and a name to. He recognised me and said hello. He was feeling sorry for himself. His mother died,' she repeated.

'You feel that's important, do you?'

'It's how I know him. I did the flowers for her funeral. It was up at Grizedale.' She spoke wonderingly, still bewildered at why the police should care about Mr Kitchener's movements.

DI Moxon nodded thoughtfully. 'We need to be sure we're talking about the same man. He's here, undergoing questioning. I'm going to go and open the door of the room, and I want you to walk past and make sure it's him. All right?'

Simmy was repeating the word *undergoing* to herself. It made the process sound painful and distressing for the poor man. 'Won't he see me? Haven't you got one of those clever mirrors that are really windows?' At least she'd managed to glean that much from her minimal interest in TV crime dramas.

'He won't be surprised to see you. He gave us your name as an alibi.'

'Alibi!' It sounded sinisterly technical and important. 'For what? I mean, what is it he's supposed to have done, then, to need an alibi?' She gave him a worried look, already on the verge of understanding what might come next. 'He's just a sad little man, who wouldn't hurt a fly. You've obviously got something very wrong.'

'I can't disclose any details. Once you've had a look at him, you can go. Preston can drive you to your car, if you like.'

'That's all right. I'll walk. Let's get on with it, then,' she repeated.

The identification was performed with some awkwardness. Mr Kitchener was sitting at a table, facing the door of the interview room, and when Simmy stood looking at him, he gave her a weak little smile and a nod.

'Yes, that's him,' she said, loudly. 'That's the man I spoke to this morning in Ambleside.'

'Thank you,' mouthed Mr Kitchener, with no visible sign of relief.

DI Moxon led her down the corridor to the reception area. He sighed and said the same words as his suspect, adding, 'You've been very helpful.'

'It wasn't very difficult,' she told him. 'Do you want me to sign anything?'

'Not at the moment. If there are any developments, we know where to find you. But it looks as if this line of enquiry has reached a conclusion.'

'A dead end, you mean.'

'You could say that,' he agreed.

She hesitated, meeting his eyes with reluctance, knowing she would regret her next question, because she thought she already knew the answer. 'So what did you think he'd done?'

He held her gaze, and she forgot that he was a policeman. He was allowing her to see well beyond his role, through to the person underneath. She understood, faintly, that this was unusual. 'An old lady was killed this morning in Ambleside. We had reason to connect her with Mr Kitchener.'

'You moved quickly,' she observed. Notions about fingerprints and DNA flittered across her mind, and the huge sinister surveillance machinery at the disposal of the police came to mind. How many CCTV cameras were there in Ambleside, she wondered? If she'd understood Julie correctly, the victim lived in a busy street in the heart of the town. 'You'll let him go now, will you?'

He nodded.

'And apologise to him?'

He scratched an eyebrow irritably. 'Don't push it,' he warned.

She could see that he was recalling the last time they had met, where her ambivalence about the obligations of the public to cooperate with the police had become apparent. 'Okay,' she conceded. 'Sorry.'

'It was a deliberate attack. The lady was in her seventies. She was in her own home, with people walking past on the pavement a few feet away. She must have let him in, which suggests she trusted him. Perhaps he never planned to hurt her, and something went wrong. Whatever his intentions, we don't want a person like that to escape punishment – wouldn't you agree?'

'Of course. Did he rob her? Is that why he did it?' She remembered Julie's idea that the killer might have been female. Seemingly the police had no such suspicion.

He smiled tightly and shook his head. 'No more questions. Get off home now – and be careful.'

She was disappointed. The warning was banal and useless. What did it mean in practice? It was already dark outside, the night set to last for well over twelve hours. A monstrous and determined killer could have his pick of thousands of defenceless women, if that was his wish. No amount of carefulness would stop him. Windows could be smashed and entrance gained to almost any house, if the will was strong enough. 'Right,' she said, and left without a backward look.

It was Wednesday, she reminded herself. Just over two weeks until Christmas. She would indeed write her cards that evening, glad that the old-fashioned habit still persisted, in the face of emails and tweets and other transient means of sending festive cheer to friends. She wanted to enclose letters for five or six old friends, telling them about her new business and giving her impressions of her new home. The Lake District had yet to fully get under her skin, with its multitude of changing views and undiscovered byways. The fells had mutated in the past weeks into mysterious grey shapes looming over the little towns. Out there, she felt, anything could happen. Unwary walkers could disappear for ever, swallowed up by the frothing becks or the bronze clumps of bracken that might somehow encase them like mummies. The near-black stone of the houses seemed to darken in the wintry light, making them look comfortless and unfriendly in the undulating streets. Further north and west, where the hills rose higher and the shelter of trees dwindled away, it seemed to her like a land from a northern fairy tale, where no right-thinking human would venture. Thirlmere, Ullswater, Haweswater – they were all within a day or two's walk of her home, and yet felt impossibly distant. She could drive to them in under an hour, but seeing them from a car was barely to see them at all. She felt an increasing duty to explore the whole region, aware that she was privileged to live in a place that the whole world regarded as being of spectacular beauty.'

Her father had expressed a vague intention to go with her on some of these walks. He had acquired his own eccentric store of knowledge about the history of the area. He focused on characters that others ignored: Baddeley, Bolton, Christopher North. He could expatiate at length on these and many others, and did so over breakfast served to unresisting guests at the B&B. He sought out little-known corners of lake and forest and showed them to Simmy on the map. But in reality, the weather was never quite right, or he had too much to do in the garden. 'In the spring,' he promised. 'We'll go and explore Elterwater and Grizedale in the spring.'

'I'd never heard of either of them until now,' she admitted. Only a few days later, the funeral of Mrs Kitchener had prompted her to go to Grizedale for a look. She reported back to her father that it was mainly a large forest full of trails for cyclists and a lot of very strange wooden statues. 'But the church at Rusland is gorgeous,' she added.

She was, however, increasingly familiar with Ambleside, virtual neighbour of Windermere. Her Troutbeck home was situated between the two, and she welcomed opportunities to walk the smaller lanes in either direction. She had watched the onset of winter on the slopes of Wansfell and considered herself to be well into the early stages of addiction to the landscape surrounding her.

'Hello again, Helen,' she wrote to her friend from college. 'How are things with you? I've had a very eventful year, leaving Worcester and starting again in the Lakes. My Windermere shop is up and running, and my little house in Troutbeck is solid enough to cope with whatever the winter brings – I hope! I've made a few new friends here, and got myself involved in a ghastly murder investigation, a couple of months ago. And now there's been another one – murder, I mean. I've just come from the police station, actually. The local detective inspector is an intriguing chap, I must say. I always seem to be arguing with him, which probably isn't a very good idea. But don't worry – I'm not planning to see him again. My parents are fit and well, and their B&B is legendary, thanks to my mother's unusual approach. She lets people bring their dogs and smoke, and tries to stop them watching television – not always successfully of course. Some people are incorrigible addicts. Everybody loves it, and they all keep rebooking, so she must be doing something right. Christmas will be quiet, I expect – just me and Mum and Dad, pulling crackers together. Let me know what's happening with you.'

She proceeded to compose similar letters to three more old friends, none of whom had yet visited her in her new home, before deciding her hand was too stiff for any more writing. Everyone else could have a few lines inside the card itself.

Shortly before nine, she had a phone call from her mother – an unusual event. 'The cat's been run over,' she began, with no discernible emotion. 'It's broken its pelvis, apparently. And leg. They're going to pin it all back together tomorrow.'

'Poor thing. Sounds expensive. Is Daddy upset?'

'Quite. It's his animal, really. He'll have to do all the nursing.'

'So?' The cat was a good-tempered male tabby that spent most of its time in the kitchen at Beck View. Health inspectors that showed up sporadically to check that the B&B was being run on acceptable lines would always raise their eyebrows and make critical comments on their clipboards, but Angie never took any notice. At least there were unlikely to be any mice contaminating the groceries, she would say.

'So he says he won't be free to go out with you on Sunday morning. Apparently you had a plan.'

'Nothing definite. There was some talk of walking to Garburn and Castle Crag, but only if the weather was right. How do you nurse a cat, anyway?'

'Goodness knows. I imagine we're about to find out.'

'Did the driver stop, then? How did you find him?'

'It was a woman. She did stop, and took Chucky to the people next door. They sent her here. She was quite upset, to give her her due. Offered to drive us to the vet, but we wouldn't let her. For a start, we haven't ever needed a vet before. We didn't know where to go. Turned out, it's barely five minutes from here. Dad carried him down.'

Simmy remembered her own lack of local knowledge, when it came to locating the police station. But she had more of an excuse – she had only lived in the area for a year. Angie and

Russell Straw were both every bit as unobservant of their immediate surroundings as their daughter was.

'Poor cat,' she said again. 'I'll come round on Saturday and
bring him some sardines, then, shall I?'

'Yes, do,' said her mother. 'Pity about the walk. I was looking
forward to having the place to myself for a bit.'

Chapter Four

HER CONVERSATIONS WITH Melanie and Julie returned to her, as she lay waiting to fall asleep. Melanie would be thrilled by the latest involvement with a murder; a response that Simmy found unsettling. The obvious explanation for it was that the girl had a boyfriend who happened to be a police constable, which gave her some sort of special interest in criminal matters. There were also the recent high-profile murders, from which Melanie had been almost entirely excluded by various accidents of timing. She had firmly insisted that if anything of the sort were to happen again, she wanted to be right in the middle of it.

'It won't happen again,' Simmy had told her repeatedly. 'Lightning doesn't strike twice.' But now, with the killing of a defenceless woman in Ambleside, and Simmy named as an alibi for a suspect, it seemed she had spoken too soon. But still she resisted any idea that she might find herself significantly involved again. She had vouched for Mr Kitchener as any passer-by would do, and that was the end of it. If his fingerprints were in the victim's house, then there had to be an innocent explanation for it. She thrust aside the niggling questions that wormed their way into her head. How did the police know the prints – or DNA, or whatever – belonged to Mr K? Wouldn't that mean they already had him on record, in their database? And wasn't there a rule that said they could only retain material from convicted criminals? She was hazy on that question, and rejected any temptation to check with Ben, who would undoubtedly know the answer.

Only by forcing her thoughts onto other matters could she close out these annoying questions. The flowers for Mrs Joseph came to mind, sent by an unknown granddaughter. That really was an interesting little mystery that she'd have liked to solve for her own satisfaction. The customer had given an address in Liverpool, explaining she had found Persimmon Petals online and thought it would be cheapest to phone her directly, rather than go through Interflora or such. She had given a credit card number that involved a confirmation that the address was valid. Her name was Candida Hawkins. 'But don't you dare tell Mrs Joseph that,' she adjured Simmy. 'She's not to know my name.' Simmy had readily given an undertaking to respect the client's confidentiality. Even so, she kept it clear in her mind. Candida was a memorable name, anyway, and one she had briefly considered for her own daughter, during her pregnancy. Tony had said it was pretentious.

She mentally tidied away the day as she waited for sleep. It had been a lot more eventful than any for some weeks. The last thought she had before falling asleep was of Ninian Tripp, and how his name conjured fairy tales and earlier times.

THURSDAY DAWNED BRIGHT and sunny, with the light flooding the hills across the lake, visible from her bedroom window.

A stirring of childish excitement at the prospect of Christmas gripped her. The carols and good cheer would make the centre of Windermere a pleasing place to be for the coming week or two. The necessity of some kind of festival to tide everyone through the winter could not be dodged. The celebration of a birth was, at the very least, a clever way of creating a sense of anticipation and possibility for the coming seasons. Even though the infant Jesus was a most unrealistic baby, whether in medieval paintings or primary school nativity plays, the idea was there. The days stopped getting shorter, and by Twelfth Night could just be perceived as lengthening again. For a florist, there was a cornucopia of spring blooms to look forward to. It was intoxicating to think of the narcissi, tulips, irises and much besides, all due to appear in a few months' time. Simmy lay in bed, quietly rejoicing in the prospects ahead.

She drove down to the shop, arriving at eight-thirty. A delivery from the wholesalers was due at any moment. Melanie would turn up sometime between nine and ten. She and Simmy were both fairly relaxed about timekeeping, especially when business was as quiet as it had been recently. So long as flowers got to funerals and weddings on time, other commissions tended to be reasonably flexible. The sense of well-being continued into the morning, enhanced by an order for a lavish anniversary bouquet, to be delivered the next afternoon to a house in Newby Bridge.

Then the shop door pinged, and Mr Kitchener walked in. He looked gaunt and embarrassed, and Simmy wished, not for the first time, that she wasn't quite so easy to find.

'Hello!' she greeted him, with a wholly excessive effusion.

'Hello,' he muttered. 'I've just come about yesterday. It was very nice of you to get me out of trouble like that. I'd probably still be there otherwise.'

'I only told the truth.' Already she was starting to share his awkwardness. 'There's no need to thank me.'

'You must have been wondering what it was all about. How much did they tell you?'

This was turning difficult. Surely he must know that she'd have been told he was being questioned about the murder? But how did you say that to someone? How did you voice the fact that he had been, albeit fleetingly, suspected of the most terrible crime?

'Oh – you know – just the basics. It was obviously all a big mistake. And I bet you could have named all sorts of people who could vouch for you, not just me. The women who run the café, for a start.'

'They wouldn't remember me. Just another faceless customer to them. It was the greatest piece of luck that you were there. I promise you, I'd have been in very hot water without you.'

'Why?' she couldn't help asking. 'What evidence was there against you?'

'The old lady knew my mother. I'd been to the house several times. She and I didn't get along, and the neighbours reported a row we had, not so long ago.' He shifted restlessly, unable to meet her eye. 'I was actually a lodger there, at one point. Ages ago now, when my wife threw me out, but people round here don't forget a thing.'

'I see,' said Simmy slowly. 'You were in the system because of the row, is that it? On the police computer or something?'

'Right,' he nodded. After a pause, he said, 'Well, I won't keep you. Just … thanks again. I owe you one.'

He turned to go, and came face to face with Melanie, who had just arrived. They sidestepped each other, and he went out into the street. 'Who was that?' asked the girl. 'I've seen him before.'

'Mr Kitchener. I told you I saw him yesterday.' It occurred to her, rather foolishly, that Melanie could therefore offer a sort of backup alibi, if required. Or would it only be hearsay? Somehow, she remembered that lots of apparently good evidence turned out to be mere worthless hearsay, because you couldn't place any trust in what people said to each other.

'You're not starting a thing with him, are you?' Melanie asked suspiciously. 'He's nothing like good enough for you. He's got funny legs.'

'It's a limp. Something wrong with one of his hips, I expect. It makes his legs look strange.' The brief scene where he kicked the chair in the café came back to her. Would any of those chattering girls have remembered him, she wondered? Was there *no one* else who could have provided him with an alibi? Suddenly, the responsibility sat heavily on her, making her uneasy. What if he had been cunning enough to make it look as if the murder had happened at a different time than it really had? Was it possible, anyway, for the precise moment to be established? How could twenty minutes in a café be enough to settle the matter conclusively? Without the full story from DI Moxon, she was doomed to ask herself questions like this, with little hope of reliable answers.

'Ben!' she said aloud. 'He'd know.'

'Know what?' Melanie looked at her as if she'd missed something. 'What are you talking about?'

'Sorry.' She took a deep breath. 'Listen, Mel – I suppose I'll have to tell you, after last time. There was an old lady murdered yesterday in Ambleside. The police thought Mr Kitchener might have something to do with it, but he gave me as an alibi because I saw him in the coffee shop. I had to go and confirm that it was the same man. So they let him go, and he came in just now to thank me. I'm probably not meant to tell anybody about it. Okay?'

Melanie kept up with this abbreviated summary with impressive ease. 'I see,' she said. 'Thanks for telling me. She was called Nancy Clark, I presume.'

'What? How do you know that?'

'It was on the news last night. Didn't you watch it? They didn't say anything much. Hinted that it might be a robbery that went wrong, somehow.'

Simmy shook her head. 'My mother phoned to say the cat was run over, and I was writing my Christmas cards. I didn't bother with the telly.'

'Is it dead? The cat, I mean.'

'No, no. It's got broken bones and my dad's going to have to nurse it better. He says he can't go for a walk with me to Garburn on Sunday.'

'Don't be daft. It's going to snow.'

'What?' Simmy's heart had done a wild lurch that was wholly uncalled for. 'Are you sure?'

'That's what they say. It won't be much, this side of Christmas. Anyway, Garburn's just a swamp. What would you want to go there for?' Melanie, despite being born and bred amongst the fells, saw little appeal in being out in them apart from the odd picnic in high summer.

'I want to see it for myself. There's a track to it, running practically from my front door. It seems all wrong that I've never gone up there.'

'Never mind that now. What about this murder? And why did you say Ben would know? *What* would he know?'

'I can't remember now.' The prospect of snow was still alarming her. 'I never got those winter tyres put on the car,' she worried. 'What if I get stuck?'

'You won't get stuck,' Melanie pacified her. 'They salt all the roads. It's only weather,' she added bizarrely. 'And snow at Christmas is *nice*.'

A customer saved the conversation from descending into mutual irritation. Simmy went to welcome the elderly man who stood staring at a garland of ivy, eucalyptus and snowberries that Simmy had made two days previously. 'I'm rather proud of that one,' she told him.

'Where would you put it?' he asked doubtfully.

'On a door, maybe. Or it could be a table centrepiece. You could stand a candle in the middle.'

'I was looking for something more ... traditional,' he said. 'Holly. Evergreens. Red ribbons. *You* know.'

She did, and produced a wreath that matched his description quite closely, albeit with the addition of some Douglas fir and a gold-coloured tassel attached to the bottom. 'I could make one up for you,' she offered. 'If you don't like this.'

'That one's good enough,' he nodded. 'It's very nice, actually. And I like the model in the window. Very clever, that is. My partner says we should do something of the sort in our garden. Is it difficult to do?'

She ran through the process with him, warning of the mess involved, with glue and bits of seedpod and stick getting everywhere. 'But it was rather fun,' she concluded. 'Why not have a go, and see how you get on?'

Melanie had drifted into the back room, to perform one of her key tasks of sorting out the latest consignment from the wholesaler.

A stickler for using everything in proper date order, she would line up the flowers accordingly, replacing the oldest stock in the shop with something a day or two fresher. Unusually for her age group, she deplored waste above everything else. If Simmy complained that hardly anything on display was really recent, Melanie would simply accuse her of over ordering. Between them, they had established an acceptable balance, with Simmy forced to admit that her assistant had a point about wastage.

The man bought the garland, referring again to his partner, who turned out to be called Jim.

'So much for gay men being supercreative,' said Melanie, who often managed to overhear conversation from the storeroom. 'He didn't seem to have the slightest idea what he was doing, did he?'

'At least he was trying,' Simmy defended. She had rather enjoyed the man's willingness to learn, despite his failure to buy the more unusual decoration. She had taken some trouble over it, worrying that the snowberries would drop off prematurely, or turn brown.

Another Interflora order popped up on the computer, for delivery the following day, which gave Simmy something to do for the next hour, selecting and assembling components for the two bouquets now on order. Only very fleetingly did images of poor Nancy Clark intrude, lying in a pool of blood in her hallway, betrayed by the visitor she had willingly admitted. Whatever she might have thought the previous evening, Simmy was resolved not to open the door to anybody she didn't know until the killer had been well and truly caught.

The sunshine outside persisted, but failed to bring shoppers onto the streets in any appreciable numbers. On such days, Melanie's presence was essentially superfluous, and Simmy would be tempted to leave the girl in charge of the shop and find some reason to get out and about. With no deliveries to make, she considered the idea of dropping into one or two local restaurants and suggesting they add festive floral decorations to their tables. There were still a few who had made vague promises to think about regular orders of flowers, but never followed through. It was an aspect of the business that she did not enjoy, but which she knew could make a big difference, if performed effectively. Melanie saw it as a way of meeting new people – something she regularly accused Simmy of failing to do.

But the timing was all wrong. Restaurants would be hectically busy with Christmas parties until well into the afternoon. Then they would be girding themselves for more busyness in the evening. They would have no time or inclination to discuss flowers. *Should have done it a month ago*, Simmy reproached herself.

So it was with undiluted pleasure that she greeted young Ben Harkness when he materialised just before four o'clock. 'Hey, Ben,' she cried. 'Nice to see you. It's been ages.'

The boy raised his eyebrows in a brief response and slung his heavy school bag onto the floor. At seventeen, he was still growing, with a thin neck and round shoulders. He spent too much time at the computer, in Simmy's opinion, but had a sort of gracefulness that she found endearing. 'Busy,' he said.

'Exams?'

He shook his head. 'Play rehearsals, mainly. I got you a ticket, if you're interested.'

'Wow! What's the play?'

'*Androcles and the Lion*, would you believe? It's been a nightmare learning all the lines.'

'Why? Have you got a big part?'

He gave her a straight look. 'Do you know it? The play?'

'Um … Sorry. I know I ought to know, but I don't think I've ever heard of it.' Drama was definitely not one of her special interests, although she had made an effort with Shakespeare at one point in her early thirties. 'Who wrote it?'

'Shaw, actually. It's about how states treat their minorities, and eccentrics. And it's terribly rude about Christianity. But it's quite short – only two acts.'

'And I suppose you're Androcles?'

'No, I'm Ferrovius. It's a big part. It's daft for me to be doing it at all, when I'm not even taking drama.' He sighed. 'But they said it would look good on my CV – which is bonkers, actually. But it is sort of fun. Makes a change.'

'Come off it,' put in Melanie, who had expressed an intention of going home over an hour before, but somehow never quite gone. 'You love it, if I know you. You'll be brilliant, obviously.'

He grimaced. 'Doubt it. And there's not much take-up of the tickets. There's only about fifteen parts in the whole thing, and the families aren't bothered if their kid isn't in it. Big mistake, but you can't tell Old Anthill anything.'

'Anthill?' Simmy echoed.

'She's called Mrs Anthony, officially, but she's got a long nose like an anteater, so that's what we call her.'

'But you said "anthill", not "anteater",' Simmy argued.

'Yeah,' he said patiently. 'Makes it less obvious, see? And quicker to say. She's okay, as a teacher. Eccentric and political – and an atheist. Makes the head nervous, which can't be bad. Keeps stopping us to make us discuss the play, as if it was English, not drama.'

'When's it on?'

'End of next week. Friday and Saturday. Dress rehearsal Thursday.'

'Great! I'd love to come,' said Simmy bravely, wondering how she would feel walking into a big strange school amongst people she'd never met, and sitting on her own in the hall. She hadn't been inside a school for twenty years or more. 'What about you, Mel? Will you come with me?'

Melanie puffed out her cheeks in unambiguous scorn. 'No thanks! I've had enough of that place. I wouldn't even go if one of our kids was in it.' She was one of a large, disorganised family, two of her siblings still working their way haphazardly through the education system. Melanie stood out as a major success, compared to the rest of them.

'Wilf's going,' said Ben, looking at the ceiling with exaggerated unconcern.

'So?'

'Just saying.'

Simmy watched in amusement. Melanie had dated Wilf, who was Ben's older brother, for a short time earlier in the year. Since then she had taken up with Joe Wheeler, a police constable. As far as Simmy could tell, there were ambivalences in the girl's heart which might yet work to Wilf's advantage.

Ben was offered a mug of tea, and while he drank it, he suddenly jerked his head. 'Oh! I nearly forgot. I saw you last night, coming out of the cop shop. I was in the car with my mum. You looked a bit ... dazed.'

'You'll have to tell him,' said Melanie.

'I was going to,' snapped Simmy. And then she did, starting with meeting Mr Kitchener in the café, and finishing with questions about evidence and forensics and police databases.

Chapter Five

BEN STAYED FOR over an hour, making Simmy late closing the shop. Melanie stayed too, afraid of missing something. Ben had heard nothing about the murder of the old lady, and was initially slow to take an interest. The incident in which Mr Kitchener had made a disturbance at Nancy Clark's house and come to the attention of the police finally drew him in. 'Well, they wouldn't have taken his prints just for that,' he asserted. 'He must have been on file for something else. Something more serious.'

'Are you sure?' Simmy queried. 'My mother says they'll grab any excuse to take people's DNA and so forth. They want everybody in their computers.'

'They *definitely* wouldn't have taken his DNA. Besides, there wouldn't have been time to do a comparison and get the results back, if the murder only happened yesterday morning. If they can be so precise about the time of death, that must mean somebody saw her alive shortly before it happened, and then the body was found pretty quickly afterwards. Leaves a short window, see? That's why your alibi worked.'

'Yes,' Simmy agreed thoughtfully. 'That does make sense.'

'And he wasn't to know you'd show up so conveniently, was he? I mean, he didn't *engineer* it in any way. He was in the café before you – right?'

'Right,' she confirmed. 'What are you suggesting? It sounds to me as if the poor man is completely innocent, and it's lucky for him that I was there. Anything else would be incredibly devious.'

'Premeditated murder *is* devious,' Melanie said. 'And it would include appearing innocent, wouldn't it? Maybe he got somebody to say they saw Nancy Clark when they didn't.'

'That would involve an accomplice, which is never a good idea. Was she robbed?'

'I don't know. He didn't tell me very much. Just warned me to be careful, which I took to imply that it was a professional burglar who'd planned the whole thing in advance, targeting women living on their own. I don't imagine he meant to kill Miss Clark. She must have disturbed him or screamed or something.'

'It didn't sound like a burglary,' Melanie said, getting carried away. 'More like a psychopathic killer, doing it for kicks.'

'Phooey!' spat Ben in a rare display of contempt. 'No such creature.'

'What? Of course there is.'

'Okay, then. One person in a hundred million. That makes it vanishingly rare.' He looked to Simmy for support. 'Think about it. The risks would be enormous, and for hardly any reward. Even the maddest mad person would have more sense than that.'

'Okay – I didn't mean it like that exactly. I guess a mad person would just stab people in the street. I was thinking more of someone who would operate to a careful pattern to make the whole thing more fun,' Melanie amended. She had taken to reading stories about serial killers in recent months.

'That's a bit closer to reality,' Ben conceded. 'Either way, there's not much point in telling people to be careful. What does that really *mean*?'

'My conclusion exactly,' sighed Simmy. 'It just makes everybody scared for no good reason.'

'Why were you in Ambleside anyway? Delivering flowers, did you say?'

Simmy nodded. 'A Mrs Joseph who's got a long-lost granddaughter, apparently. It was her birthday, and the message said "From a granddaughter you never knew you had". She said she did know – it was her daughter's baby, who got adopted at birth. Presumably the girl thought the whole thing was a secret.'

Ben frowned attentively. 'How interesting,' he said. 'What a mystery! Wasn't she excited?'

'Seemed a bit cross about it, if anything. I suppose that's understandable. At that age, you don't really want strange grandchildren turning up and rocking the boat, do you?'

'Don't you?' Ben looked blank. 'I'd have thought it would be thrilling, however old you were. Like finding the missing piece of jigsaw.' He shrugged. 'Nothing to do with the murder, anyway. The only imaginable link is you.'

'Don't be too sure of that,' Melanie interposed. 'Ambleside is a small place. And I happen to know there's a connection between the Joseph family and the Clarks.' She gave a complacent smile. 'Like me to explain?'

'Go on then,' Simmy encouraged.

'Of course, it might not be the same people at all, but it goes back to sometime after the war, when my gran was about twelve. I was going through her old photos with her on Sunday afternoon, and she was reminiscing about her schooldays. She made me write names and little notes on the backs of the pictures. We didn't come close to finishing, so I'm going back there this Sunday. It was fun, actually. There was one of her class at school, in Ambleside. Only fifteen kids in the whole class, and she told me about all of them. There was a girl called Penny Clark, and a boy called Matthew Joseph. She remembered him because he was half Jewish, but because it was his father's side, he wasn't technically a Jew. He married a girl three years older than himself, which was unusual in those days. That might be your Mrs Joseph. She'd be the right age. Matthew died in an accident when he was sixty or so.'

'I'm amazed you can remember all that,' Simmy said. 'But if it's the same people, why is the Clark girl called Penny and not Nancy?'

'Aha! That's why I remember it so well. They were twins – Penny and Nancy. But Nancy was very clever and got packed off to a better school after a couple of years with the others. Caused a lot of ill feeling, Gran said. She did some sort of fancy nursing when she left school, which sounds a bit of a disappointment, when she should have been a surgeon or astrophysicist or something. Penny gave up trying to compete and just sat at the back in all the lessons chewing gum and looking out of the window. She married a farmer up in Carlisle and had loads of children.'

'We can find out whether it's your Mrs Joseph easily enough,' said Ben, practically. 'With that much to go on, we can find out just about anything.'

Simmy felt oddly fluttery. The central fact of a link between the two elderly women was unnerving. She tried to rationalise it. 'In a place so small, you could find links between almost anybody,' she insisted. 'It doesn't mean anything.'

'And it isn't exactly a *link*, anyway,' Ben pointed out. 'In the same class at school sometime in the 1950s hardly constitutes a proper connection, does it?'

'I bet it's more than the police would ever have worked out, all the same,' flashed Melanie.

'They wouldn't be looking, would they? They're not going to be interested in Mrs Joseph, just because Simmy took her some flowers.' Ben's reasonable tone verged on the patronising.

When annoyed, Melanie's artificial eye became more noticeable, although the new one – that she had had fitted only six weeks previously – was remarkably convincing. Nonetheless, it could not match its mate for piercing scrutiny of an opponent. Ben put up his hands and apologised. 'That came out wrong,' he claimed. 'Don't get cross.'

'I'm not,' she denied.

'That's enough for now, anyway,' decreed Simmy, like a mother announcing bedtime. 'Get off home, will you.' She often felt as if the youngsters were her surrogate offspring, even though they treated her very much as an equal. Their earlier experience had been traumatic for Ben in particular, but he had recovered within days, boosted by universal praise for the way he had conducted himself.

'Wait,' Ben resisted. 'We should check this business about the unknown granddaughter. Do you have any more details? Names of Mrs Joseph's children?'

Simmy ransacked her memory. 'Davida and Nicola,' she announced with some pride. 'Mrs Joseph's daughters. Davida gave up a baby for adoption and Nicola ... didn't, I suppose. You can't find records for an adoption, can you? Surely that wouldn't be allowed?'

Ben gave her a pitying look. 'There are ways,' he said mysteriously.

'You don't know, do you?' Melanie challenged. 'I think Simmy's right. They wouldn't just give out the details to anybody who asked.'

Ben was on Simmy's computer before she could stop him. She watched as he brought up the government website pages about adoption and the form to be filled in by a person requesting information. 'You have to state that you're the person who was adopted,' he said. 'But there's no identity check, look. You just sign it at the bottom. Anybody could do that, and then say they got it wrong, if there was any bother. After all, everybody thinks they were adopted, don't they, at some stage. Usually when they're about fifteen,' he added loftily.

'Maybe so – but you have to know names and dates and places before you can start to fill in the form. And it's none of our business,' Simmy finished forcefully. She elbowed him aside and closed down the computer. 'Now go home, both of you,' she repeated. 'Ben, you must have lines to learn.'

'I know them already,' he boasted, nonetheless gathering up his school bag and drifting towards the door. 'See you sometime. You will come to the play, won't you?'

Simmy locked up and paused to admire the Christmas lights strung across the dark street and the various imaginative decorations in the shop windows. There was a timeless feel to it all, with the snowflakes and robins and grinning Santas all at their best now daylight had gone. At thirty-eight, she was already noticing how the years flew by, with Christmas coming round far too quickly – and yet every time it felt fresh and genuine, with everyone willing to throw themselves into it. Although Ben's drama teacher seemed to have badly failed to capture the spirit, if his brief description of the school play was anything to go by. Perhaps it had a redeeming message at the end, with a nod to brotherly love or the turning seasons of the year. She would ask her father, who she faintly recalled had a soft spot for George Bernard Shaw.

'Hello again,' came a gentle male voice behind her. She spun round, alarmed. In that fraction of a second, she had time to assure herself that there were still a few people on the pavements, that she was in no danger from whoever it was, that she could scream if she had to.

When she recognised the potter, Ninian Tripp, she felt ashamed of her stupid fear. 'Oh – hello,' she smiled.

'Did I startle you?' The very softness of his voice was what had done it, she realised. Almost a whisper, it carried hints of secrecy and unsettling undercurrents. If he had boomed out his welcome, she would have found him much less unnerving.

'A bit,' she admitted. 'I was thinking about Christmas.'

'Ah!' he said, with a sad expression. 'Lots of family to go to, I suppose?'

'Just my parents. How about you?'

'They exist, but I won't be seeing them. It took a long time, but we finally came to the position where we all know we're best off apart.'

She sifted this convoluted statement with a little frown. 'That's a shame,' she said.

'It's a total failure on all sides. After years of therapy, we still can't abide each other. The best we can manage is to agree that it's really nobody's fault.'

Simmy belatedly remembered Julie's remark about a break-down. The man appeared to be more than confirming the truth of this now. She imagined a schizophrenic outburst at the age of nineteen, where he ran at his mother with a knife or bashed his father with a hammer. His current gentleness was probably the result of medication. She guessed him to be about forty, probably never properly employed, in and out of mental hospitals or inadequately supervised in the community. Then, looking at him again, she discarded all these automatic stereotypes and experienced a sudden wish to know the real story.

'So, what do you do – on Christmas Day, I mean?'

He lifted one shoulder in a boyish show of unconcern. 'Nothing much. Just carry on as usual, if I can. There's always something to be fired, or glazed, or a new pattern to play with. I do tiles mainly – did I mention that?'

'No, but I heard about it on the grapevine. What sort of tiles? I mean, for bathrooms or kitchens, or what?'

He laughed. 'Anywhere you like. In Portugal they put them on the outside of their houses. They're mad about tiles over there. And there's always floors, of course.'

Simmy had never taken much interest in home decorating, although as a florist she knew she ought to think about it rather more than she did. Flowers were part of the whole business, after all. She found herself picturing a kitchen floor covered with ceramic tiles on which were painted roses and tulips. It really wouldn't work, she decided.

'And you do pots,' she reminded him. 'Vases.'

'A new line,' he nodded. 'Can I bring you some in? How about tomorrow? You did say I could.'

She couldn't remember exactly how she had left it with him the day before, but it all seemed to be moving rather rapidly. They'd been interrupted by Mrs Weaver, and then Julie had turned up, quickly followed by DI Moxon, and the vases had been forgotten. 'Did I?' she said.

He pouted reproachfully. 'Have you forgotten?'

'Not entirely. Yes, bring me some nice big ones. Maybe someone will get one for a Christmas present. You never know.'

'Thanks! I'll see you tomorrow.' And he walked away, with an uncoordinated gait that reminded her oddly of Mr Kitchener.

Chapter Six

FRIDAY MORNING WAS generally not one of Melanie's days at the shop. Her college course in hotel management included a busy timetable of lectures and tutorials on that day. The end of term also fell on this particular Friday, with none of the whirl of excitement and relaxation of schedules that Simmy remembered. 'There's a lecture in the morning, and a meeting with one of the lecturers after lunch. He's going to give us the project for next term,' she told Simmy. 'And talk over our progress so far.'

'You've got good marks, haven't you?' Simmy had occasionally helped with a piece of coursework, noticing with some concern the girl's shaky grasp of spelling and punctuation. At the same time, Melanie showed real determination to do well, regarding the eventual qualification as a reliable route out of the limited world inhabited by her family.

'Pretty good,' had been the modest response.

So Simmy juggled unaided with two new orders, five customers, decisions about the wholesale delivery and a fresh display in the window for the weekend. Every time the shop doorbell

rang, she expected to see the detective inspector, or Mr Kitchener, or someone accusing her of getting something wrong. She
felt jumpy and defensive, but unable at first to account for these
feelings. She couldn't readily identify any cause for guilt, other
than the very vaguest sense that she had overstepped a mark
with Mrs Joseph on Wednesday by asking too many questions.
This led to a slow realisation that she had stepped across it even
further by telling Melanie and Ben about the unknown granddaughter. She had betrayed a confidence, and at the time never
even noticed. The fact that an old lady had been murdered in
the same small town had somehow lifted the prohibition against
talking about customers' personal business – and that was sense-
less. No wonder she felt so uneasy, she told herself, having finally
niggled out the reason for it. If Mrs Joseph had heard the three
of them, the previous afternoon, she would inevitably have been
upset. Simmy had carelessly broken her own moral code, and
deserved to suffer for it.

She was still reproaching herself at half past ten, when the fifth
customer came in. It was Wilf Harkness, brother to Ben and one-
time boyfriend of Melanie. Simmy had barely met him, and had
to think for a moment before she could remember who he was.
'Hi,' she said cautiously, thinking it might be better to pretend
ignorance, at least to start with.

He looked past her to the back of the shop. 'Is Melanie here?'
he asked.

'Not on a Friday. She's got lectures.'

'Ah.' His disappointment was palpable.

Simmy examined his face. Grey eyes, deeply set, and a beaky
nose combined to make him look melancholy even when he
smiled. Any resemblance to Ben lay only in the shape of the head

and tone of the voice. Wilf was two years older and worked in the kitchens at a major local hotel. He had a towering ambition to be a chef, according to his brother.

'Can I give her a message? She'll be in tomorrow.'

'No, not really. I'm Wilf, in case you didn't know. I came here with Ben once.'

'I remember,' she nodded. 'It's nice to meet you again.'

'Ben thinks a lot of you.' He sounded almost wistful, and it occurred to her that he might be feeling somewhat left out, after the dramatic events in October. 'He's always talking about you.'

She laughed. 'That sounds bad. I worked out that I'm easily old enough to be his mother.'

'You don't look it,' he said gallantly. 'Ben's a geek, which means he's old before his time. You've probably noticed.'

'I don't think I'd have put it quite like that, but I know what you mean. Can you come back tomorrow, if you want to catch Melanie? She usually gets here by nine-thirty.'

'I'm not sure I'll have the courage to try again,' he said glumly. 'She's still with that Joe Wheeler, isn't she?'

'As far as I know, yes.'

'You'd know if she wasn't,' he said sagaciously. 'She'd tell you all about it, blow by blow.'

'I imagine she would,' Simmy agreed, lost for anything to offer him by way of consolation. Joe Wheeler was a ginger-haired police constable, with roughly half Melanie's IQ, as far as Simmy could tell. It seemed obvious to both her and Ben that Wilf would be a considerably better bet. In the long run, Simmy was hopeful that Melanie herself would come to realise this. Meanwhile, Wilf could very easily find somebody else – although that didn't look likely just for the moment.

'But she does love being involved with the police,' he went on. 'I can't offer anything half as exciting.'

'Exciting!' she moaned. 'That's not the kind of excitement any right-thinking person could wish for. I don't think Melanie wants anything of the sort. She might like to feel *involved*, I suppose, with a connection to what's going on—' She stopped herself, horrified at the direction her words were taking her. 'Listen to me, talking as if it was a regular occurrence. I didn't mean that at all. All that business is over with now.'

'Is it?' His grey eyes held hers. 'Ben says there's been a murder in Ambleside this week, and you three have been discussing it. If Mel can get some inside information from Joe, that's going to … you know … strengthen the bond, sort of thing.'

'It might,' she admitted. 'If Joe really did know anything, and if he was daft enough to pass it on. Sounds like cause for dismissal to me, actually. Besides,' she added emphatically, 'we none of us has any connection whatever with this new murder. We don't have to give it any thought or worry about it, or talk about it.'

'That's not what Ben says,' said Wilf.

THERE WERE TWO deliveries to be made that day, in diametrically opposite directions. Simmy had decided to leave them until lunchtime, closing the shop for an hour or so. It was something she tried not to do, but there were days when it was inevitable. The first was a traditional but expensive sheaf of red roses from a man to his wife on their anniversary. They lived just north of Newby Bridge, which would take a minimum of ten minutes to reach, and much more likely to be over fifteen. But then she could zoom along the main roads to Staveley, where the second delivery was due. It would in theory be possible to perform both visits within an hour.

The second bouquet was composed of the more exotic and flamboyant end of the floral spectrum. Gerberas in red, pink and orange were teamed with clusters of red holly berries and two peach-coloured roses. Encircling the flowers were glossy evergreen leaves. It was unsubtle, but perfect for the season. The occasion was a sixtieth birthday, but the order had added a note: 'Make it as Christmassy as you like.' Simmy had taken this as permission to go overboard on the reds.

Simmy had a liking for Staveley, where she often found herself heading for flower deliveries. The encircling hills gave the village an atmosphere of settled security and permanence that she enjoyed, and once there, having made excellent time on the roads, she habitually lingered over the task as long as possible. Only when a car tooted its horn at her, did she realise she had been driving at twenty miles an hour, peering up at the fells and generally admiring the wintry scene in the continuing sunshine.

She accelerated moderately into the village centre and found the designated house after a brief search. Making the first deliveries since that to Mrs Joseph, she was inexorably reminded of that episode. The door of the Staveley house opened inwards, she noted. The woman told her no personal details, but grasped the flowers with unambiguous delight. 'They are good to me,' she rejoiced, with no further elucidation. 'Thank you very much. Did you make it up yourself? The bouquet, I mean?'

'Yes I did.'

'It's gorgeous. You *are* clever. The roses are absolutely perfect. And the *colours*!'

'I'm glad you like them.'

'Thank you again,' said the woman, and the door was gently closed.

And a happy birthday, Simmy belatedly and silently mouthed. She still wasn't getting this delivery thing right, she suspected. Probably she should remain faceless and anonymous, just two legs on which to convey the flowers and nothing more. People didn't want anything beyond that. They wanted to revel in the scents and symbolism of the tribute, savouring the sentiment behind it, and closing out anything extraneous to that.

She drove back only slightly less slowly, convinced there was no real cause to rush. For some reason she thought of her father, nursing his injured cat. Russell Straw was a kind man, good with animals and children. She remembered that they'd been planning a walk to Garburn, which was near Kentmere, which was approached via Staveley. It all connected, both geographically and psychologically, and explained the sudden intrusion of her father into her thoughts. The area was crying out for exploration, and she had let far too many months pass without any serious efforts to gird up and get going. Now it would all have to wait, and she was annoyed with herself.

Perhaps there would be a crisp cold winter, in which walking would be perfectly feasible. And then she remembered Melanie's unsettling prediction of snow, and she sighed. However much she tried to shrug it off, she could not deny that snow frightened her. It concealed landmarks and lured people into crevasses. It fell off hillsides and buried you. It smothered sheep and cattle, and caused barn roofs to collapse. Simmy somehow knew these things, without ever having come close to experiencing them. If it hadn't been so ridiculous, she might have believed that in a previous life she had met her death in a snowdrift. As it was, she had no livestock to worry about, and even if the road from Troutbeck did become impassable by car, she could still walk down to Windermere in an hour or two. The fear was foolish, but nonetheless real for all that.

She was hungry, she noticed. Eating quite often got left out of her schedule during the week, with cooking for herself a depressing exercise best ignored. Shopping for food was a disorganised business, with no regular slot for a supermarket visit, much less ordering groceries online. She knew she was thinner than she ought to be, but saw no reason to worry about it. There was always an apple handy at this time of year, since her father passed on the surplus from his fruit trees, carefully wrapped to keep them edible through the winter. She often bought sandwiches in the high street, to have for her lunch, but had neglected to do so this morning. She could yet get something, she supposed – but found herself preferring the idea of something hot. Soup or fish pie – the sort of thing you'd get in a pub.

There wasn't really time for anything like that, unless she put on some speed. She would pass the Elleray on the way back to the shop, so that seemed the best option. With luck they'd manage to produce something quickly. Otherwise there was the Brookside, close to where her parents lived. That would take longer, as would using any of the local hotels which also offered bar and dining rooms. She was unaccustomed to dropping into pubs unaccompanied, but had no qualms about doing so. People knew her, and seemed to like her. She might find someone to talk to.

In the event, she met someone she knew even before she'd got inside the building. The stretch of street where parking was permitted offered a convenient space, and she quickly grabbed it. Then she became aware of a blue Volvo that parked behind her. A man got out and waited for her to do likewise. 'Hello again,' said DI Moxon.

'Were you following me?'

'Of course not. Or only for the last minute or two. I remembered something else I wanted to ask you.'

'I'm in a rush. I've only got twenty minutes at most. The shop's already been shut for over an hour.'

'Come on, then. We'll have lunch together. This a regular watering hole for you, then?'

'Actually, no. I've only been a few times. I was hoping they might have some fish pie. I got a craving just now.'

He gave her a look that could only be described as quizzical. She could not imagine what had brought it about. 'What?' she said.

'When a woman mentions a craving, I always imagine she must be pregnant.'

'Huh!' she snorted, trying to quell the flash of pain caused by the remark. Insensitive beast, she thought. He knew about her stillborn baby – she had told him about it on their very first meeting. Obviously, he had forgotten all about it.

'Time for my lunch, too,' he went on obliviously. 'Can I join you?'

'I suppose so. But I really do have to be quick. I can't close the shop for long without risking losing customers.'

The man behind the bar clearly knew exactly who the detective was, and became galvanised when he said they hoped they could provide a swift lunch. 'Lucky there's no Christmas party on today,' Simmy remarked, looking round at the numerous empty tables. 'I hadn't thought of that.'

'There's one this evening,' said the barman. 'Local undertaker and all their staff.'

'The undertaker's ball,' said Moxon with a laugh. 'That should be a riot.'

'They're lovely people,' said the man, with a slight sniff. Simmy was glad to see that Moxon was managing to annoy others as well as her.

They sat at a corner table, Simmy drinking beer and Moxon sticking conscientiously to fruit juice. She had been cheered to find they could supply a fish pie, and he ordered steak and chips. They carefully paid separately, in advance. He was already questioning her, long before the food arrived. 'Has the Kitchener man approached you?'

'Actually, yes. He came into the shop yesterday to thank me. He didn't stay long.'

'He owes you.'

'Anybody would have done just as well as me. He was lucky I remembered him.'

'He was, wasn't he?' He leant forward. 'Is there any chance at all that he could have known you'd be going to that café in advance, and positioned himself where you'd see him?'

'None whatsoever. I didn't know myself. Normally I'd just have driven straight back here after making a delivery. I just fancied a quick coffee, for once.'

'Hmm.'

'You really want to pin this on him, don't you?'

He shook his head reproachfully. 'It's not like that. Not at all.'

'So why this persistence? It obviously wasn't him. Ben says—' She stopped herself with a gulp. What was she thinking of? At best, Moxon would think her an idiot for discussing police procedure with a seventeen-year-old boy.

But it was too late. 'Ben? Would that be young Mr Harkness, by any chance? You've talked this over with him, have you?'

'He saw me leaving the police station, and wanted to know what it was all about.'

'And you told him.' The detective sighed.

'Why shouldn't I?'

'We do try to keep these things under wraps. It doesn't help the investigation if it's common knowledge who we've been questioning. We've had very good cooperation from the press so far.' He sighed again. 'Not that it's a very newsworthy murder, I suppose.'

'Ben won't tell anybody. And he might even help. He is very clever.'

'So what were you going to say, when you stopped? Something that the boy said.'

'Well – just that you must have information about Mrs Clark's being alive that morning, shortly before you found her. I mean, you must know the time of death quite accurately.' She found herself struggling for words. She couldn't say *the body must have still been warm* or anything so graphic. Ben would have had no such hesitation, with his predilection for gruesome TV series and forensic interests. When Simmy let herself think about even the peripheral realities of a murder, she felt sick. Crushed skulls, flowing blood, gasps for air or shrieks of pain all made her shudder.

'You know her name?'

'Didn't you tell me?'

'I might have done. But she was *Miss* Clark, not Mrs.'

'Right. I remember. Melanie said it was on TV last night, in the news. They gave her name. And her granny was at school with her sister,' she added, unable to resist scoring a point.

'What? Whose granny?'

'Melanie's. They all know each other, apparently. Penny Clark was in the same class as Mel's mother's mother. Nancy was her twin, but she went to a different school.'

'Penny is Mrs Hopkins now. Married to a farmer with five children. One of them's in jail.'

'Really? What did he do?'

'She, actually. She killed a child on the road. Drunk driving. Got three years for it.'

Simmy winced. 'How awful!'

'Miss Clark was her aunt.'

'Yes. I see.' A thought struck her. 'The child wasn't Mr Kitchener's, was it?'

Moxon smiled and gave a slow head shake. 'No connection with him at all. The connection with Miss Clark was through his mother.'

'Who died a few weeks ago.'

'Right.'

The food arrived and they ate quickly. Simmy reviewed their conversation. 'What else did you want to ask me? Surely it wasn't just whether Mr K had seen me again?'

'I was wondering what you thought of him. How well you knew him. Exactly what he said to you on Wednesday morning. We got a bit sidetracked,' he apologised. 'As we so often seem to do.'

'Do we?' The *we* gave her pause. Did he think of her as in some special sort of relationship with him? Was there more going on than she had suspected? She had no idea whether he was married or not; she had liked him to start with, although there had never been anything of a sexual attraction. He had told her she was unusual, with a useful approach to police enquiries. Did he think she was encouraging him? *Was* she?

'Well?' he prompted.

'Oh! Well, I felt sorry for him. He took his mother's death very hard. I get the impression he's lonely. He's divorced and there was no mention of anyone else on his flowers. I mean, they were just from him. He spent a lot on them. He looks thin, don't you think? And a bit grubby. Not looking after himself too well. He was

Mrs ... *Miss* Clark's lodger for a while. Then I assume he moved in with his mum, maybe because they both felt they needed to be looked after. He'd do the DIY jobs and she'd do the ironing and all that sort of thing. How am I doing?'

He made a face, suggesting it was much as he'd expected. 'He's not the only one who looks thin. That fish thing's good, is it?'

She had finished it within five minutes, as well as draining her beer. 'Lovely, thanks. Now, I really have to go. Good luck with everything. It sounds like rather a muddle.'

'It is,' he agreed. 'And I can't pretend you've helped at all.'

'I did my best,' she defended, before grasping that he was joking. Or was he? She probably *hadn't* helped, if he was still hoping to pin the crime on Mr Kitchener. But it had been an essentially amicable conversation, until this last remark. Was she angry with her? It was difficult to read him, as he continued to sit at the table when she got up. Even after several encounters, he still seemed alien, a man from another world. She could not imagine touching his skin or handling his clothes. There was an invisible patina to him that was not quite greasy or repellent, but which put him beyond any wish for closer contact. It was, she believed, mainly due to his job. Just as you hesitated to shake hands with an undertaker, you were reluctant to get inside the mind of a man who devoted his life to catching criminals. They both inhabited a shadowy realm that ordinary mortals preferred to ignore. She thought again of Melanie and her Constable Joe, and wondered whether the girl had come close to any of these same resistances. And if not yet, would she ever?

'Thank you,' he said heavily.

'Bye, then.' She left him finishing his chips and trotted hurriedly to her car.

NOBODY WAS WAITING on the doorstep when she got back to the shop, which made her feel she had rushed for no good reason. Where was Ninian Tripp with his vases, for one thing? She admitted to herself that she had been anticipating his return ever since she'd opened at nine o'clock. His grey eyes and clear skin had made a far more positive impression on her than DI Moxon had done. Ninian was somehow *wholesome*, despite his troubled background and undercurrents of desperation. He had a sweet smile and scruffy clothes, and a faintly earthy scent that was probably clay. Ninian made things come alive under his hands, like God fashioning Adam. Moxon sniffed out guilty secrets and confronted people at their worst. While knowing it was unfair to compare them, Simmy found herself doing exactly that.

The next person to come into the shop was a complete surprise on a number of levels. Simmy's initial reaction was to anticipate reproach of some sort. The next was acute curiosity. Finally, she felt concern. Here was trouble, she realised. 'Hello,' she said quietly. 'Mrs Joseph, isn't it?'

Chapter Seven

THE WOMAN LOOKED older and sadder than she had on Wednesday. Then she had shown an animated array of emotions, one of them being a kind of excitement. She had permitted Simmy to share some of her personal details, at least at first. Now she stood pathetically just inside the door and blinked as if unsure of where she was, or why.

'This is Persimmon Petals?' she quavered. 'I came on the bus, you see.'

'Is there something the matter?' She wanted to add *with the flowers*, but stopped herself. That would be too defensive, as well as much too trivial. Mrs Joseph was worrying about something far deeper than the condition of a bunch of flowers. And yet they *had* been substandard. Comprised of week-old carnations and dahlias, with lacklustre greenery, she had known from the start they were unworthy. Just because the Candida girl had insisted on spending less than twenty pounds, Simmy had lowered her own standards unforgivably.

'Well, in a way.' The old lady lifted her chin in an valiant attempt to be dignified. 'The flowers – do you remember? From my grand-daughter, it said.'

'And you thought they were from the one who was adopted? Yes, I remember.'

'It seems I was wrong. That girl died. My daughter has known for years, but never told me. My granddaughter got breast cancer and died, when she was thirty-six. She'd be forty-two now. Imagine that!'

Again, Simmy wrestled with the mental arithmetic. Mrs Joseph's daughters were likely to be mid to late fifties at most. If one of them had a daughter forty-two years ago, she'd have been about sixteen at the time. Not so terribly unusual, of course, but highly likely to carry elements of real tragedy hidden in the detail. 'How old are your daughters?' she found herself asking. Any more of these calculations, and she'd give herself a headache.

'Davy is fifty-nine and Nicola is fifty-three. Davy had the baby when she was seventeen. Nobody forced her to give it up. I wouldn't like you to think that. It was not especially shameful or secret. Her father was upset, of course – what man wouldn't be, even now? She was so young, still his baby girl, in his eyes. The boy wasn't much older. He'd nothing to say for himself. Davy saw right through him, and knew he'd never be any use. She wanted to be a radiographer. She'd wanted it ever since she broke her leg when she was ten, and got so fascinated by the x-ray machines. The baby went to a good home, and nothing more was ever said about her.'

'Did Davy have more children?'

'A boy, when she was thirty-one. Stephen.'

'And Nicola?'

The old lady's face tightened, her mouth a thin line. 'I don't see a lot of her. She's opted for a very unsavoury way of life. I'm afraid I no longer know what to say to her.'

Simmy could think of no constructive answer to this. 'Oh dear,' she mumbled.

'The thing is, dear, I've come to ask for your help. Davy says there's been a mistake somewhere and the flowers came to the wrong person. She says there's no way in the world that I can have an unknown granddaughter. She vows black and blue that it has nothing to do with her – quite cross about it, she was. And Nicola – well, let's just say she'd never have come close to getting herself in the family way. The idea is simply ludicrous, as Davy said.'

'A mistake?' Simmy shook her head. 'I really can't see ... I mean, couldn't it be that Nicola was, well – *forced*, somehow?'

'Raped, you mean? And made pregnant? I did think of that. But I would have *known*. I would have been told. I've gone over and over it in my mind, and there really isn't any way that she could have gone through a pregnancy. She only lives in Keswick and my brother lives a few streets away. She gets on well with his wife – always has. She's a real peacemaker, is Sally. A very dear woman. She'd have let me know if there'd been anything ... I phoned her yesterday, just to make sure. She *vowed* there'd never been any hint of a baby. They've seen Nicola at least once a month since she left home. Sally laughed at the very idea.'

'All the same ...' Simmy floundered. 'I suppose it could have been some awful kind of joke.'

Mrs Joseph seized on this eagerly. 'Yes! It could, couldn't it? People do horrible things like that sometimes, don't they? Will you tell me, then, who it was that ordered the flowers? You must have a name, or phone number or something. How did they pay? You *have* to tell me something. It's driving me mad, you see. I can't sleep. And they weren't even very *nice* flowers,' she added, with the long-expected note of reproach.

'I can't tell you anything. I'm really sorry, but it would be the most outrageous breach of confidence.'

'I do understand that. But, you see, I've been thinking about it. Surely she *wanted* me to trace her? Why would she make such a gesture in the first place? And how did she know it was my birthday? It's all so mysterious. I had an idea. Do you think you could forward a letter to her, from me? That's what the adoption people do, you know. Then she can reply to me directly, if she wants to.'

'I don't think I've got her address,' lied Simmy, feeling terrible.

'But you could get it, I'm sure.'

'Besides – she's got *your* address,' Simmy remembered, in relief. 'I think she'll approach you herself, if she's genuine, and it's not just a trick or a joke.'

'But her *name*. You know her name.'

'I can't give it to you.' It was anguish to be so unaccommodating. She felt like a stiff public servant brushing off an importunate applicant for extra funds. 'I really am very sorry. I can understand how you must feel, but if you're absolutely sure that it isn't possible that you've got a granddaughter, then you should try to forget all about it. There is a chance, I suppose, that it's part of a confidence trick – that she's out to get your money or something. You probably ought to be careful.'

This wasn't helpful, she realised. 'You mean, I should tell the police about it?' Disbelief made Mrs Joseph's jaw go slack. 'Surely not!'

'Well, it's up to you. Perhaps not unless something else happens.'

'If I did, and they took it seriously, they'd question you about it and you'd have to give the person's name to the police, wouldn't you?'

'Probably,' Simmy said, impressed at the clarity of the old woman's thinking. She wondered whether she herself would have been so competent under the same circumstances. 'But I'm not sure they would take it very seriously, as it stands. After all, the only thing that's happened is that you've been sent some flowers. I'm just saying you might be wise to watch out for anything else that might happen.'

Mrs Joseph went very pale. 'Like being murdered, you mean,' she said in a muffled voice. 'I heard what happened to Nancy Clark.'

'Did you know her?'

'Not really. I think there was some vague connection between my husband and her sister Penny. Nancy sent a rambling letter of condolence when he died. Something about a school reunion in the 1970s. I had no idea what she was talking about. It almost sounded as if she was hinting at an affair between them.'

'How very nasty.'

'She never married. I think she must have got bitter and twisted. Some women do, you know.'

Simmy made a mental resolve that it wouldn't happen to her. Mrs Joseph went on, 'Perhaps that explains why she got herself murdered, don't you think? She must have been rude to somebody and they lost all control. If that was what happened, there'd be no need for anyone else to worry, would there? No need to keep looking over our shoulders, waiting for a madman to attack.'

'I'm sure there isn't,' said Simmy confidently. 'I didn't mean that, anyway. The flowers can't have anything at all to do with Miss Clark, can they?'

'Of course not,' the woman agreed. 'I don't know why I brought the subject up. It's just all those policemen in town, you can't get away from it.'

If anything, Simmy was quite glad of the diversion. She had managed to fend off Mrs Joseph's demands for information, while letting her speak freely about her situation. The old lady had grown in stature and confidence during the conversation, showing herself to be fully functional mentally, and quite robust physically. She had been landed with a major mystery, and had tackled it intelligently. Simmy decided that she liked Mrs Joseph and she suspected the feeling was mutual.

'Well, I won't keep you any longer. You've made a lovely job of this shop, haven't you?' She looked around with little nods of approval. 'And if you do change your mind about giving me that person's name – well, you know where I am.'

'Right.'

Simmy watched her go with a sense of having allowed principles to dominate normal human decency. She wasn't sure what she might have lost by giving Candida Hawkins' name to the woman she claimed was her grandmother. It might even have been what the girl wanted and expected – a devious way of making contact, for which she could subsequently disclaim responsibility. If so, then Simmy had no wish to act as go-between, without knowing a lot more of the implications.

All the same, it was a preferable mystery to that of who had killed Nancy Clark, and why. Even if it was a scam of some kind, it had the merit of originality. And she had no serious qualms that Mrs Joseph ran any risk of becoming the next murder victim.

BEN CALLED IN again that afternoon, talking almost before he was inside the door. 'That adoption business,' he began. 'I've been thinking about it.'

'Well don't. I've had the granny lady in today, and she says there's no chance whatever that it's really a grandchild of hers. One daughter swears blind that it's not hers, and the other apparently never had anything to do with men, and couldn't possibly have got pregnant.'

Ben blushed briefly, but was undeterred. 'But what if it's her *husband's* grandchild? I mean – that would more or less make her the grandma, wouldn't it? He's quite likely to have unknown children somewhere.'

'He's dead, Ben. He's been dead for years and years.'

'All the more reason they'd go to her, then. They'll be after the inheritance. She'll have got his money, won't she?'

'If there was any. It's only a small house. She doesn't look very rich to me. Plus there are two daughters who'll get everything when she goes. Although she might have left Nicola out of her will, by the sound of it. She doesn't seem very fond of Nicola.'

'Well, it's still a good theory,' he insisted.

'I don't think it is. Why now?'

'Maybe the old girl's been ill lately.'

Simmy did her best to give the matter her full consideration. For one thing, she had no wish to hurt Ben's feelings by dismissing his ideas, and for another, she found herself intrigued by the whole experience. 'Actually,' she said, 'it *might* have some mileage to it. Mrs J said there was something between that Penny Clark Melanie told us about, and Mr Joseph. Something about a school reunion in the seventies, and a card that came after he died.'

'There you are, then!' he triumphed. 'So this is a secret love child, coming to claim its rightful dues.'

'It has to be the child of the love child,' Simmy corrected him. 'Which seems rather remote to me.'

'No, no,' he argued. 'Think about it. If you suddenly discovered that your parent – mother, probably – had been adopted, after a lifetime of secrecy, you'd want to know who the original parents were, wouldn't you?'

'Um … Would I? I'd probably think it was none of my business. And where's the adopted mother in all this, anyway?'

'She could be dead, or emigrated or something. *Plus*,' he added with great emphasis, 'it leads straight to a connection with the murder! You'll have to tell the Moxo man about it.'

'No, wait. What if the daughter that was adopted – that is, Mrs J's granddaughter, child of Davida – had a child? That would be possible. It would fit quite easily, in fact. Then this would be a *great*-granddaughter.'

'Hey – that's brilliant! I bet the cops would never think of that.'

'They would, if they thought it was important. But it's not, Ben. It's our own private little mystery, nothing to do with the police. I mean, what would I say if I did go to the inspector with it? You think I should tell him about the message on the flowers, I get that. But there isn't anything else, is there?'

'I suppose the rest of it is all hearsay,' he agreed thoughtfully. Ben was especially interested in the nuances of evidence and the delicate game the law required police prosecutors to play. 'But they can check most of it,' he concluded.

'How can they? The only hard fact is Mrs Joseph's name and address. I think it would be mean to bring her to their attention. Poor old thing – she's obviously got nothing at all to do with the murder.'

Ben ignored her. 'I wonder whether she knows your Mr Kitchener?' he mused. 'That would connect everything up beautifully.'

'*How* would it? We already decided, with Melanie, that in a small town everybody's going to be connected, anyway. None of it helps catch a murderer. If you go back fifty years, you'll probably find that everybody in Ambleside has got some sort of motive for killing everybody else in town.'

'We're not interested in *everybody*. Just a few. After all,' he said patiently, 'somebody really did kill the old girl. They must have *had* a reason.'

In spite of herself, Simmy knew she was hooked. She admired her young friend's cleverness; even his unemotional approach to events that she found wrenching helped her to get some perspective. But a dash of compassion would not have gone amiss, all the same. Ben was clearly destined for a great career as a forensic pathologist or something of the sort – no doubt achieving brilliant results, thanks to his great intellect. It would just be nice if he acknowledged that there was pain and fear, disgust and despair somewhere in the story as well.

'We shouldn't be getting ahead of ourselves without Melanie,' she decided. 'She'll never forgive us if we leave her out. Besides, we need her for all the background stuff. That's where her real strength lies. She *knows* everybody.'

'So do I,' he said. 'I've lived here all my life, same as she has.'

'Yes, but she's actually related to most of them.' *And she's much more interested in the personal stuff*, she could have added, but didn't. Instead she said, 'Wilf was here this morning, you know. He was looking for her.'

Ben groaned. 'Don't tell me,' he pleaded, in a poor attempt at adult cynicism. Then he performed another change of subject. 'I got you that ticket. For the play on Saturday, remember?' He rooted in his school bag for some time, before producing a crumpled scrap of paper.

'Oh, thanks. How much is it?'

'Have it on the house,' he said. 'You're in the second row.'

'Great. I'm looking forward to it. It's the only thing I've got booked between now and Christmas.' She remembered DI Moxon's joke about the undertakers' ball, and thought whimsically of a florists' party, with everyone in fancy dress representing some kind of flower.

'My parents are throwing a big bash next week,' he said gloomily. 'With about fifty friends and neighbours. It'll be madness.'

'Do they make you serve the canapés?'

'No way. They make me *talk* to people. And all anyone does is ask me about school, and which universities I've applied to and what career I've chosen. Then they glaze over when I tell them.'

'Why? What *do* you tell them?'

He looked at her. 'Don't you know?'

She frowned. 'Come to think of it, I'm not sure I ever asked you for details. I just assumed you'd applied for various science courses.' She had a faint recollection of some sort of enquiry when she first met him, but had no memory of the reply.

'I've got a firm place at UCL to do forensic archaeology, from next October. Got the letter this week.'

'Blimey! And you never said anything. Isn't that very early to get accepted? I seem to remember it all happens in February and March. Has it all changed since my day?'

He shrugged self-effacingly. 'It's a sort of fast-track thing. I did all the paperwork last year, and ... well, sidestepped a few of the procedures. It's complicated.'

She cocked her head at him. 'You're telling me you're so darn clever they've accepted you a year earlier than anyone else. Does Melanie know about this?'

'More or less. I keep telling you about *Bones*, remember? Well, I wanted to go and study in the States, so I wrote to a couple of places. They said I should at least do the first degree here.'

'I see,' said Simmy, not entirely truthfully. 'All this is because of a TV series? What do your parents think about that?'

'They're cool about it. Why wouldn't they be?'

She knew when she was beaten. 'Home time,' she announced. 'Have a nice weekend.'

Chapter Eight

ON SATURDAY MORNING Melanie was waiting outside the shop when Simmy arrived to open up. So was Mr Kitchener. 'Am I late?' she asked, already quite sure she was not.

'Not really,' said her assistant. 'I got a lift from my dad, because Pete's got the car, and Dad wanted to get somewhere.'

Mr Kitchener had evidently shaved carefully and chosen a clean set of clothes. He smiled nervously at her, and stood back while she unlocked the door and deactivated the alarm.

'What can I do for you?' Simmy asked him briskly. The word *stalker* had whispered itself into her mind's ear, at the sight of him. Melanie plainly had something of the same suspicion.

'Miss Clark's funeral,' he said. 'I should send some flowers.'

'Okay. But there won't be a date set for it yet, surely? Don't they delay it for months after a murder?'

'Not if it's a burial,' he mumbled. 'As far as I know, they generally release the body soon after the post-mortem. That's if they feel sure there won't be any further need for examination. I think that's right.'

'Even so – with Christmas coming, I very much doubt whether it'll be before the New Year. And you know it'll be a burial, do you?'

He shook his head. 'I don't even know who'll be arranging it, for sure. I thought – perhaps you could let me know, when you have the date? I discovered when my mother died that the under-takers tell the florists the date and time. Makes sense, when you think about it.' He forced another uncertain smile.

'It'll be her sister, won't it?' said Melanie. Simmy tried in vain to flash her a warning look. It struck her as ill-advised to volun-teer any information concerning the murder victim – especially to a man who had been under police investigation as the possible killer.

But it was too late. 'Sister?' he said quickly. 'You mean Penny? But she's practically bedridden with Parkinson's. I doubt if she'd be up to it. She's got plenty of children, of course. They could take some of the responsibility.'

Melanie raised her eyebrows, replying airily, 'And for all we know, the Clark lady's got a son or daughter somewhere. Who can say?'

'She was unmarried and in her late seventies,' he said. 'I hardly think that's very likely.'

'Well *somebody* will make the arrangements, I'm sure,' said Simmy. 'I suggest you phone me during the first week of January, and see if I've heard anything. Of course, it's quite common these days for funerals not to accept any flowers.'

'And why do you want to send some anyway?' Melanie blurted. 'It sounds as if you barely knew her.'

'I knew her very well, actually, several years ago.'

'You were her lodger,' Simmy remembered. 'Of course!'

Melanie threw a furious glance at her boss, who grimaced in apology. She must remember later to tell the girl that Mr K himself had revealed this fact. Melanie hated to be left in ignorance. Mr Kitchener nodded vaguely. 'Well ... thank you,' he mumbled. 'If you'd just let me know, then?'

'Yes, all right,' Simmy agreed.

When he had gone, she and Melanie exchanged looks. 'Was that a bit weird?' asked Simmy. 'He knows the family, so why ask us about the funeral?'

'I don't like him,' said Melanie. 'He's creepy.'

'I feel rather sorry for him, actually. I can't believe there's any harm to him. But I do wish people would stop coming here about Nancy Clark.' She sighed. 'It really isn't any of our business. I'm more interested in Mrs Joseph, to be honest. I'm a lot more involved with her – and I *like* her. I want to help solve her mystery. It might actually have a happy ending, which makes a nice change.'

'Okay,' said Melanie, with surprising compliance. 'Then we should try and find the daughters. The unmarried one should be possible to track down. Where does she live? How old is she?'

Simmy supplied answers to both questions, feeling rather pleased with herself, although the 'tracking down' remark worried her. 'We can't just follow people about and demand to know their personal details,' she objected.

'Obviously,' scoffed Melanie, 'but we can ask my gran what she knows about them.'

'She sounds miraculous,' Simmy marvelled. 'How many people does she know?'

'She can rattle off names, ages, jobs, offspring, place of residence for *hundreds*. I tried to add them all up, a little while ago, but it was hopeless. Everyone she was at school with or worked with; the entire WI membership; neighbours; all my mum's friends' families – and all the rest. People she meets in shops will tell her their life story while they wait at the checkout. And she remembers every detail. It's what she does – a sort of life work. She's just madly interested in everybody.'

'I should meet her sometime.'

'Oh, you *have* met her. She's been in here a few times, for flowers. But she'd never have said who she was. She's shy like that.'

'But ...' Simmy was lost for words. Which old lady could it have been, she wondered? Various candidates flitted past her mind's eye. 'Well, just tell her to make sure she introduces herself another time.'

'I can't make her. She'll worry that you'll talk about me, and she wouldn't like that.'

'Why on earth not? What does she think I'll say?'

'She'd be embarrassed whatever it was.' Melanie made an impatient gesture. 'I don't think I can explain it to you. She's old-fashioned, that's all. People around here don't like to hear praise of their family. It's like bad luck or boasting.'

Simmy knew when to give up. She had some grasp of Melanie's family situation – the brightest child of a large brood, accustomed to having to fight for everything she had. The car she shared with an older brother; the clothes she had to hide from a predatory younger sister. Her mother barely functioned and her father, while nominally present, was actually away on building projects a lot of the time. Melanie had stuck at schoolwork to an unprecedented degree, and was now causing wholesale amazement in Todd circles by doggedly attending a course at a college that was so awkward to reach that she sometimes did the journey by bicycle.

'I see,' she said. 'Sort of.' She cast around the shop for a new topic, hoping a customer might come in and divert them. Her gaze fell on the tiers of bright poinsettias near the door and she was reminded of something. 'Hey! That Ninian chap never came back. He said he was bringing some vases, yesterday. He never showed.'

'You told him he could, then?'

'I couldn't see why not. It sounded quite a nice idea. He was so *keen*. I wonder what happened to him.'

'Unreliable,' said Melanie succinctly.

Before Simmy could defend the man she had instantly liked, the shop doorbell pinged and three women walked in. They comprised a crowd in the narrow space between displays and Melanie automatically retreated towards the back room. 'Good morning,' Simmy greeted them, thinking they'd come for funeral flowers. There was that sort of air about them.

'Are you the proprietor?' asked the foremost one. She was slim, a faded blonde, wearing a black coat well covered with white hairs. Owner of a moulting dog or cat, Simmy concluded.

'That's right. What can I do for you?'

'It's about my mother. Mary Joseph.'

A suppressed giggle told Simmy that Melanie was still close by, listening eagerly. 'Mary – her first name's Mary?' Perhaps it was only because of the season that the name seemed so laughable.

'Yes it is. As if that had any bearing. We've come to ask you about those damned flowers.'

'You must be Davy,' said Simmy thoughtlessly. 'Is that right?'

The woman clenched her jaw. 'She's been telling you all about us, then, has she? When will she ever learn?'

'Too late now, Dave.' A second woman had spoken up, and everyone looked at her. She was more substantial than the first, and darker. Her hair was curly and unkempt. 'I'm Nicola,' she explained. 'And this is Gwen.' Gwen was tall and smartly dressed, older than the other two. There was a look of intelligence about her, as if she were a legal advisor or impartial observer. She gave a generalised smile in Simmy's direction.

'Gwen's my partner,' Nicola went on, with a faint suggestion of challenge that told Simmy she meant life partner, rather than business.

'Anyway,' continued Davy, 'we need you to tell us exactly who it was who sent those flowers. They've caused untold trouble in the family. Somebody's making mischief for some reason, and you have a duty to disclose their identity.'

'I don't think I do.' Simmy stood her ground. 'It strikes me that that would only cause a lot *more* trouble. The best thing would be just to forget all about it.'

'Not possible. The genie is out of the bottle. That baby I had adopted has come back to haunt us, after all these years. She died, you know. Can you imagine how that makes me feel?'

Simmy resisted the urge to tell her own tragic story, in direct response to the question. It was, after all, very different. 'Not really,' she said. 'Neither does it persuade me to break my customer's confidentiality.'

'You told my mother it was probably some kind of swindle. Somebody after her money – what there is of it. Or trying to get back at her for something in the past.'

'If there's no possibility of a granddaughter, then that's the only explanation I can think of.'

Davy fell silent. Gwen stepped forward, a hand on Nicola's shoulder. 'How did this person know it was Mary's birthday? How did they know her address? Why would they single her out? What possible *reason* could there be?' She stared intently into Simmy's face, as if willing the answers to fall from her lips.

'What about your father? Mr Joseph? It occurred to us that it might be about him – a child he had without realising.'

'You accuse my father of adultery,' said Davy softly.

Simmy spread her hands in defeat. 'It makes sense as a theory.'

'Except he was the most dearly devoted husband any woman could ever wish for. And any suggestion like that could only upset my mother even more deeply than she is already.'

'Poor old Mum,' sighed Nicola. 'She thinks I had a baby without telling her, somehow. She's been imagining all sorts of nonsense about rape or drunken orgies when I was twenty. However she thinks I'd have found time to produce a sprog, I have no idea.' She gave a choked sort of laugh. 'It's not funny, I know, but it certainly is ludicrous.' Gwen patted her shoulder.

'Well, I'm very sorry to have been part of this whole mess, but I'm still not prepared to give you the name.' With a pang of guilt, Simmy thought about how close she and Melanie had come to googling the flower sender themselves. That now struck her as a very wrong thing to have done. 'I honestly can't see that it would do any good to anybody. If she's genuine, surely she'll get in touch again, anyway. The flowers might have just been a sort of advance warning.'

All three women pulled sceptical faces. Gwen gave a faint snort. 'She's *not* genuine,' said Davy. 'We're certain of that. At best, it's mistaken identity. You know how easy it is to get the wrong person these days, on those ancestry websites. It's all so horribly public – you can apply for birth certificates and adoption information for absolutely anybody. This poor girl might have been given false facts at the outset. The central point is, she is not my mother's grandchild, and she's caused a lot of distress by claiming that she is.'

It was a long and forceful speech, which Simmy listened to carefully. Somewhere deep down, she was still grappling for a link between Mrs Joseph and Nancy Clark that would bring the two apparently distinct stories together. Melanie and Ben had both seized on this, almost automatically. And yet there didn't seem any real logic to it. The two women only peripherally knew each other. The only present-day connection was Simmy, who had seen the former shortly before meeting the man suspected of killing the latter. That was ridiculously flimsy as a link – except that the mystery of the self-professed granddaughter carried so many sinister implications that it felt important.

She became aware of Melanie rustling something behind her. The girl had been uncharacteristically quiet throughout the conversation, but there was no doubt that she had heard it all, and would have plenty to say at some stage. When a new customer came in, Mel quickly moved forward to greet him. It was a man in his fifties, wanting a poinsettia, uninterested in any discussion about it. He edged past the group of women in the middle of the shop, and paid with cash. He left with his head down, as if embarrassed at having entered a florist shop at all. It was a far from unusual pattern. Men and flowers were an abidingly uneasy mixture, which Simmy mainly found amusing, but sometimes regarded with exasperation.

She returned her attention to Davy. 'It is quite public,' she agreed, picking up on the detail that seemed most likely to let her off the hook. 'We'll have to hope she's gone back to her searches and realised her mistake.'

Again, a triple expression of scepticism greeted her, but she stood her ground. 'I'm afraid I really can't help you any further,' she said.

'It's much as I expected,' said Nicola. 'I told you, didn't I?' she addressed her sister. 'At least we tried.'

'Poor old Mum,' Davy sighed. 'Thank goodness there's Christmas to take her mind off it. We'll have to make a special effort this year.'

'Of course, if we went to the police, they could force you to reveal the person's identity,' said Gwen.

'Oh, no!' Nicola protested, with a look at Simmy that was almost pleading. 'We don't want to start making threats like that, do we? Can't we keep it all civilised?'

'And without some very good grounds for suspicion, they wouldn't do that anyway,' said Simmy tightly. 'Simply sending flowers to somebody isn't a crime. The message carries no hint of a threat. I wouldn't have agreed to deliver it, if it had.'

'We're not *accusing* you of anything,' Davy snapped, losing patience. 'We'd just really like to know what this whole fiasco is about. It's a big thing, after all, being told you've got a close relative you knew nothing about.'

'We're not getting anywhere, Davy,' Nicola said. 'We've done all we can. Let's leave it now, shall we?'

'It's all right for you, isn't it? Nobody seriously imagines that *you* had a secret child. All attention's on me, because everybody thinks if I could do it once, I could do it again. I can see Mum thinking exactly that. Bernie and Stephen are going to start acting all suspicious, if they get to hear about it. I can deny it until I'm black in the face, and they'll never be entirely sure.'

'So don't tell them,' said Gwen calmly. 'Just let it all fade away naturally. If this pest doesn't make any more approaches, then we'll know it was either a stupid joke or a mistake, and we can forget the whole thing.'

Nicola put a hand on the older woman's arm. 'Thank you, love. You always say the most sensible things. She's right, Davy, you know she is.'

'Doesn't look as if we've got much choice,' grumbled Davy. She looked hard at Simmy. 'Since we've not had any cooperation here.'

Simmy smiled weakly and said nothing. She kept reminding herself that she would probably behave in much the same way if the roles were reversed. She worried that if they stayed much longer, she would hand over the darned name just to see an end to the matter. She was trying not to repeat 'Candida Hawkins' to herself, for fear the words would slip out into the open air of their own accord.

But they were leaving. First Nicola made for the door, followed by Gwen and Davy. Not one of them looked back, until the first two were outside. Then Davy turned and nodded, in a wordless valediction that contained reproach, frustration and a smidgeon of respect.

'Phew!' sighed Melanie. 'You were awesome, Sim. Really stuck to your guns. I don't suppose they'll be back any time soon.'

'I hope not,' said Simmy, feeling rather shaky. 'I just wish that damned girl hadn't chosen me to deliver those wretched flowers.'

Melanie gave a sympathetic grimace. Then she said, 'And then Mr Kitchener wouldn't have got his alibi, and we wouldn't have given a thought to the murder. Ben wouldn't like that. So one person is happy, anyway.'

'It's not really on for Ben to interfere with real murder investigations,' Simmy worried. 'I never should have told him about it.'

Melanie did a rare but unnerving trick of rolling her good eye, while the prosthetic one simply wobbled slightly. It left a person in no doubt that they were being treated to censure. 'Come on, Sim!

Ben's in his element. He's not *interfering*. The police have no idea he knows anything.'

'I might believe you if he hadn't marched into the middle of everything last time. As it is, I wouldn't put it past him to go knocking on doors and asking questions.'

'Whose doors? We don't know anybody who was connected with Nancy Clark.'

'What about her sister? And all her offspring?'

'Yeah, but they all live miles away. And who else? There's nobody else. And Ben doesn't even know the precise cause of death.'

Something in her expression alerted Simmy. 'But you do, right? Joe's told you?'

'Not really. It wasn't anything as crude as a bash on the head, though. It was nastier than that. Something sneaky and clever. He's dying to tell me, but they've told him not to.'

'Oh dear. Why are we talking about it again? I don't even want to think about Mrs Joseph and her annoying grandchild, either. I quite liked those daughters. I hate being part of something that's got them so upset.'

Before Melanie could argue, a couple came in, wanting to order flowers for a spring wedding. For twenty minutes, Simmy was immersed in their wild ideas for a hundred lilac rosebuds and lavish sheaves of ripe corn, trying to explain that the former would be extremely expensive and the latter unobtainable in May. 'I know that,' said the bride, about the expense, but looked blank about the natural season for wheat and barley. 'But I want it to symbolise fertility and abundance,' she said without a blush.

'We could probably find some grasses that had gone to seed,' said Simmy doubtfully. 'But they might have to be imported.'

The future bridegroom looked weary and bemused. 'I think it'd look daft anyway,' he muttered. 'I keep telling her.'

'*All* flowers symbolise fertility,' Simmy tried to explain. 'And a spring wedding is usually a time for blossom and buds, suggesting future fruitfulness.'

'Well, I've *got* the buds,' whined the bride. 'But I want something *unusual*.'

Simmy ran a long list of suggestions past her, some of them even wilder than the out-of-season corn. They finally arrived at a shortlist, which the couple agreed to go away and consider. By the time they left it was half past three – later than the shop usually stayed open on a Saturday.

'Go home,' she told Melanie. 'You've been here too long as it is.'

'I'm in no rush. It's even worse than usual at ours, with Christmas on the way. The little ones are crazy with excitement already, and that makes them fight. We've had the decorations up for weeks and Mum's got a CD of carols she plays non-stop. It's like being in Tesco all day long, only louder. Please God, let me be out of there by this time next year.'

'Is that likely?'

'Yeah, course it is. I finish at college in the summer. Then I'm getting a live-in job in a hotel. I've started looking round. I *told* you.'

Melanie's ambitions had always been clearly spelt out to Simmy. Floristry was a part-time stopgap, a means of earning extra cash between lectures and tutorials. 'You're the only place in town with the right hours,' she had said frankly. 'And it's not *completely* irrelevant.'

But nothing specific had been said about when her availability would end, and Simmy realised that over the past month or two she had come to value the girl more and more. Her manner with customers could be impatient, and her flair for flowers was limited to an acute sensitivity to wastage. She would fiercely resist throwing away anything with a hint of a brown edge or a wilting leaf, despite Simmy's frequent explanations that it was bad for business to offer stuff that wasn't fresh. Melanie liked strong scents and flamboyant colours, but had very little ability when it came to arrangements, even in a roughly assembled bunch, such as they sold for people to compose their own final bouquet.

Now the prospect of losing her in another eight or nine months' time made Simmy feel sad. 'I'll miss you when you leave,' she said.

'Well, it won't be for ages yet,' sighed Melanie.

Chapter Nine

SIMMY BRIEFLY CALLED in on her parents once she'd locked up the shop. They lived in Lake Road, where Simmy often left her car as an easy place to park for the day.

Her father answered the door quickly, putting a finger to his lips to tell her to be quiet. 'Don't disturb my patient,' he whispered. 'Just go quietly into the kitchen, will you.'

She had forgotten the injured cat. 'How is he?'

'Mending slowly, poor old boy. He's a wonderfully good patient.' Russell Straw smiled bleakly, his eyes moist. Simmy couldn't remember seeing him so emotional about an animal before. They had always owned a motley assortment of rescued dogs and cats; ill-disciplined creatures who jumped on furniture and stole food that was left out. Angie's B&B was run on dangerously unhygienic lines, as a result. And yet very few visitors objected and the bookings diary was nearly always full. It was a surprisingly good living, especially as neither Russell nor Angie seemed interested in spending money. She was busy cooking, changing bedding, vacuuming carpets, while he was a keen gardener and avid reader. Once in a while they would go out to see a film, if they could escape their responsibilities.

The cat was confined to a large makeshift bed at the end of the passageway from the front door to the kitchen. A fireguard had been erected, and the space filled with old blankets. In the middle of this a half-naked animal lay curled. Much of his hair had been removed from all around his pelvis and back legs, and black stitches were visible. 'Don't touch him!' warned Russell.

'I wasn't going to. He does look a mess.'

'You should have seen him when it happened. They've done wonders with him, considering.'

'What happens when he needs to pee?'

'I carry him out to the garden, and he squats down on the bean patch. He's amazingly good about it. He seems to understand what's going on.'

'Nine lives,' she murmured.

'He'll need them.'

'I never knew you were so fond of him.'

'Me neither. But he's always been such an inoffensive creature, and very affectionate. I hate to see him in such a state. The dog's been worrying about him as well.'

The dog was a small elderly Lakeland terrier who spent most of his time in a basket in the kitchen. He had been acquired from a rescue centre when he was already in middle age, and showed every sign of contentedly living out his days as peacefully as possible. He had never caused the slightest trouble, which explained why the Straws had seen no reason to register with a vet. Russell sporadically walked him around the local streets, but his chief source of occupation was digging in a half-made rockery that Russell had been forced to abandon to the dog's craving for excavation. When his feet got sore, he would turn to chasing a semi-resident squirrel across the garden, which he did almost every morning. Simmy and he largely ignored each other, in a fond sort of way.

They moved into the kitchen, leaving the cat in peace. 'So what's what?' Russell asked, as he often did. 'How's business?'

'Not bad. A new wedding turned up this afternoon. She seems keen to spend a lot of money.'

'That's good.' He nodded comfortably. As far as Simmy could ascertain, her father had never much worried about her. He had been saddened by the death of the baby, making no secret of the personal loss he felt at being thwarted of grandfatherhood. He had winced at Simmy's separation from Tony, and then welcomed her with undemonstrative ease when she opted to move to the same town as her parents. He had listened to her plans and offered advice, and never once criticised anything she did. He provided a broad chest on which she had cried a few times in recent turbulent years, with no hint of embarrassment. If anybody ever asked her about him, Simmy would assert with complete confidence that he was the perfect father in every respect.

'Where's Mum?'

He looked round as if half expecting his wife to be lurking in a corner of the kitchen. The large cooker, dishwasher and fridge took up a lot of space. Preparing full English breakfasts for up to ten people at a time required a lot of equipment and considerable efficiency. The kitchen was the heart of the operation, with high-quality equipment and only the best ingredients. Racks of eggs stood in the pantry, with locally produced bacon, sausages, black pudding and mushrooms all stockpiled in great quantities. 'We ought to offer kippers and haddock as well,' sighed Russell. 'But we decided that was asking too much.' The freezer was carefully stacked with sliced bread and emergency cartons of milk, as well as the bacon and sausages. Boxes full of breakfast cereal and jars of marmalade and jam occupied a sideboard in the dining room. Simmy was still marvelling at the logistical challenges required to accommodate and feed a constantly changing succession of guests, and the apparent ease with which her parents had risen to meet them.

'Out, I suppose. I can't remember what she said.'

'Any customers tonight?'

'Of course. When are there not? We've had to be ruthless to turn them away over Christmas – I told you.'

'I feel sorry for people trying to escape from their families. Where are they supposed to go?'

He laughed. 'I don't care. All I know is, we're not prepared to shelter them. You sound as if you'd like to escape yours as well.' He gave her a look from under his bushy eyebrows.

'Not a bit of it. Where would I go? I escaped *to* mine, remember?'

'Tony used to be your family,' he said in a sad, soft voice.

'Don't, Dad. I can't even bear to think about this time last year. You can't imagine how awful it was, and how much better it is here. I'm going to bring crackers and balloons and a big jigsaw, and we're going to be silly and irresponsible for two whole days.'

'Sounds exhausting.'

The back door opened and Angie strode in carrying an assortment of bags. 'Where did you go?' asked her husband.

'Kendal. I told you. Christmas shopping.'

'On a Saturday afternoon? Are you mad? Isn't that when everybody else goes?' Her husband stared at her.

'Not entirely everybody. But I like the crowds. It's a wonderful atmosphere with all the decorations and carols. Gets me in the mood very nicely. Oh – P'simmon, you're here. Don't look at my parcels. I'm going to go and hide them.' She hugged the bags closer and went up the stairs two at a time.

'Such energy,' moaned Russell. 'She makes me feel so ancient sometimes.'

Simmy gave him a close inspection. 'You *do* look tired,' she noted. 'Are you okay?'

'Not sleeping as well as I used to, that's all. Latest expert opinion says it doesn't matter, and nothing to worry about, but it does leave me in need of a nap, come teatime. Not always possible, of course.'

Her mother was back in under ten minutes, rolling up her sleeves. 'Staying for supper?' she asked Simmy.

'Yes, please.'

'How's business?'

'Not bad,' she repeated.

'A new wedding,' put in her father. 'Lots of money to spend.'

'That's good,' said Angie. 'It'll soon be a whole year, won't it?'

'Since I moved here, yes. But the shop didn't open till March, if you remember. Gosh, that was chaotic, wasn't it. I don't know how I did it, looking back.'

Angie shrugged. 'Oh – I've got a message for you. That boy, Ninian something. He was in one of the shops just now. Said to tell you he got called away and couldn't bring his pots as arranged. He'll try again one day next week.'

Simmy blinked. 'How do you know him?'

'Oh – I don't remember. He has stalls at the craft fairs, that sort of thing. I've chatted to him a few times.'

'He's hardly a *boy*. He must be at least forty.'

'No, no, he's thirty-six. He told me. His birthday's the same as mine.'

'I'm amazed.'

'How could you think he was as old as that? He looks about twenty-five to me.'

'How did he know you were my mother?'

'I told him, of course. I suggested he show you some vases. It looks as if he followed up on it.'

'He never said.' Simmy was left feeling oddly exploited, knowing there'd been a plan forged behind her back. 'Are the pots nice?'

'Gorgeous, obviously. You'll love them. Big black matt things, with blobs and swirls stuck on. Terribly tasteful. They need to reach a wider public. If I had space, I might have been tempted to put a little display up here somewhere.'

'He doesn't seem very reliable.' Resentment was bubbling gently in the depths, for reasons that remained obscure. Ninian Tripp had changed for her in those few seconds, now he turned out to be her mother's discovery. 'I was expecting him yesterday.'

'Don't be petulant, pet,' cautioned her father. It was something he said quite often. 'Who is this bloke, anyway? First I've heard of him.'

'He's a potter,' Simmy said.

'That much I already gathered. A potter born under the sign of Leo, with appealing wares. Must be dozens of them.' He waved an airy hand. 'You haven't asked after the cat,' he reproached his wife.

'You'd have told me if it was dead. I assumed there was no change.'

'Quite right,' he agreed peaceably. He addressed Simmy. 'You heard the weather forecast, did you?'

It was the first time she'd thought of weather for at least a day. 'No,' she said warily.

'Light snow,' he said. 'Nothing to panic about. But you shouldn't leave it too late to get home.'

She swallowed the childish urge to plead for a bed with them. She couldn't just abandon her own house at the first hint of difficulty. 'Oh,' she said. 'Right.'

'Is your heating on?' Angie asked. 'You don't want the pipes to freeze.'

'They're well lagged. I'm more worried about roads than pipes.' She visualised the route home, with all the hilly bends and narrow junctions. The likelihood of sliding sideways or backwards on an invisible sheet of ice made her shudder. It seemed impossibly difficult from the comparative security of a Windermere street.

'You'll be fine. It won't be bad until sometime tomorrow. Just a sprinkling,' Russell assured her. 'You *live* up there, Sim. You've got to get used to it. You'll enjoy it in the end, young and strong as you are. It's good to have a bit of hardship around the edges. We've all got much too soft.'

It was a familiar refrain, and she had always vaguely agreed with him. But she also suspected it was based much more on theory than practice. Russell Straw had not known a lot of hardship in his life, and he only walked the fells in sunshine. He had no more resilience than the next man when it came to snowy slopes or power cuts in icy weather. Simmy gritted her teeth and said nothing.

A meal was quickly produced and eaten. B&B guests came and went, summoning Angie to query a dietary detail for their breakfast. Simmy registered, for the hundredth time, how utterly disruptive to normal life it was to throw open one's home to a constant succession of strangers. They used lavatory paper at a prodigious rate; they stole towels and soap; they ate sausage rolls in their rooms and left greasy crumbs all over the bed. They shouted at each other and let doors slam. But Angie persisted in liking them and tolerating their quirks. She had allotted a downstairs room to them, where they could play games or watch TV in a communal fashion that generated friendships and fierce political arguments in equal measure. Children formed alliances, adults compared notes and walking maps. A constant low level of chaos prevailed at Beck View, especially when guests came trailing dogs and young babies. Angie permitted smoking, as a final act of defiance, even though she scarcely indulged the habit herself. Some unwitting guests found this quite extraordinarily perverse, and made loud complaints. Most of them found their way eagerly to Beck View for this very reason.

At seven-thirty, Simmy was ready to brave the elements. She went to the back door and looked out. The air was still and only faintly chilly. 'No snow yet,' she reported, back in the kitchen.

'Off you go, then,' encouraged her father. 'While the going's good.'

Her car was parked close by, its windows free of frost. There was no reason to hesitate, or to quail at the prospect of driving home. Her house was four miles away by road, less by footpath. She had walked it many a time. It was practically next door by Lakeland standards. She set off with a backward wave at her father, who stood watching her from his front doorstep.

Before she reached the turn off to Troutbeck, there were tiny white specks in the beam of her headlights. A mile further on, at Thickholme, the specks had become swirling flakes. At the turning by the church, where the road became little more than a track rising steeply up to the main street of her village, she could see a faint white frosting on the hedges. When she finally pulled in beside her little cottage, the ground was already changing colour. Doggedly, she repeated her father's mantra, *We've all got far too soft*. Mankind had survived an ice age, after all. The human body, given a modicum of warm insulation made of wool, could withstand astonishing degrees of cold. So what was she afraid of?

The answer was always the same. She was afraid of the claustrophobia of being trapped in a snowdrift, of losing control of her car, and – most shamefully – of being dependent on other people. It came, she supposed, from being the only child of self-reliant parents. They had expected her to carve her own way through life, and only offered help on the most minimal of terms. She did not want a local farmer to tow her out of a snowy ditch. She didn't want some team of Troutbeck stalwarts to bring her bread and milk. She should not, by rights, be living there at all.

The solution to these concerns was to maintain a well-stocked freezer, to lag the pipes properly and keep the most sturdy of tyres on her car. All these she had done. And besides, she persuaded herself, this was only a sprinkling of dusty snow, not enough to cause more than a fleeting concern. She tried to turn her thoughts around, whereby the snow created a cosy blanket around her and her neighbours. They would be closed to visitors, forced to accept some inactivity. Life would reduce to essentials. She would light a log fire and bake potatoes in the embers. The phone would still work, and the electricity probably stay connected. Only in the harshest of storms did the power go off these days. Everything would look pretty – especially the fells – after a moderate snowfall. Children would have snowball fights and dogs would dash round in delirious circles. And then it would all go away again, and everyone would be happy.

She let herself into the house and turned on all the lights. She closed the curtains and switched on the TV. The next day was Sunday and she did not have to be anywhere. She could read, write more Christmas cards, perhaps phone Julie, and generally be a slob for a day. If there was an inch of snow on the roads, it would have been driven over many times before she had to brave it on Monday. Everything would be fine – not just her father had said so, but Melanie, too.

Chapter Ten

AT FIRST WHEN she woke on Sunday, it seemed that her optimism had been justified. She could hear voices outside, as well as a car driving past. The world had not frozen to a standstill, then. There were not six-foot drifts burying all the cars and imprisoning the population in their homes.

But the voices sounded oddly urgent, a man shouting and a young woman replying in a high pitch. Simmy went to the window of her bedroom and looked out. There definitely was snow. It was on roofs and cars, trees and stone walls. But the road had snowless tracks that revealed the dark surface, blessedly free of ice. Only the middle was still snowy. The people were standing on the other side of the narrow road, looking down the slope to the east, where there was a gap between walls. Simmy couldn't see the object of their attention, but she heard a man say, 'We'll have to see if we can push it.' Another man replied, 'Better to get a tractor.' A vehicle, then, had left the road, and was somehow stuck. The slope was gentle at that point, the accident apparently not serious. *But it could have been me*, Simmy thought with a shiver. She closed the window and quickly got dressed. The view from her bedroom was of the fells to the east, the church tower just visible in its hollow, crags mistily to the north. There was snow up there, its depth hard to gauge. Kirkstone might be closed; Garburn an unthinkable exercise. Her father's projected walk now seemed close to insanity.

Hesitantly she went outside, to see what was happening. The moment she came into view, one of the men called to her. 'Hey, Mrs Brown – any chance of you lending a hand?'

She looked at her feet, clad in loose-fitting shoes. 'Let me get my boots,' she called back. The idea that she might become one of the rescuers came as a major surprise. In under a minute she was striding towards the troubled car, flexing her inadequate muscles. Two men and a woman were attempting to find enough traction to heave the silver-grey Mondeo back onto the road from its crooked position. Muddy grooves gave witness to frantic attempts to drive it out, dirty snow splashed all around. 'Simmy. Call me Simmy,' she said, as she found a space and laid her bare hands on the cold metal.

'Haven't you got any gloves?' the woman – or, more accurately, girl – asked.

'I forgot them. I'll be okay.'

'You'd be more use at the front,' said one of the men, who she recognised as living at Town Head. 'Open the driver's door, and steer, will you? You can push at the same time.'

It felt like a very responsible job, surely one generally adopted by a man. Awkwardly, she obeyed, worrying that if the car slid in the wrong direction, she might fall underneath it, or be squashed between it and a nearby wall. Did they regard her as dispensable, then? The least valuable member of the team?

'One, two, three,' chanted the man, and they all heaved in unison. Simmy's right foot locked against a convenient stone, and she felt the whole car shift forward. 'Again!' ordered the man, and this time Simmy was required to pull the steering wheel round, to guide the wheels out onto the road. The car hesitated and lurched and was then moving freely. It was all over very quickly. 'Jump in, will you?' the man called to Simmy. 'Pull it up just down there.' She assumed he meant a slightly wider stretch of road, fifteen yards away. Feeling impressively agile, she made a graceful leap onto the driving seat, and pulled the door shut after her. Steering could have been impossible, she realised, in most modern cars, with the ignition off. But this one did as it was told, and she gently directed it as instructed, braking delicately once it was properly straight, and in no danger of being stuck again.

Everyone clapped their mittened hands together, and smiled at each other. Simmy got out. 'Oh, thank you, everybody,' said the car's owner. 'What a fool I was!'

Only then did Simmy recognise her. It was the girl from the Giggling Goose, on Wednesday morning. The one whose chair Mr Kitchener had accidentally kicked. 'Do you live here?' she blurted, without thinking.

The girl tilted her head as if to suggest politely that the question might be a trifle abrupt. 'Actually, no. I'm staying in Windermere for a few days, and decided to come and explore. Stupid, obviously. But I have to get back later today, and I wanted to fit as much in as I could.'

'You were lucky to get up Holbeck,' said the man from Town Head. 'If that's the way you came.'

'I followed a tanker. It made some useful tracks,' she laughed. 'Then I met a big van and went skewing off the road. It was terrifying.'

'You could have done some damage if you'd hit the wall,' said the other man. Simmy remembered him calling her *Mrs Brown*, and wished she could think of his name. She had not been as sociable as she might, she admitted, since arriving in Troutbeck. Everyone in the village shop had always been friendly and interested. They mostly knew she ran Persimmon Petals in Windermere. Some had promised to patronise her next time they needed flowers. She had been invited to join a variety of clubs and groups, but never quite taken the plunge. Perhaps over the winter, when there was little else to do, she would make the effort.

'So I see,' grimaced the girl. 'I chose a daft time to come exploring, didn't I. Somebody told me to have a look at the east window in the church, and I was looking for it. I thought I might join in with a service, if there is one today.' She looked brightly around at the faces of her rescuers.

'I saw you in Ambleside on Wednesday,' said Simmy, with a sense of needing to establish some degree of truth. A wild suspicion was taking root in her head, and she saw no reason to hold back from trying to pin it down.

'Help!' squealed the girl, appealing to the two men. When they showed no sign of responding, she made an exaggerated show of capitulation, bending her knees and spreading her hands. 'Where did you see me?'

Simmy was badly wrong-footed, she realised. Although the men were starting to drift away, nodding blandly and glancing at their watches, they were also giving her strange looks. 'Sorry,' she said lightly. 'I was just surprised to recognise you. I thought I knew your face, you see, and then it came back to me. Quite a lot has happened since then. It was in the Giggling Goose café,' she added, belatedly answering the question.

'Oh … right. The one up that lovely little hill, by the river. It's gorgeous, isn't it.'

'It's a ghyll,' said Simmy. 'Stock Ghyll. Bigger than a beck, but smaller than a river. I think.'

One of the men looked back and snorted. 'A ghyll's a ravine, by rights.'

'Not a bit of it,' argued the other. 'It's a stream, just as Simmy says.' He threw her a supportive glance, proud of himself for getting her name right.

'I went up to see the waterfall,' interrupted the nameless girl. 'It was fantastic.'

'Even better after this snow. Worth a picture or two,' nodded the arguer. 'Now it's time I shifted myself. I only came out for a paper.' The shop was still some distance away, its existence a vital beacon in Simmy's life. 'Mind how you go,' he adjured the car driver. 'Best not try to get down to the church from here. It'll be slippery.' Both men walked away, chatting softly together.

'Is your name *Simmy*?' queried the girl. 'What's that short for, then?'

'Persimmon. And you are …?' she said boldly.

'Candy. Short for Candida. We've both got weird names, haven't we. I never heard of a person called Persimmon before. It's a fruit, isn't it?'

Simmy's lurking suspicion, based on nothing more than a husky voice heard over the phone, was dramatically confirmed. But she was beaten to the post by a mirroring realisation from the other. 'Wait a minute … Are you the flower woman? Persimmon Petals? My God!'

'That's me. Why?' A need for caution was suddenly pressing upon her. She kept a blank expression, giving nothing away.

'Oh, it just seems such a coincidence. I saw your shop in Windermere … that tower thing in the window. It's not so surprising really, I suppose.' She squared her shoulders. 'I'll have to go. Shame about the church – but the snow's beautiful, isn't it. I do love snow.'

Evidently the same wariness was gripping Candida. She wasn't going to admit to ordering flowers from a mysterious granddaughter, just as Simmy was hiding the fact that she remembered those flowers and who they had been delivered to. Or her understanding of the fact that the same granddaughter had been sitting in a café, barely a hundred yards from the old lady's house. Something wrong was happening; something sinister and worrying. And yet the girl's face was perfectly frank and open, with no hint of a secret.

Suddenly, Simmy wanted Ben. Young Ben Harkness would extract the logical thread from this confusion and make everything clear.

But then all concealment fell away, and Candida said, 'You won't tell her, will you?'

'Tell who? What?'

'The old lady. She'll probably ask you who sent the flowers. You knew it was me, didn't you? I saw it in your face when I said my name. But I really don't want you to give me away just yet. It's all terribly delicate, you see.'

Obfuscation seemed futile. 'She already did ask me for your name. And no, I didn't tell her. You asked me not to.'

'That's really nice of you. I don't suppose it was very easy.'

'You should go and see her, and explain. That's if you really are her grandchild. She's convinced that you can't possibly be.'

'And you want the mystery solved, I see.' She gave Simmy a sideways look, as if reading her mind. Simmy felt a surge of resentment. This child was nearly twenty years her junior. She shouldn't be cleverer in any way. Then she remembered Ben, who was cleverer than almost everybody.

Candida laughed. 'I've had a lifetime of secrets, so I've had lots of practice. They're just starting to crawl out of the woodwork now.'

Simmy frowned. 'They couldn't have been *your* secrets, though. I mean – if there's a mystery around your birth, that's other people's doing, isn't it?'

'You'd think so, wouldn't you? But ever since I was about twelve, I've known I couldn't be the biological child of the woman I know as mother. We did genetics at school, and the teacher said it was impossible.'

'How very irresponsible!'

'No, it wasn't. I mean, it was all quite impersonal. I just knew I was adopted, from then on. But they still wouldn't tell me the whole story until I was sixteen.'

'And Mrs Joseph really is your grandmother?'

'Right.' She paused. 'Look, I really must go. It's all so complicated, and I can't tell you more than that. I've already said far too much. I expect the old lady was upset by those flowers. I didn't think it through very well, but when I found out it was her birthday, I couldn't resist it. It was stupid.'

Simmy said nothing. She had as much of the story as she wanted or needed. Her hands were blue with cold, and she was hungry for some breakfast.

'And I'll have to make sure the car's all right. I borrowed it, you see. No way I can afford a car.'

'But you *have* passed your test?'

'Oh, yes. I was seventeen and two months,' she boasted. 'My dad taught me when I was sixteen, on an old van. We drove across the fields in it. I'm really a good driver.'

Simmy supposed that that explained the girl's bravado in tackling steep, snowy country lanes early on a Sunday morning.

'Fields?' she echoed. Hadn't Candida's address been somewhere in the urban wastes of Liverpool?

'My dad's brother and family live on a farm in Cheshire.'

Simmy heard the automatic reference to 'dad' and wondered at the complexities of adoption, where a person didn't know quite what to call the assortment of parents that they were liable to end up with.

'I see,' she nodded. 'Well, bye, then.'

Candida Hawkins got into her borrowed Mondeo, and Simmy went back into her cottage, her head stuffed with half-answered questions.

Chapter Eleven

'BUT WHERE'S THE link with Nancy Clark?' persisted Ben, when Simmy phoned him and told him the whole story.

'There isn't one. There never *was* one. We were daft to think there might be. It's quite illogical.'

'My gut tells me otherwise,' he said sonorously. 'There *is* something connecting them. The Kitchener man proves that. He knows everyone, from all sides. I think he deliberately got himself seen by you, so he'd have an alibi. I bet he killed her, all along.'

'He couldn't have done that. Don't get into conspiracy theories, for heaven's sake. If you start thinking like that, you can dream up any wild notion. Stick to facts, okay. Isn't that what you're always telling me and Melanie to do?'

The boy was undaunted. 'We ought to go and retrace your steps from Mrs Joseph's house to the Giggling Goose, and check the timings. After all, that girl was in there, too. And that's crazy! She must have been watching out for you, to make sure you delivered the flowers as she wanted. Maybe she was lurking round the corner, to get a glimpse of her old granny. And Kitchener was there as well. Maybe they *know* each other. It's definitely sinister, Simmy. You must see that.'

'It's mysterious,' she conceded. 'But things always are, once you start delving into people's lives. And Ambleside's a small town. Everyone knows everyone else. Melanie understands all that side of it.'

'So – let's go and have a look,' he encouraged.

'I'm not going anywhere with all this snow,' she objected. 'I might never get home again.'

'Snow?'

'Haven't you got it?'

'Not a flake. Serves you right, for living up there in the mountains. Your weather is way worse than ours.'

'But it's only three miles away!'

'And a hundred and fifty metres higher. That makes a difference.'

'It doesn't sound much,' she said obstinately, trying not to think of the long climb up to Troutbeck from the lakeside road.

'How much snow is there, anyway?'

'At least an inch.'

He laughed. 'Wow!'

'It's scary, Ben. Look how that girl skidded off the road, right near my house.'

'And that's another thing,' he responded swiftly. 'Why was she there? She was stalking you, I bet. Wanted to see where you lived and what you looked like. You should be worrying about that, not a few flakes of snow.'

'She came to look at the church. People do, you know. That window's famous.'

'Huh!' he snorted. 'Nobody under forty goes to look at churches. Be realistic. What was she like, exactly?'

'Pretty. About nineteen. Big mouth, small eyes, dark hair. She had a woolly hat on today, but not on Wednesday. She seems nice,' she finished feebly.

'But you do have to wonder what exactly was she doing in the café, so close to Mrs Joseph's house? There must have been more to it than a random place to have coffee.'

'I don't know. She said she was staying here for a few days and wanted to explore.' Simmy tried to recall every word of the conversation. 'I suppose she must be a student on vacation.'

'Which university, I wonder?'

'Why does that matter?'

'It doesn't,' he agreed easily. 'She's *here* now. That's the main thing. We ought to warn Mrs Joseph, at the very least. She might be in for another nasty shock.'

Simmy had a sensation akin to how she imagined a rider felt when their horse bolted. 'I wish I'd never told you,' she grumbled. 'You're going far too fast.'

'So – what? We just sit at home and forget the whole thing? Leave the cops to struggle all on their own?' His ironic tone was one of the things she knew she would never forget about Ben. Most people would find it annoying, she supposed – a teenager acting as if he knew so very much more than people twice his age couldn't fail to get backs up. But she rather liked it. In some ways it reminded her of her mother, who was another person who held scant respect for the brainpower of the population in general.

'I wasn't aware that we were helping the cops. I thought we were helping Mrs Joseph work out what happened in her family.'

'Not at all,' he said forcefully. 'That wouldn't be any of our business, would it? We're much more interested in the murder.'

'But you said we ought to warn Mrs J.' Inconsistency was one of the less appealing aspects of a high IQ, she was discovering. It probably meant she had failed to catch a subtle implication, or a jump in the boy's reasoning.

'Only that there's a dodgy character hanging around. You can't betray Candida Whatsit's confidences. You've been clear on that from the start.'

'Yes,' she agreed uncertainly. 'I'm sorry, Ben, but I think you just lost me.'

'Never mind. Listen – you know Wilf?'

'Your brother. Yes.'

'He's got a mate that he hangs out with sometimes, called Scott, who works at the hospital. He's a porter. Takes the bodies down to the mortuary, among other things. And gets to see what's going on down there. Picks up the gossip. All the stuff about post-mortems and pathology. Anyway, Scott told Wilf there was a real buzz about the way the Clark lady was murdered. Some sort of lethal injection, so the story goes. They found the site where it went in – right into a vein. Dirty great needle it must have been.' His voice was breathless with excitement, and Simmy wondered how he had managed to let her prattle on about cars in the snow when he had something so thrilling to impart.

'And the police want to keep it secret,' she said, feeling uneasy. 'Scott shouldn't be gossiping about it. Don't they tell him to keep his mouth shut?'

'I doubt it. Nobody ever thinks about the porters. They're just part of the furniture. They probably assume they're all foreign or too thick to understand what they hear. Scott's actually rather bright. He says he's gathering material for a book. He wants to write thrillers, so he needs to know all the ways people can be killed.'

Simmy sighed inwardly at this new glimpse of the world of young men, where reality merged uncomfortably with fantasy. 'I wouldn't have thought that was Wilf's kind of thing,' she said. 'He seems very grounded to me.'

'He likes to keep abreast of things.' Ben sounded offended at her lack of enthusiasm. 'And this is important. It means the killer had some sort of medical connections – access to hypodermics and toxic substances.'

'Maybe he robbed a GP surgery – or a vet. They have stuff to put animals down, don't they? And dentists,' she added wildly. 'Novocaine and so forth. Would a big dose of that kill someone?'

'That's better,' the boy approved. 'Now you're getting into the spirit of it. Dentists – I never thought of that. I bet their security is nowhere near as good as doctors or vets. They have all sorts of people wandering about unsupervised at the one I go to. If you knew what to look for, you'd easily be able to grab a couple of phials when their backs were turned.'

His imagination was irresistibly infectious. 'That would definitely make it premeditated, and not a burglary that got out of control. That's horrible. Poor old lady. And *why*? What could anybody have against her?'

'She must have been in the way somehow. Or done something to make somebody really hate her. But we don't know what she was like. Was she nice or nasty? What did she do for a job? All that sort of stuff is missing. We need Melanie,' he went on decisively. 'And her granny. I'll call her now, and see if she's up for a get-together. We can all go and chat to the granny this afternoon.'

'Ben – I told you, I'm not driving anywhere in all this snow.'

'Look out of the window. The sun's shining. It's about seven degrees out there. I bet you every morsel of snow'll be gone by eleven. Don't be so soft.'

She swallowed down her protests at being spoken to like that. Ben was her friend, even if he was twenty-one years her junior. They had fallen into easy conversation within moments of first meeting and had enjoyed a mutual liking ever since. Besides, he was almost certain to be right about the weather. In true geeky fashion, he was always well aware of the elements and what they would deliver next.

'My dad said it would snow again today, worse than before.'

'Well, he's wrong. The forecast has changed drastically since this time yesterday.'

'Even so, we can't just descend on Melanie's gran without warning,' she objected weakly.

'Which is why I'm going to call her now and see if she thinks it'll be okay.' The exaggerated patience was definitely patronising. 'Can you be down here at two, and we'll take it from there? I'll get back to you if it's not going to happen, right? If you don't hear anything, assume that's the plan.'

'Where, exactly?'

'My house. You can find it, can't you? Helm Road. House with yellow door.' He added the number for good measure, and she confirmed that she could easily find it. 'But I haven't said I'll come yet,' she remembered crossly. 'I've got things to do here.' The last was not really true. Sunday afternoons could stretch boringly slowly, occupied only by housework, if there was no prospect of a walk or shop-related paperwork.

'You'll come,' he laughed. 'If you don't hear back from me, assume it's all fixed. Right?'

'Don't tell Melanie what Scott said,' she urged. 'She might pass it back to Joe and that'd cause trouble for Scott.'

He was silent for a few seconds. 'Wilf said the same thing. But she'll be furious when she finds out. We ought not to have secrets from each other. We're a gang, after all.'

'Are we?' Was it possible for a thirty-eight-year-old florist to be in a gang? It sounded ridiculously childish, the way he said it. And at the same time, it gave her a ridiculously childish thrill.

'Definitely,' he asserted. 'See you later.'

WITHOUT BEN, LIFE would be very different, she reflected, over her solitary lunch of lamb chops. Her mother had somehow befriended a smallholder in Coniston, years ago, who sold her whole carcases for the freezer at rock-bottom prices. Since Angie's freezers were always uncomfortably full, Simmy was used as an overflow – which meant she always had more than enough meat to eat. Not to mention all the apples that accumulated through the autumn, to be stewed with blackberries or plums and used for pies all through the winter. Seldom enticed by the lavish displays on supermarket shelves, Simmy was glad to keep things basic, seasonal and cheap.

Ben was a dynamo, a hothouse of ambitions and theories. He had eagerly involved himself in solving the investigation into the violent deaths of two men back in October, putting himself in sufficient danger to warrant a warning from Detective Inspector Moxon not to be so cavalier in future. At the same time, he had earned gratitude and admiration from the relatives of the victims. Not to mention envy from Melanie and bewilderment from his parents. He relished the intellectual puzzle that lay at the heart of any but the most straightforward murder. He reminded Simmy and Melanie that a significant proportion of homicides were never solved. Killers escaped without punishment and families remained stuck in agonised frustration.

None of which was of much help to Simmy as she tried to establish her own role in the Ambleside murder. By any reckoning, she was being inexorably drawn in – first by the accident of being able to give Mr Kitchener an alibi, then by her lunch with DI Moxon in the pub and now by Ben's increasing conviction that there was a definite connection between Mrs Mary Joseph and Miss Nancy Clark. This last was still hard to believe, based, as it seemed to be, on the most tenuous of links.

But Ben had been right about the snow, and Russell had been wrong, which was not unusual. Although the fells were still white, the roads were clear and there was no sign of ice. So long as she got home again by about five, she supposed she could make the short trip down to Bowness and back without undue risk. With a host of very mixed feelings, she drove carefully down the twists and turns of Holbeck Lane and out onto the main road a mile or two south of Ambleside.

Ben met her on the doorstep of his parents' house, and jumped into the passenger seat without a word. He then directed her back the way she had come, to Oak Street, not far from the station. Melanie's gran lived in a two-storey terrace house, made of the ubiquitous dark stone, Simmy discovered. There was a narrow strip of front garden, hardly big enough to turn round in. A dead-looking shrub pressed itself against the wall of the house. Simmy found herself feeling idiotically shy.

'Hiya!' Melanie carolled from somewhere behind them, as they stood at the door. 'Brill timing, you two. Gran's ever so excited about all this. She can't wait to show you her old photos. Brace yourselves.' She pushed open the door, which was obviously not locked, and led the way into a dark little hallway.

The existence of a grandfather came as a big surprise to Simmy. She was sure she had never once heard Melanie mention him. But there he was, in a deep velvet reclining armchair, his feet almost level with his head, turning an indifferent gaze upon them. 'Barb!' he called. 'They're here. Melly and her friends. Let themselves in as bold as brass, they have.'

A coal fire was smouldering in a generously sized grate, throwing out heat that had to negotiate the old man's legs before reaching the rest of the room.

A tall woman with silver hair came through from a door at the back of the room, carrying a substantial wooden tray laden with mugs of tea and heavy dark cake. Her back was straight and her eyes clear. 'How lovely!' she breathed. 'I'm ever so pleased to meet you properly. I'm Barbara Ellis. Call me Barb – everyone does.'

She was addressing Simmy, who held out a hand, and smiled as broadly as she could. 'I hope we're not intruding,' she said. 'It does seem a bit of a cheek.' She found that she did recognise the elderly woman, from occasional visits to the shop. The soft accent and intelligent gaze had made an impression on her, but she had never made a connection between the customer and Melanie. Probably because Melanie had never been there when her grandmother called in.

'Not a bit of it. Melly explained it all. How you've met up with Mary Joseph, and this boy here wants to practise for his studies, asking me questions.' She faltered slightly, and busied herself with handing out the tea and cake. Nobody was offered sugar, and milk had already been added without consultation. Simmy resolved to tell her mother that here was a woman she would find highly compatible. 'Have I got that right?' the hostess asked, after a moment. 'About his studies?'

'Quite right, Mrs Ellis,' said Ben heartily. 'I'm afraid I'm going to use you as a guinea pig, if that's okay. I need to see what sort of questions to ask, to help you remember things from your past. It's just practice, you see. Nothing important's going to come of it. But I just thought that seeing as how you've lived here all your life and know so many people, it would be a very interesting experiment.' He took a large bite of cake and beamed his approval.

Simmy blinked. If Melanie's gran understood a word of that, she was doing a lot better than Simmy. As far as she could tell, it was pure gobbledygook. For the first time, she wondered what in the world DI Moxon would make of it, if he knew what they were doing.

It seemed that Mrs Ellis was no fool. 'Doing the police's job for them, is that it?' she asked with a wink.

Simmy frowned. 'Well, actually, the police aren't at all involved with the Joseph side of things. It's only Melanie and Ben who keep thinking up wild theories about a connection.

'Well, I've no argument with that. The police are always six steps behind when it comes to understanding local business. Just look at that boyfriend of Mel's, Joe Wheeler, who might not be too happy for her to go ferreting out people's secrets, maybe, but he's no detective, now is he?' She laughed, not quite kindly. Ben joined in, ducking his head conspiratorially.

There followed an hour and a half of total recall. Photos were produced and used to spark anecdotes that dated back to the 1950s and beyond. But the big surprise came early on, with a picture of two girls aged about ten, standing arm in arm, with tidy hair and wide smiles. 'That's me with Lilian Smart. She was my best friend for years. We met when we first started school, and stayed together till we were fifteen. We both failed the eleven-plus,' Mrs Ellis laughed. 'Best thing that could happen to us. Gave us all the time we needed for having fun. Never had much in the way of homework or exams. We used to feel so sorry for those girls at the grammar, with their round shoulders and glasses. We both got jobs the minute we left. By the time we were all twenty, we were like people from different planets. Take those Clark sisters – never stopped trying to make something of themselves and where did it get them?' She was plainly lost in the 1950s world of home perms and handmade frocks, Friday evening dances and the pursuit of a likely lad.

Melanie leant forward. 'Gran – slow down a bit, okay? Where's Lilian Smart now? And I thought you said Nancy Clark was never much good at school. It was her sister Penny who got all the qualifications.'

'Dead. She's dead. Just a few weeks ago.' The old lady shook her head sadly. 'Lovely funeral, though. Saw your flowers, of course.' She looked at Simmy. 'Melly told me to look out for them.'

Simmy quickly went through all the funerals she'd done flowers for recently. 'Was her name still Smart?'

'Oh, no. Kitchener. She was Lilian Kitchener.'

'Oh!' said Simmy faintly. 'Yes, I remember. What a coincidence.' She seemed to be saying that quite a lot these days.

'Coincidence? Why?'

'Well – I met her son last week.' She had no intention of explaining the connection, and why Malcolm Kitchener had been such a presence over the past four or five days. She threw a warning glance at Ben and Melanie, who both gave tiny nods of compliance. 'He's taking it hard, missing her badly.'

'What was she like, Gran?' Melanie asked.

Mrs Ellis had a deep voice, and now it got even deeper. The words seemed to come from far back in her throat. 'She had a difficult life,' she said. 'Her husband was a swine. The boy had an awful time when he was growing up. There was a girl, as well. Brenda. She got out early. Emigrated to Australia. Never even came back for the funeral.'

'Her father's funeral?' asked Melanie.

'Neither of them.'

'She sent flowers,' said Simmy. 'It was an Interflora order.'

Lilian Kitchener had become a martyr, it seemed, while her brutish husband was alive. A man who began as a suave charmer, sweeping the girl off her feet at the age of seventeen, and turned nasty before the first bed sheets had been changed, as Mrs Ellis quaintly put it. 'Lucky for her, he died before he reached fifty. Fell in front of a train, the damn fool. Drunk, of course. Made a terrible mess.'

Ben snorted, trying to suppress a laugh. Melanie's gran smiled at him. 'Feel free, lad. It was the best thing that could happen. Gave her thirty years as a merry widow. She'd earned it, bless her.'

Another snort came from the horizontal reclining chair. 'Don't get ideas, my girl,' said old Mr Ellis. 'I'm good for a few years yet.'

'You're no bother,' his wife told him flatly. 'Never out of that bloody chair, are you? Can't even sit up straight when there's visitors.' Simmy had inwardly noted the rudeness implied in this, from the outset.

'You know why that is,' he defended himself. 'It'll break if I keep doing it.'

Everyone laughed at this. It was true he was a heavy man, but the chair looked quite capable of managing a good number of transformations yet. 'It's what it's *made* for, you fool,' said his wife. 'You've only had it three months.'

Ben lifted his chin, waiting for a chance to speak, picking up another photo from the array spread across the coffee table. 'Is this Nancy Clark, did you say? Could you tell us what you remember of her?' he invited. 'She never married, did she? Wasn't that rather unusual?'

'Career girl. It was *Penny* that I knew, not Nancy.' She pointed a finger at Melanie. 'You got it wrong, girl. Wrong way round. Nancy was the clever one. She did some sort of special exam and got top marks so they sent her off to the grammar. Never saw much of her after that.' She got up from her place on a three-seater sofa and tipped more coal onto the fire. Her husband sighed his contentment.

Melanie was frowning. 'Did I get it wrong?' she asked Simmy.

'Not the first time. Last week, when you told me about it, you said Nancy was the successful one. Penny married a farmer and had umpteen kids.'

'Five,' said Mrs Ellis. 'She and Nancy were twins, and she had a pair of her own. It goes like that in some families,' she said knowingly. 'Three boys and then twin girls. Lovely they are. I saw one of them at the harvest, back in October. Got their own kiddies now, of course. Most of them, anyway. The girls are good with poor Penny, now she's got that Parkinson's thing.'

'Not the one who's in prison,' said Simmy, looking round smugly at having held onto that snippet of information.

'That was a travesty,' old Sam Ellis spat, to everyone's surprise. 'Could have happened to anyone. Poor girl, ruined her life it has.'

Ben was looking immensely interested. 'What?' he demanded.

Nobody spoke, until Simmy said, 'Moxon told me. She got three years for dangerous driving. Killed a child. That's all I know.'

'Well, it has nothing to do with anything,' said Mrs Ellis, with a placatory glance at her husband. He settled down again, after a few angry sniffs.

Ben spoke carefully but persistently. 'So they all still live in the area, then? Penny's children, I mean?'

Barbara Ellis read his mind, and swiftly headed him off. 'Don't you go suspecting any of them of killing their old auntie,' she cautioned him. 'Not one of them would have the gumption, nor any reason to do such a thing. Maybe they had precious little love for her, but that's a very long way from murder, as even a scrap of a boy like you would understand.'

Ben took this put-down very well, but Melanie protested. 'Hey, Gran – he's not to be sneered at, you know. I told you about all those awards he's got, and how everyone thinks he's going to be a star one day.'

'I'm sorry, lad. But it won't do to start imagining things, will it?'

'Not at all,' the boy shook his head. 'So can we go back to Nancy and find out a bit more about her? She didn't work as a dentist, did she?' he asked hopefully.

'Pardon? Who – Nancy? No, she was at some fancy private clinic. There for years. Chief nurse, or something of the sort. Hobnobbed with the doctors and rich philanthropists, or whatever they call themselves. Never a sign of getting married. Story was she was mistress to one of the top consultant blokes. Wouldn't have surprised me.'

'Did Penny tell you that?' Melanie asked.

'Might have done. Could have been Lilian, even. Come to think of it, most likely that's who it was. Lilian was always a great gossip. Nobody's secrets were safe with her, and she'd have enjoyed putting down the poison about Nancy. Never did like each other, those two. Of course, we're talking thirty years since. Not sure I can recall just who said what, after all that time.'

Simmy could see Ben having the same idea as her own sudden suspicion. 'How did she die, exactly? Lilian, I mean?'

'Heart. Out like a light on the kitchen floor. Never knew what hit her, poor old love. People say that's a good way to go, but it would never suit me. I'm hoping for a bit of warning first.'

Ben gave a little shrug, before pressing on. 'What about the Joseph man? Melanie says he was in your class as well. Married a girl called Mary.'

Mrs Ellis looked blank, interrupted in the expression of her wishes as to how she might die. Then her face became more animated. 'Matthew? Oh yes, a beautiful boy. Dark, curly hair, fabulous eyelashes.' She rummaged amongst the photos, in vain. 'Never did like having his picture taken, though. There *was* one of the whole class, but he was blurred at the back. Can't find it now. Anyway, everybody was in love with Matthew Joseph. He went off to Leeds, and worked his way up in the printing trade. Did very well. Mary she was called – the girl he married. A bit older than him, they said. They came back here later on, with the two young girls. Matthew set up his own works in Keswick. But he died too young. I never saw much of him; just heard his name now and then. Saw her out and about a few times, over the years. Got a daughter with a daft name.'

'Davy,' nodded Simmy. 'It's short for Davida.'

'Anyway – why do you want to know about Matthew?'

'Simmy's had some business with his wife, that's all. Another coincidence, sort of.'

'Listen, lad,' said Mrs Ellis firmly. 'All these so-called coincidences, they're nothing of the sort. Think about it, why don't you.

Anyone who's lived here – Windermere, Ambleside, Bowness – since they were born, they're bound to know each other. It's just plain fact. The incomers, well, that's different. They struggle to understand who everyone is.' She threw a kindly look at Simmy. 'But there's still enough of us in the place to make a kind of … *foundation*. Do you see? The farmers, butchers, schoolteachers, doctors, shopkeepers – most of them have always lived here, and they stay after they retire. This place is all they know. They've got *roots*. And they all know each other. Most of them have married each other. Look at Melly's mother. She's got eighteen cousins, and a good many of them live less than ten miles from here.' She reflected for a moment. 'And one of them married Matthew Joseph's sister,' she finished in triumph. 'She's called Beulah, of all things. She was younger than us. Cross-eyed, poor girl. Sam's young brother married her. Never had any kids, though.'

'That's Mum's uncle, not her cousin,' said Melanie, irritably. 'And they live down south. I never even *saw* them. I can't remember who all those cousins, are. There are too many of them.'

'How many have *you* got, then?' It was evident that Mrs Ellis already knew the answer to that.

'Six.' The sense of a contest lost was clearly in the air. 'So far.'

'You still think that useless Robin's going to settle down and start a family? He must be forty-five if he's a day.'

Again, Ben took charge. 'They had two girls – the Josephs,' he prompted. 'Did they ever have anything to do with the Clark twins?'

'How d'you mean? Sam – give us a hand here, will you? Penny Clark's eldest. What's his name … Edward, is it? Didn't he have a bit of a thing for that Nicola Joseph, years back?'

'Broke his heart,' confirmed the old man with a minimal nod. His chin was already pressed into his neck, from the angle of his chair, which somehow arranged for his face to be pointed towards the television while much of his body was horizontal. 'She never would have truck with him.'

Simmy bit back the explanation for this, unsure of the Ellis couple's reaction to lesbianism. She could see Ben mentally filing away this flimsy connection, for further analysis later. She also found herself entertaining a rogue theory about a brief experimental encounter resulting in a child that got itself hurriedly adopted, in total secrecy. Despite the emphatic denials from Nicola, the possibility remained. What the implications might be for the murdered Nancy Clark remained stubbornly obscure.

Ben tried one more time to get more of a grasp of Nancy Clark's life and character. 'So she worked at a clinic,' he summarised. 'A private place, you mean?'

'As far as I can recall, yes.'

'And she had an affair with the top consultant there?'

'That's what they said.' Barbara Ellis drew a deep breath. 'The main thing about Nancy, you see, was that she was a very nasty person. Had been from a small girl. Never worked out why. Always sly and unkind, she was. Selfish, too. Scowled the whole time and was a devil for pinching. I never did like a girl who pinched.'

'Did she pinch you?' asked Melanie.

'She certainly did. More than once. It was a relief when she got sent up to the grammar and we didn't have to bother with her any more.'

Another forty minutes passed, in which more names were thrown out, forcing Ben to extract a notepad and ballpoint from the small rucksack he'd brought with him, and start writing down some of the blizzard of information. His questions were becoming more sporadic, his face flushed from the warm room and the futile efforts to draw anything resembling a logical thread from Mrs Ellis's recollections. At last, Melanie called a halt. 'Gran, we'll have to go,' she said. 'It's dark already, and there's been snow up at Troutbeck. Simmy's scared of the drive home. I'll wash those mugs for you, shall I, before we go?'

'You will not. But you're a good girl for offering.' The proud grandmother patted the girl's back. 'You were always the special one, our Melly. But don't go boasting to the others about it, will you? No good can come of it. Just remember your old granny when you're rich and famous.'

The departure took a few more minutes, with Ben solemnly shaking hands with his informant, and Simmy expressing effusive thanks. The man of the house had slipped into a deep sleep half an hour before, and was oblivious to everything around him.

'Still don't know what it was all about,' sighed Mrs Ellis. 'All this digging into the past. What good's it going to do you? But I must admit it was nice, for a change. Nice to know I can still dredge it all up when I try. Makes a life worth something, if you know what I mean.'

Simmy entertained slippery thoughts about identity and the meaning of any individual's span on earth. When it came right down to it, she supposed that all a person really amounted to was the sum of their memories. 'I know what you mean,' she said.

Chapter Twelve

THEY ALL PILED into Simmy's car, without even thinking about it. 'So where does that leave us?' asked Ben, blowing out his cheeks. 'What a woman! My granny can hardly remember what day it is. She's never told me a thing about her early life.'

'It's just the way she is,' said Melanie proudly. 'I did tell you. That was nothing to how she can be sometimes. It's not just the past. She remembers everything that happened last week as well.'

'We ought to tell DI Moxon about her,' said Simmy, aware of a stab from her conscience. 'She could solve all his crimes for him. She's wasted as she is.'

'She's not too keen on the police, as you might have gathered,' said Melanie. 'Especially since they stopped Grandad on the dual carriageway for eating a sandwich when he was driving. We've never heard the end of that one. She's quite funny about it some-times, but I'd hate to be that constable if she meets him again. She's got quite a temper on her.'

'She was wonderfully welcoming,' said Simmy. 'She must have wondered what we were there for. Not that she seemed flustered or anything.'

'She's never flustered. Plus she's glad to have someone to eat all the cakes she makes. She's got tins and tins of them. It's not just at Christmas. If you go there in the middle of summer, she'll give you the same thing. I think she and Grandad live on it. She never seems to cook a Sunday roast or anything like that.'

'I'm worried about Mr Kitchener,' Simmy changed the subject. 'I can't get him out of my mind. He saw Candida in the café. He kicked her chair. She looked at him.'

Ben made a choking, squawking sound. 'What? You never told us that.'

'It was nothing at the time. But when I saw the girl again this morning, it came back to me. What if there was some sort of plot between them? The kick might have been a signal, that they'd prearranged.'

'Stop!' Melanie ordered. 'This isn't your sort of thing. You're talking about a conspiracy between Malcolm Kitchener and Mrs Joseph's granddaughter – what, to kill Nancy Clark? But *why*?'

'I can't imagine.'

'Yes, but ... no ... but,' said Ben wildly. 'It *does* make sense. I mean, the alibi does. If the girl did the killing, under his instruction ... no, that doesn't work. Simmy's alibi covers both of them, doesn't it. And if the cops have got their times wrong, then it could just as easily have been Mr K all along. Where does this Candida person fit in?'

'What's she like?' Melanie asked, as Ben had done, earlier in the day.

'Confident. Pretends to be ditzy, but isn't really.' It was a different answer to the same question.

'The cops thought Kitchener did it,' said Ben slowly. 'They must have come up with some sort of motive, as well as means and opportunity. It's only Simmy's alibi that wrecked it. But *crucially*, we've got a link!' He raised a hand in triumph. 'A proper link this time, between the two old women.'

'Have we?' Melanie, on the back seat, seemed to be peripheral to the main conversation. She leant forward, pushing her head between the front seats. 'Explain.'

'The man suspected of killing Miss Clark was seen in a café with the self-proclaimed granddaughter of Mrs Joseph. They *looked at each other*. That can't be a coincidence. We've already established that there really aren't any coincidences here at all. It's all quite logical.'

'Simmy's a link, as well,' said Melanie. 'Plus she did the flowers for Mrs Kitchener. That could have made her son think of flowers as a way of getting at Mrs Joseph – if we're thinking that's what he did. Don't forget that's why she was in Ambleside in the first place. Flowers that the girl sent. The girl that was in the café at the same time as Mr K. It's starting to come untangled, now. One step at a time, and there's a definite thread to it.' She made string-pulling gestures with her hands that went unseen by the others in the fading light.

'Melanie, that's brilliant!' Ben congratulated her.

'Getting at Mrs Joseph?' Simmy repeated. 'Where did that come from?'

'What if Mr Kitchener is one of those conmen who goes around getting money out of old ladies?' Melanie was in full spate. 'He worms his way into their confidence, visits them in their house, gets them to tell him where their valuables are, and then bashes them on the head.'

Ben cleared his throat. 'There's about ten things wrong with that, Mel. It doesn't fit the facts. For a start, he's local, so everybody knows him. If it *is* him that did it, he's after something other than their valuables. It's my belief it has to do with his mother. What if he's taking revenge for something that was done to the old girl years ago? What if he blames them for her bad heart? You heard how interconnected all these people are, since about a hundred years ago.'

'But getting at Mrs Joseph?' Simmy persisted. 'I still don't see it. How can sending a bunch of flowers be getting at her?'

'Come on, Sim,' urged Melanie. 'Look at how worked up you said she was when she came into the shop. The whole family's in meltdown because of it. It's not the flowers so much as the message that came with them. It's a brilliant way of unsettling somebody.'

'It would be a nifty bit of revenge, in fact,' claimed Ben.

'But she really does think she's Mrs Joseph's granddaughter,' Simmy insisted. 'She knew she was adopted, because of some genetic thing at school. So she must have got the details from the adoption people, just like you said, and found Mrs J's birth certificate so she knew her birthday, and sent the flowers on that day.'

'Some genetic thing?' Ben queried. 'You never told me that. What was it?'

'I have no idea. Hair colour, or eyes or something, presumably. Or blood group. She said she couldn't possibly be the biological child of her mother, for some reason.'

'Garbage!' said Ben. 'There's nothing you could glean in school science that would prove anything like that for certain. You'd have to do a DNA test.'

'So maybe she did.'

'She'd have said, wouldn't she? And how would she get a sample from the old lady for comparison? I'm not sure that story holds any water at all. I think she's just a stooge for Mr K. I think she lives locally somewhere and made the whole granddaughter story up. She was in Troutbeck this morning looking for you. The thing is,' he concluded solemnly, 'you can't believe everything people say. You have to trust your own senses – and you saw them together in the café, at the same time as Miss Clark was being murdered. That's the fact of the matter.'

'Yes,' breathed Melanie. 'That's right. Which means it can't have been Mr Kitchener or Candida who did it.'

Simmy rubbed her temples, feeling old and slow-witted beside these youngsters. 'I don't think they can be so absolutely precise about the timing as that. That's the whole trouble with alibis – especially if it's all in the same little town. It's barely five minutes from one place to the next.'

'Exactly,' said Ben, which got them nowhere.

Simmy tried to grasp all the implications. 'So do we think Mrs Joseph is in danger? You said before that we should warn her. She'll be there on her own in that cottage, same as Miss Clark was. She probably doesn't lock the door. Nobody seems to around here. She won't see any reason why she should. Poor old thing. I *liked* her. I don't want to be the instrument of some nasty bit of revenge.' She looked up at the sky, which was dark but cloudless. 'I think I'm going to go there now and see that she's all right. I'll tell her to keep her door locked. And maybe I *should* tell her Candida Hawkins' name, after all. Now I've met her, I really think she's genuine. I think she's just scared to make the final approach. It might be doing everyone a favour if I help it along a bit.'

'That's a pretty big change of heart, isn't it? What happened to professional ethics?'

'Well, it's different now, you see. I met her as an ordinary person, not a professional anything.'

'Too subtle for me,' said Ben. 'I think you were right the first time. Except, it *might* move things along a bit. Make something happen.'

Simmy shivered. 'And it might not be anything good. Maybe I'll just play it by ear, and if it seems reasonable I'll do it, but only if I'm sure. How's that?'

'Why not just phone her?' said Ben. 'Instead of going all the way up there in the dark.'

'That wouldn't work. What would I say? I need to lead up to it gradually, testing the water as I go. I need to watch her expression. It might turn out that she's perfectly all right. She might have somebody with her, or have gone to stay with one of the daughters.'

'Or she might already be dead in her hallway,' said Melanie. 'And then you'd spend all night in the nick, answering questions.'

Simmy winced. 'Don't say that. Of course, she might not let me in. She's not awfully keen on me as it is. But I really think I ought to make an effort. I feel responsible.' She glared at Ben on the seat next to her, trying to convey that most of her unease was his doing.

'Nothing so far has been your fault,' he said, as if this was too obvious to need voicing. 'But if you tell her the girl's name, you'll have got yourself more deeply involved. You see that, don't you?'

'I suppose so. But it would stop them being so cross with me.' She could hear the childish desire to be liked in her own voice, and felt foolish. But it was true, for all that.

'Do you want us to come with you?' Melanie asked. 'Because if you do, it'll have to be quick. I'm seeing Joe this evening.'

'And I'm rehearsing my lines,' said Ben.

'No, no. That would be all wrong. We don't want to look like a deputation,' Simmy assured them. 'I'll just say I was in Ambleside, and thought I'd drop in to say hello.'

'She'll think that's very strange,' said Melanie. 'It's not as if you're her friend.'

'I don't care what she thinks. I just want to be sure she's all right. I'll say I've been worrying about her, and felt bad about not cooperating when she came to see me. It's true, after all.'

'Go on, then,' said Melanie, as if Simmy needed her permission.

'You won't be home by five,' Ben observed. 'There might be a frost later on.'

'Shut up,' said Simmy. 'Only this morning you were telling me I was being scared for nothing.' She tried not to visualise the steep winding road back to Troutbeck, where treacherous patches of ice could so easily lie in wait for her. 'I'm taking you home, and then I'm going to Ambleside.'

'Not me. I'll walk,' said Melanie, already opening the door. Simmy had never yet seen the Todd house, and suspected that her assistant was ashamed of it.

TEN MINUTES LATER, she was heading north on the road to Ambleside, rehearsing exactly what she would say to Mrs Joseph, if and when the old lady opened the door to her.

Parking was complicated in the poor light, with very few available spaces in the twisting streets at the northern end of the town, but eventually she tucked it into a quiet yard not far from the Unicorn pub, hoping nobody would object on a Sunday. She automatically took her shoulder bag with her and locked the car, before making for the upper reaches of Ambleside. This entailed a walk up Peggy Hill, having negotiated the short white-painted tunnel that curved around and up the lower part of the hill. Christmas lights twinkled from the surrounding shops and houses, but it was still uncomfortably dark in the narrow streets. For a few moments, she lost her bearings, unsure of whether she needed to traverse another row of houses before locating the one she wanted. She tried to remember the number, in vain, but a distinctive shrub beside a front porch jogged her memory, and she knocked on the door of the adjacent whitewashed cottage. Most of the houses up here were white, as were several in Troutbeck. It was the only permitted colour, it seemed, other than the natural dark grey stone.

There was no reply to her knock and she tried again, remembering to stand well back from the outward-opening door. She felt the usual irrational rejection that came with the situation. After she'd gone to so much trouble, the least the woman could do was to be at home. It was no time to be out – unless, of course, she was at church. That was all too possible. There might be a special carol service going on somewhere. The thought had not occurred to her until that moment. Even if it had, she would not have known the usual time for Sunday services. It was just after five, and the word *evensong* flitted into her mind, with images of candlelight and angelic children singing 'Silent Night'.

She turned to go, pressing into the stone wall opposite the cottage to allow a car to creep past. These streets had never been designed for modern traffic, and vehicles were forced to park at all kinds of awkward angles, with no suggestion of garages or carports. Once in, there was often no choice but to go out again in reverse – which was why Simmy never even considered bringing her own car this far up the hill. The car pulled up a few yards further on, but nobody got out. Simmy assumed it must be a couple, using the car as an undisturbed place for a kiss and a cuddle, or an intense conversation. She could dimly see two heads in the front.

Slowly, with a dragging sense of disappointment, she retraced her steps down the hill. Perhaps if she dawdled enough, she would meet Mrs Joseph coming towards her, and be invited back for tea. Stock Ghyll dashed past on her right, deep in a cleft between the buildings. In summer, customers at the Giggling Goose sat outside, overlooking the stream. A stone ledge provided a high seat for children, held tightly by their parents, so they could see the water below them. On a winter night, the ghyll was more sound than sight, the water loud and urgent. There were no people visible, and Simmy paused to absorb the distinctive atmosphere. It pleased her that there was no need to walk up onto the fells in order to savour the elements that made up the whole region. Hurtling water, implacable stone, a sense of timelessness – they were all right there in the little town. She leant her forearms on the stone ledge, and gazed down at the flickering shadowy water twenty feet or so below her. Her coat was thick and warm, but her feet were slightly cold, despite the ankle boots she was wearing.

When a hand was placed firmly on the back of her neck, her first fleeting impression was that some friend had crept up behind her, to surprise her. She waited for an explanatory voice, unable to turn round, even if she tried. But she did not try. She waited trustingly even when the hand pushed her head and shoulders forward. Then another hand somehow scooped her legs, below the knee, and lifted them high. Then she tried to kick and twist. Her hands tried to grip the stone, only to slither over its smooth cold surface. She was moving forward, horizontally, to the edge, the drop. It wasn't possible, her brain insisted. It was a joke, a game. The concept of a deliberate act, in which an innocent woman could be pushed over a ledge into a dark, cold river, was beyond acceptability. She sailed head first onto the hard rocks of the river bed still unable to process the idea. No protest, no fear or attempt

to save herself had time to surface. She was still asking herself
who it was, and what unthinkable dislocation in the pattern of
the universe could be taking place, when she lost consciousness.
She never even noticed how cold the water was, as it carried her
downstream towards the town's main car park.

Chapter Thirteen

SHE DID FEEL cold some time later. She was aware of violent shivering, inside the impossibly heavy coat. Her head hurt with a pounding agony that wouldn't let her think. There was something hard pushing against her chest, and her feet were rising and falling in a fractured rhythm that brought a sweeping black terror with it. She was nothing but a powerless, tormented body. Pain and fear swamped everything else. No questions formed; no determined efforts to survive. She lay inertly, all movement created by external forces. Until she found her fingers. They were curled tightly against her chest, trapped by the hard object, and cold. But they moved when she wanted them to. They twitched and twisted, and finally opened. They were bare of gloves, stiff and sore, but they worked. She used them to push, and found herself moving bodily as her arms straightened, a frightening floating movement. Volition brought dawning consciousness with it. She could still use her own will, which meant she must be alive. Where, when, why, how, who – they were all still beyond her reach, but she could sense them approaching.

Water. She was in cold running water that had hard things in it. There were sounds somewhere close by. An engine. A voice. There were yellow lights, one of them directly above her. So her eyes and ears were functioning, she noted with astonished relief. She must be breathing, then. Her heart must be beating. Such fundamentals acquired immense significance, and acted like magic to repel the towering pain in her head. She made a faint gurgling sound of pure joy, which was cut off when it turned into a choking cough and an understanding that there was water inside her where it ought not to be.

'Mummy – there's a person in the water,' came a clear angelic voice, miraculously close by.

'Don't be silly, darling.'

'There *is*. Look! Right there.'

So Mummy looked, and screamed and slowly recruited people who felt equal to the arduous task of wading into the shallow edge of Stock Ghyll and heaving the sodden object that was Persimmon Brown onto the comparatively dry surface of the Ambleside main car park.

She coughed again, and stretched her arms, but uttered no words. More people appeared, after a long cold time, who lifted her into a warm vehicle and removed her ruined coat. They wrapped her in shiny stuff that made her think she must in fact be dreaming. Then, after another long time, in which she shivered so much her teeth clattered together loud enough to frighten her, she was in a room, full of voices and machines and faces that came and went in a strange dance that formed no comprehensible pattern. Somebody asked insistent questions, but her head was too painful for there to be a chance of processing an answer. Her main worry continued to be *Where?* It was a hospital, she understood – but which one? It mattered immensely to her, to know where in the world she had been taken. The nearest town of any size was Kendal, which did have a hospital. Somehow she knew that, deep beneath the awful pain. People died there. People dying was the main thing she knew about hospitals – not people being wrapped up warmly and given injections and asked impossible questions.

But the pain was becoming more muffled, subdued by the attentions of the people. It turned into a rhythmic throb that felt as if it *should* hurt, but strangely didn't. 'Tell us your name, dear,' urged a new face. 'We need to tell your family where you are. They'll be worrying about you.'

'Simmy,' she croaked. 'Where am I?'

'Sammy? Samantha? Is that it? Or Jimmy?'

She shook her head hopelessly, inwardly blaming her mother for giving her such a ridiculous name. 'P'simmon,' she whispered. 'P'simmon Brown.'

'Brown!' The young woman – more than ten years younger than Simmy – latched onto the syllable with relief. 'And you live in Ambleside, right?'

'Troutbeck. Where am I?'

'Ms Brown from Troutbeck,' announced her inquisitor to the room in general. 'Is that enough to go on? I couldn't catch the first name. Sounded foreign.'

Simmy experienced a powerful wish for Ben Harkness to materialise. He would explain everything to these people. He would understand what had happened to her, much better than she did herself. Gradually, the word *forensic* came into focus, followed by a murky idea that nobody knew how she had come to be in the water. They might think she jumped in on purpose. It mattered that they should not think this, but they had other things on their minds, it seemed.

'Miss Brown – your pelvis is broken, and your skull might be cracked. Now the hypothermia is under control, we need to x-ray you.' It was a Chinese man speaking. His accent was soothingly sing-song, the words entirely unworrying as a result. X-rays didn't hurt, after all. And a cracked skull sounded almost funny. *Like an egg*, she thought. Already she had forgotten the part about her pelvis.

'Yes,' she said. It sounded pleasingly clear inside her muffled head. 'Yesss,' she said again, lingering on the sibilance.

They wheeled her, bed and all, into another room. There was then some disagreeable manoeuvring that taught her how limp and unresponsive much of her body had become. She still had no idea where she was, or what time it might be, or which detail should be the most concerning out of a host of possible candidates.

After that she fell asleep and missed a lot of procedures. She finally woke in a different room, with something tight round her head. Just about everything she had ever known was lost and forgotten, including the worrying questions. Her throat was dry and scratchy when she tried to swallow. There was a stabbing pain in her hand. When she tried to wiggle a foot, it only minimally obeyed. It was a while before it occurred to her to open her eyes. When she did, she saw a small window high on a pale-green wall, revealing a pale-grey sky. 'Is it morning?' she gasped.

A woman was standing by her feet. 'Hello,' she smiled. 'Don't worry – you're doing fine.'

She hadn't known she was *doing* anything. 'Am I?' she said, in puzzlement. 'I need water. Please.' The words scraped their way through the sore throat and swollen tongue. She did not expect them to have the desired effect.

But by some magic, they did. The smiling woman brought a plastic cup to her lips and carefully poured some drops into her mouth. 'Better?' she asked.

Simmy tried to nod, but the tightness around her head made it feel dangerous. 'Tell me,' she pleaded.

Again, by a miracle, her request was answered. 'You're in Barrow-in-Furness. They brought you here last night, after you were found in the ghyll in Ambleside. You had hypothermia, severe bruising, a broken pelvis and a fractured skull. You had surgery to alleviate the pressure on your brain, and to put a thing called a fixator around your hips – and you were then sedated for the rest of the night, to give everything a chance to settle down. You'll probably need another operation on your pelvis in a day or two.'

She had never been to Barrow-in-Furness, despite its being only thirty miles or so from Windermere. She had been to Kendal, Whitehaven, Keswick and Carlisle – but the big coastal town to the south remained unvisited. She imagined it as somewhat smoky and uninviting. 'How will I get home?' she whimpered idiotically.

The woman laughed. 'Don't you worry about that. We'll get you home – and in plenty of time for Christmas, too. Now, listen – there's somebody here to see you. He's been waiting quite a while. I'm going to go and tell him you're awake, and he can stay ten minutes. Okay?'

Ben. It would be Ben, she knew. She was about to nod when she remembered the effect it would have. 'Yes,' she said.

It wasn't Ben, but a much older man. He swept into the room like a doctor on an urgent errand, and stood looking down at her. His face was foreshortened, the chin too big and the hair scarcely visible. 'What happened to you?' he asked.

It was DI Moxon. The voice confirmed it. She sighed at the prospect of more questions, the answers to which barely concerned her. She didn't care enough to make the necessary effort. 'I don't know,' she breathed. 'Could you sit down, do you think?'

He narrowed his eyes, and nibbled his lower lip, and went to fetch a chair from a corner of the room. When he spoke again, it was with obvious restraint. 'We think you must have gone into the water somewhere upstream of the car park, to get so many bruises. And the most likely place is the bridge just above the Giggling Goose. Do you remember that? Did you fall in by accident?'

'A person threw me in,' she said regretfully.

'Where?'

'Over that ledge. Where you said. I don't remember much.'

'Do you know what time that was?'

'About five, I think. Evensong.'

He smiled uncertainly. 'You went to evensong? Where?'

'No, I didn't. Mrs Joseph might have done. I thought she might. She wasn't in.'

'You were in the water for an hour, then. It's incredible you survived.'

'It was cold,' she agreed. 'With hard rocks.'

'Do you know who it was? Who's Mrs Joseph?'

'She's an old lady. It wasn't her. I don't know who it might have been. Just a pair of hands. They tipped me over. Like a doll. Or a model from a shop window. You know? I just shot right over. I can see myself.' She frowned cautiously. 'Like a doll.'

'Man or woman?'

'Don't know.'

'Did they say anything? Was there any noticeable smell? Perfume, or cigarettes, or alcohol? Can you remember?'

'Sorry.'

'Your parents will be coming soon. We managed to let them know what had happened late last night.'

'Oh.' She gave this some thought. 'That could have waited until the morning. Did you wake them up?'

He smiled ruefully. 'Very probably.'

'But this is Barrow, isn't it? They won't want to come to Barrow.'

'It's the nearest A&E department. Only forty minutes or so from Windermere. Some people get taken to Lancaster. That's twice as far.'

'I broke my pelvis. They don't seem to think that's very serious.' As she spoke, she wondered where that impression had come from. Her lower half was invisibly encased in a sort of cage, and she had not yet attempted to test how much she could move.

'I think it's quite serious,' he argued mildly. 'They'll be worried about internal damage, as well.'

'Really? I suppose I bashed it on a rock, same as my head. I can wiggle my toes, though. That's good, isn't it?'

'Ask the doctor,' he evaded. 'I could tell you all wrong. My job is to find out why somebody tried to kill you.'

'Is that what they did?' She felt nothing but weariness at the idea. Everything that was happening was utterly exhausting, including answering a detective inspector's questions.

'Isn't it?' He shook his head in something that looked like despair. Then, he took a deep breath and raised his chin. 'Who's Mrs Joseph?' he asked again.

The realisation of how much he did not know drained Simmy even further. Scraps of conversation from the previous afternoon returned to her, with connections and suspicions that floated away when she tried to capture them. She felt sorry for the policeman in his blinkered quest for the killer of Miss Clark. And her sympathy stirred her to an effort. But first she needed to adjust her position. Something somewhere was stiff, another area was aching. Pressing her elbows into the bed, she began to haul herself further up the pillows.

A vicious pain shot through her, radiating north and south from her hips. 'Aarghh!' she shouted, before a great trembling gripped her. All her deepest organs were quivering from the attack. She felt as if she was helplessly dissolving into a watery sludge, which would never function as a body again.

'Nurse!' yelled DI Moxon.

MUCH LATER, SHE was restored to something more human, thanks to chemical intervention, and her parents were sitting on either side of the bed. She remembered her father's cat, whose pelvis was also broken. 'Can you nurse me as well as Chucky?' she asked weakly.

Her mother put on a grimly cheerful manner and pointed out that the timing could hardly be better. She said there would be no B&B guests for the next two weeks at least, which left her perfectly free to take care of her daughter. 'You'll have to use the playroom,' she sighed. 'You won't manage stairs for ages.'

The 'playroom' was a well-stocked lounge, specifically for the use of guests. It had games, a TV, books and spare clothes for wet walkers. There was no space for a bed without major reorganisation. Glimpses of the implications of her condition gave Simmy reason to quail and whimper. 'I'm so sorry,' she wailed.

Angie had never taken easily to the inevitable disturbances that came with parenthood. She had snarled dreadfully every time little Simmy had fallen ill and stayed off school. She made great commotions when the bus was late returning from a school trip, causing her such inconvenience. She had moaned about the impossible decisions over curfews and boyfriends and which A levels to take. Russell had gone unheard when he tried to remind her how lucky they were – how Simmy had been an extraordinarily easy daughter compared to most.

But now Angie was doing her utmost to rise to the occasion. She meant it when she said the timing was good. She pointed out that a small bed could quite easily fit into the corner where the clothes chest stood. Hardly any major shifting around would be needed. She attempted to reassure her daughter that it would all work out quite well. 'And if there's more snow, you won't have to worry about driving up and down the road from Troutbeck,' she concluded.

Neither parent seemed much interested in the cause of Simmy's injuries. The absence of questions struck her as unnatural. 'Have you been speaking to Mr Moxon?' she asked them.

'Who?' said her father.

'The detective investigating the murder of Nancy Clark.' The sentence tired her, by taking her back to the complications and threats that formed a thick, dark backdrop to everything else.

'Who?' repeated her father blankly.

If he was acting, he was doing it well. She tried to see into his mind, testing him for subterfuge. 'What have they told you?' she finally asked. 'About what happened to me?'

'They don't want you to get upset,' said Angie uncomfortably. 'We're to keep things positive.'

The surge of anger was almost as disabling as the earlier pain had been. She wanted to express it, but couldn't find the words. Instead she made a sound that was part growl, part moan. A silence followed that seemed to be full of effort and resentment. 'What about my shop?' It was the first time she had given it a thought. Now it seemed like a safe and not-very-important subject.

'Melanie's putting a sign on the door saying it's closed until the New Year,' said Russell.

'But there are orders for next week. She'll have to find someone else to do them, and check the computer every day for new ones.'

'She says she can do that from home. Lots of businesses will be closing for Christmas, anyway.'

'Yes, but …' She trailed off, not caring about lost orders or flowers left rotting in the storeroom. Melanie might have the wit to cancel further deliveries, she supposed.

'I wish Ben would come and see me. Will you ask him?'

'Who?' said her father for the third time.

'That boy,' Angie told him quickly. 'P'simmon's geeky friend – *you* know. The one who got so involved last time.'

Last time. The words swelled significantly in Simmy's head. It had of course occurred to her that she was currently entangled in a second murder investigation, but the details and circumstances were so different that she had refused to link them in her mind. To do so was to admit the dreadful possibility that there could perhaps be a *next time* as well. And *this time* was turning out very badly indeed.

'Ben can't come all the way to Barrow,' Angie told her. 'School doesn't finish until the end of the week.'

'The play!' she bleated. Ben's play was the only engagement she had in her metaphorical diary for the foreseeable future. He had given her a ticket. She wanted to go and see him perform. 'Will I be able to go to the play?'

Angie's eyes widened. 'When is it?'

'Saturday.'

'Not a chance,' said her mother flatly. 'Friday's the absolute earliest they'll let you out of here, according to the doctor.'

'We brought you a couple of nighties, pyjamas and a book and the local paper,' offered Russell, rummaging in a plastic carrier bag at his feet. 'Your mother didn't know which was best – nightie or jim-jams. We'd better go now. You'll be having more tests and things soon. They'll tell you everything. We told them you're a big grown-up girl and can take the truth, whatever it is. We'll phone to see how you are this evening, and be back tomorrow.'

A big grown-up girl. She was thirty-eight, so it must be true. The fact that she felt about twelve was simply a consequence of being clucked over and patronised. But the prospect of being told a terrible truth that until then she had not even remotely anticipated sent icy waves through her veins.

IN THE EVENT, nobody told her anything until the following morning. Then an Indian doctor appeared at her bedside and started to explain about the construction of the pelvis and the nature of her injury. She watched his long, soft eyelashes intently. He could be Pakistani, she decided, with such fine bones to his nose and jaw. He was small and kind and conscientious. She made a token attempt to understand his message, but it remained obscure. All she grasped was that she had been lucky. Blood loss had been minimal, and internal damage entirely absent. 'No blood in your urine,' he announced with a smile. There would be another operation that afternoon, to insert a small metal plate that would hold the broken bones together. Then something about ten or twelve weeks in which no weight-bearing could be permitted. There was an elusive implication in those words that frightened her. When he invited questions, she simply sighed and shook her head.

IT WAS TUESDAY, she calculated with dismay. Somebody had tried to kill her on Sunday, and now it was Tuesday and her attacker could be in Australia for all anybody knew, free to continue a life of liberty and ease. Was that what murderers did, though? As a deliberate exercise, Simmy tried to imagine herself into the brain of a killer. It would divert her from worries about the ban on weight-bearing, if nothing else.

But before she got far, a nurse came in, holding a phone. 'Call for you,' she said.

It was not her own phone. That was inside her bag, which was probably at the bottom of Lake Windermere by now. And for the first time she thought about her car, which was illegally parked in a yard in Ambleside. Another thing she had totally forgotten about. What would they do to it? She liked her car and hated to think of it being hauled off to a pound somewhere and finally crushed into scrap metal.

But the call was waiting. She took the phone, holding it awkwardly to her bandaged head. 'Hello?' she said.

It was Ben. 'What happened?' he breathed in a childlike voice.

'Hasn't anybody told you?'

'Sort of. Melanie called last night. I had no idea,' he complained.

The day before, she had wanted to speak to him, more than to anyone else. Now he was far from the right person for her needs. She wanted a woman who would keep her warm and safe and shielded from worry. Or a very kind strong man who would settle everything in a calm, practical fashion. Neither of her parents quite fitted these requirements. Ben was a million miles short of meeting them.

'I can't tell you about it now,' she said. 'It's too scary. Too complicated. I might have *died*.'

'I know. So the person has to be caught, before they do it again.'

Only moments before, she had been planning to meditate on the motives and personality of the mysterious killer. Now she cringed at the prospect. 'Easy to say,' she whined.

'I'll have to go to the police and tell them all that stuff about Mrs Joseph and her daughters. You *were* there, weren't you? At her house? Did you see her? What *happened*?'

'Oh, Ben,' she moaned. 'That would be such a relief if you did it, instead of me. I wanted to tell Moxon, yesterday, but it was too hard. You explain it all to him. The granddaughter stuff. And Mr Kitchener's mother.'

'I will,' he promised stoutly. 'Leave it to me. Because ... Simmy ...'

'What?'

'It has to be one or other of them that did it. Hasn't it?'

Her mind thickened and clouded. 'One or other of who?'

'The granddaughter or Mr Kitchener,' he repeated loudly. 'I've thought the whole thing through, and that's what it comes down to. One of them did it – Miss Clark and now you. Don't you know if it was a man or a woman who attacked you?'

She forced herself to think, conscious that she owed it to Ben to try. 'There was a hand on the back of my neck.' She felt it again.

'Was it bare or wearing a glove? Was it *strong*?'

'I don't know. It was through my coat collar and hair. I was leaning forward anyway, so it was easy to push me.'

'Where were you, exactly?'

'Looking over that bridge, by the Giggling Goose.'

'I can't remember what it's like. How high is it?'

'Chest height, more or less. The person lifted my legs and sort of *shot* me over.'

'A man, then,' said Ben with certainty. 'Only a man could have lifted you so easily.'

'Or could be there were two of them,' she mused.

'You think? Didn't anybody *say* anything?'

'Not a word. That made it so much worse. More inhuman.'

'Poor you,' he said, with such sincerity she felt tears prickling. 'Does it hurt?'

'My head just aches, but the pelvis is agony if I move. They're doing another operation this afternoon. I'm quite a mess, actually. I'll miss your play. I'm really sad about that.'

'Oh, well,' he said bravely and she could hear how much it mattered. 'No big deal.'

'It's a bummer,' she insisted. 'I was looking forward to it.'

'At least you're not dead,' he said, with unarguable force.

Chapter Fourteen

SHE CAME ROUND at six on Tuesday evening, to meet the eyes of her father, patiently sitting by the bed. He smiled and she moaned. 'Does it hurt?' he asked softly.

'I don't know. What's happening?'

'They've patched you up, and confirmed there's no damage internally. You can start learning how to use the crutches tomorrow. It's all miraculously fast, compared to the olden days. Same as the poor pusscat, actually. Must be improvements in the anaesthetics, I suppose.'

'Crutches?'

'That's right. They said they told you about not putting weight on it.'

'I didn't realise that meant crutches. Can I have a drink?'

There was a nurse in the room somewhere, and as before, the request was quickly obeyed. Then her vital processes were checked on the machine behind her head, and her father given an encouraging smile. It was all reassuringly *human*, Simmy thought comfortably – unlike the cruel impersonal attack on her. Even if nobody actually felt for a pulse with a warm fingertip any more, there was a kindness in the air. Perhaps she was just lucky. The news was always running reports of neglected old people dying of thirst in hospital.

'They're nice here, aren't they?' she said.

'As good as good can be,' he said, using one of his many catchphrases.

'How's the cat?'

'Coming along brilliantly. He's walking already. Still not allowed out by himself, of course.'

'He can sleep in with me. You can set up a sickroom for us both.'

'I was thinking that Bertie will probably want to cuddle up with you, as well.'

Simmy grunted. 'Or maybe not. He's too smelly.' The Lakeland terrier's reputation for bad breath was legendary. He also had permanently muddy feet from his digging operations at the end of the garden.

Russell shrugged and moved on to the next item on his mental list. 'Your friend Ben phoned us. He's been to the police, this afternoon. Caused quite a stir, apparently. I think you might get a visitation again tomorrow, if you're well enough.'

'From Ben?'

'No, silly. From the police. They seem to think you've got a great deal that you can tell them. They wanted to come today, but the medics vetoed it. I've got to go in a minute, as well. I just wanted to make sure ...' He stopped and gave an artificial cough that did nothing to hide his emotion.

'Oh, Dad.' Tears ran down the sides of her face, and he managed a watery laugh.

'Didn't mean to set you off,' he said. 'But you can imagine the effect on your mother and me. It's going to be all right, though. No lasting damage, they said. You'll be back to normal by the New Year.'

'Really?'

'Nearly,' he amended. 'No driving for the foreseeable future, unfortunately.'

'So how can I go back to Troutbeck?' Implications began to chip through the barrier she had unconsciously erected in her mind. 'How can I run the shop? I won't be able to make deliveries.' Her breath began to catch. 'I'll go out of business.'

Her father put a hand on her shoulder, pressing her into the bed. 'Stop it,' he ordered. 'You've got nearly three weeks to sort it all out. Melanie can drive, if she has to. There are all sorts of things we can do, between us. Now get a good rest, and I'll see you again tomorrow.'

She passed a long tormented night, in a different room, containing two other women. Her recovery was so good, it seemed, that she no longer warranted the solitude she had come to take for granted. One of the women alternately snored and moaned, while the other clearly had no idea of where she was or why she was there. 'Maisie!' she called, approximately every thirty minutes. 'Where are you, Maisie?' Everything had suddenly become much more like the hospital stories so beloved of the media. Simmy felt sick, thirsty, sore and scared. When she slept, she dreamt that all the flowers from her shop were being hurled into Stock Ghyll by a hooded, faceless figure. Then she dreamt that a huge cat was sitting suffocatingly on her chest. When she fumblingly tried to push it off, she woke enough to understand that it was her own hands, pressing on the painful bruise that she had not noticed until then. Experiment showed her that it spanned an area including her breasts and extending down to her navel. Next morning, she would have to undress and have a good look at herself, however appalling it might be. Nobody in the hospital seemed to be aware of that aspect of her injuries at all, presumably because bruises were so much less interesting than broken bones.

The first signs of morning were the raised level of lighting and a clattering of metal equipment in a nearby room, since the room had no windows. A nurse appeared, who proceeded to tinker with a plastic tube that mysteriously led from under Simmy's blankets to something invisible on the floor. 'What *is* that?' she asked.

'A catheter. Why do you think you haven't had to go for a pee in the past two days?'

This took a moment to process. 'Oh!.You mean, it's in my bladder? I had no idea.' Her ignorance struck her as culpable in some way. It was, after all, her body. She should be taking more notice of what was being done to it.

'It's coming out soon. You're to get walking later today. The sooner we get you out of here the better.'

'Oh,' said Simmy again, feeling alarmingly frightened, not least by the unfriendly tone. 'On crutches?'

'That's right. You'll soon get the hang of it.'

'I hope so. Are you pushed for bed space, or something, to want me out so soon?'

'Not specially. It's the police guard in the corridor that we don't much like.'

'Pardon?'

'Didn't anybody tell you? You're a security risk or something. Nobody allowed in to see you unless they satisfy the man on the door.'

For a mad moment, she imagined DI Moxon sitting there all night, faithfully watching over her in case she was dragged from her bed and thrown once again into a freezing Lakeland river. 'How long has he been there?' she asked.

'Half an hour, and we're already fed up with him.'

The nurse faded away, without making any further disclosures. Simmy rather missed her, feeling she might be due some further ministrations. She might have quite liked that warm finger on her pulse, and the briskly shaken thermometer that patients once had inserted under their tongues. Where was the upside-down watch for counting heartbeats, and the black rubber stethoscope? All gone, it seemed; replaced by digital read-outs on a screen on the wall above the bedhead. She had wanted to say something about her bruising, and the dressing on her head, that felt so weird. A delicate fingertip exploration suggested that much of her hair had been shaved off, which gave her another lurch of panic. There was every prospect that the day would bring a succession of such moments, as she was forced to abandon her passive horizontal position and return to some sort of normality.

It made sense, she supposed, to have the police watching out for further attempts on her life, but it was unnerving to think such an attempt might happen in a hospital. Was it not far more likely to be when she was at her parents' house, where the door was seldom locked and all sorts of people came and went? Her mother would not react well to a constant constable sitting outside in his steamed-up car, or – even worse – inside her hallway, with a rustling newspaper.

Gradually, a belated sense of outrage took hold of her. She had been singled out from the start, with no say in the matter. All she had done was deliver a cheap bunch of flowers to an old lady, and listened to why the flowers could not have come from the person claiming to have sent them. And *then*, as an added insult, she had been cited as an alibi to a man suspected of murder. She had been twice victimised, even before being half killed. As Ben had said, there was every reason to suppose that the attack had come from one or other of those individuals who had already used her in some complicated plan to create an alibi, for reasons that remained stubbornly obscure.

Candida Hawkins was tall, young, well muscled. She had added her weight to the strenuous heaving of her car back onto the road. She might be a black belt judo practitioner for all Simmy knew. All that had been required was to catch Simmy off balance, and gravity did the rest.

Mr Kitchener was an inch or so shorter than Candida. He had a funny leg. He seemed to be vaguely unhealthy and definitely unfit. But he was a man, and men had a natural strength to them that automatically qualified them for physical aggression.

The problem for Simmy was that she had believed that both Candida and Kitchener had *liked* her. She liked both of them, and the thought of either trying to kill her was abominable. How could either of them have turned so cold-bloodedly vile as to do such a thing, after showing such warmth beforehand?

She was brought a melancholy breakfast of cold toast and tasteless cereal swimming in far too much skimmed milk. Weak tea eventually followed, very nearly stone cold. Nobody had asked her about any preferences. The old woman who had called all night for Maisie was now in a deep sleep, only to be roughly aroused to consume the unappealing meal. She gazed blearily at Simmy and made no attempt whatever to feed herself.

The morning passed in a jerky alternation between dozing boredom and sudden activity. She was hauled out of bed and into a chair while the sheets were changed. Then two nurses took an arm each and effectively carried her to the bathroom where she finally had a chance to inspect herself in a mirror, having been subjected to an astonishingly undignified procedure during which she was positioned on the lavatory and expected to urinate despite tight dressings holding her pelvis in place. Everything hurt, including one knee, her head and the bruises on her chest. But the nurses were adamant, and gradually she confirmed that both hip joints were intact and worked well enough to enable her to sit down. The idea of a broken pelvis gained substance, as she examined the extent of the damage. Her left side was wadded with taped-on dressings, just above the hip. 'You must not put any weight *at all* on that side for at least a month,' said one nurse. The bone was badly cracked, she explained, and needed time to heal.

'But even with crutches, you have to put some weight on your legs,' she argued, trying to visualise how life would be.

'That'll all be explained to you later today,' said the nurse.

The bruise on her chest was already a nightmare mixture of black, purple and green. The green was on her breasts, and made her gasp in horror. 'Look at me!' she wailed.

'Breast tissue always looks dreadful when it's damaged,' said one of the nurses. 'You've got a cracked rib, apparently, but it's nothing to worry about.'

'What about my head?' She'd been right about the shaved area, although it was smaller than she had feared.

'We'll have a look in a minute. Your vitals are fine, so it doesn't seem to be causing any concern.'

A doctor turned up sometime later and told her she was lucky. The pelvis had survived remarkably well, under the circumstances, and all she had to do was keep it straight and let it mend. It was an awkward bone to deal with, but she was young and healthy ('and blessedly slim,' he added boldly) and should have no lasting effects. 'We'll probably send you home first thing Friday,' he added casually.

It seemed sadistically irresponsible to Simmy. She couldn't walk. She had a wound in her head. Her breasts were green and a rib was cracked. How in the world could she possibly go home like that?

And yet it was no fun in hospital. She was already dreading the coming noisy night. The only hope was to be so exhausted by all the demanding daytime activity that she could sleep through anything.

Nobody visited her before midday, but then a steady stream developed. First was DI Moxon, pulling rank and ignoring official visiting hours. He leant over her, with real concern in his eyes, and asked her how she was. When she managed to convince him that she was dramatically improved, he slowly came to the point. 'Your young friend Mr Harkness came to see me,' he told her. 'Had quite a story to tell.'

He expressed reproach via his eyebrows. 'Couldn't you have come to me sooner with your suspicions?'

'Um ...' she began. 'I'm not sure ...'

'Those flowers, from a granddaughter who the family never knew ever existed, for a start. Wasn't it worth telling me about that?'

'I don't see why.' She was rallying in the face of his unreasonableness. 'It couldn't have been anything to do with the murder. At least ...'

'Perhaps it could,' he supplied heavily.

'Ben told you what Mrs Ellis said, did he? How Mr Kitchener's mother was her best friend, and the Clark twins were at different schools? Penny married a farmer and had five children, while

Nancy never married and worked in a clinic. She carried on with the consultant there, according to rumour. Did Ben tell you all that?' She gave a weary exhalation after the long speech.

Moxon had a notepad on his lap. 'You're telling me everybody knows everybody, right? Kitcheners, Clarks … what about these Joseph people?'

'Matthew Joseph – her husband. He was at school with the others. Not her, though. She came from somewhere else.'

'Why do you think you were attacked?' he blurted suddenly, cutting through the complex network of local affiliations. 'What had you done? What did you know?'

She had still not expressed the questions to herself in quite such terms. 'I have no idea,' she said. 'I've been wondering whether they've been using me all along, somehow. It's a horrible feeling.'

'They?'

'He. She. Whoever's behind all this.'

'She?'

'I thought perhaps a person called Candida Hawkins might have done it.' There – she had committed the betrayal that she'd resisted so earnestly a few days before. 'She's the granddaughter who sent Mrs Joseph the flowers. Or says she is. But it might have been Mr Kitchener. Something to do with the alibi I gave him. Or both of them together. I think they might know each other. But of course if you've got the timing right for Miss Clark's murder, then it couldn't have been either of them, could it? Because they were in the café with me.'

Moxon closed his eyes. 'This is not the way murder investigations generally go,' he complained. 'As a general rule, the police officer has at least some idea of what the witness is trying to tell him.'

'Sorry. Which bit didn't you understand?'

'More or less all of it. You obviously know far more about this whole case than I do – which is tantamount to obstructing the course of justice, if we're being particular about it.'

'I'm doing my best. What's wrong with what I've just told you? What's wrong with me, that you get so cross?'

'You're unusual,' he told her. 'You don't seem to have any idea about rules of evidence, for a start.'

'That's true. It's never occurred to me to pay them much attention.'

'You'll have to if you're ever called for jury service.'

'I expect I will,' she said. 'Except you'll have explained it to me before that, I imagine.'

His lips tightened. 'This is the first time I've heard the name Candida Hawkins. Do you have an address for her? Any other details? Reasons for your suspicions? What car does she drive?'

The mention of a car triggered a memory. 'There was a car on Sunday,' she said. 'At the top of Peggy Hill. It had two people in it.'

'And?'

'It might have been them who threw me over the ledge. They could have followed me down the ginnel and crept up behind me.'

'Describe the car.'

'Pale colour. Middle-sized. Quiet engine.'

He waited, with little sign of anticipation. Simmy tried to capture more descriptive detail in vain. 'Isn't there a CCTV camera up there anywhere?' she asked, eventually.

He shook his head. 'One further up the hill, that's all.'

'Nothing in the ginnel? That might have been useful. It would have shown anybody following me.'

'There's one at the Unicorn pub, which has a shot of you,' he said. 'On your way up to Peggy Hill.'

She shivered at the idea. 'How beastly,' she said. 'And how use-less.' Her mother's abiding rage at being so constantly monitored and surveyed flickered in her own breast.

'You'd have been glad of it, if the attack on you was on film.'

'Not really. It wouldn't have saved my poor pelvis, would it?'

'But it would stop the attacker hurting anybody else.'

That thought had never crossed her mind. 'Somebody else? Who?'

He sighed. 'If we knew that, the case would be solved. We have no idea what's behind all this. We don't even know if the same person is responsible. There's no forensic evidence whatsoever sur-viving from your hour in the water. It was a very efficient crime.'

'Nancy Clark was killed by a lethal injection – is that right? I'm lucky I didn't go the same way, then. I wonder why that was.'

His eyes bulged. 'How do you know that?'

'Grapevine,' she shrugged. 'What does it matter? That murder sounded pretty efficient as well.'

'The cause of death is meant to be totally confidential. If the means is kept out of the public domain, it gives us a better chance that someone will give themselves away.'

'Like I just did,' she said, with a stab of anxiety. 'It could have been me that killed Nancy Clark. I was in town at the right time, after all.'

'Yes, you could,' he nodded. 'Except that alibis cut both ways. Mr Kitchener is yours, the same as you're his. And I can't for one second imagine what possible motive you could have had.'

'She doesn't sound very nice, does she?' Simmy was feeling slightly giddy, from a new throb inside her head, and a returning ache in her chest. 'Nancy Clark, I mean. Nobody seems to have liked her.'

'Not many friends,' he agreed. 'But we learnt about the con-sultant. It often happens, don't you find? A woman who carries on with a married man forfeits most of her female friends. They don't approve.'

'That's rather outside my experience. Were they still carrying on, then, up to when she died?'

'Oh, no. He's ninety now and in a home.'

'Do you think they had a secret love child?'

He shook his head. 'The post-mortem showed she's never had a child.'

'You should talk to Mrs Ellis,' she said, feeling again the guilty stab of treachery. Melanie's gran had no love for the police, and would not be pleased at being questioned. 'She seems to know most people's secrets.'

Moxon looked doubtful. 'Why would anybody care enough to kill Nancy Clark *now*? That's one of the first questions we ask, you see. Why now? What changed?'

'Old Mrs Kitchener died,' she suggested. 'That seems to have some significance, don't you think? It sounds very sudden.'

He made a note, but continued to look doubtful. 'It could be anything,' he muttered. 'Something nobody's thought of.'

Simmy felt sorry for him. His hair still looked greasy, his shoulders slightly dingy. She remembered their lunch in the Elleray, as if it had been months ago. Most murders had totally obvious perpetrators, she understood. There would be a distraught husband standing over his dead wife with the kitchen knife still in his hand. Or the dazed boy nudging his lifeless friend in disbelief that a blow from a tyre iron could actually kill anybody. Devious plans involving hypodermics fell well outside the usual pattern, as did pitching harmless florists into the freezing waters of Stock Ghyll.

'You've put a guard outside,' she said. 'That's very scary. What do you think might happen?'

'There was an attack on your life. We don't want that to happen again.'

'The hospital people don't like it. They want to be shot of me.'

'Too bad,' he said unfeelingly.

'And how would anybody know how to find me, anyway?'

He sighed. 'It was on the news. It named the hospital.'

'Did it name *me*?'

'It said you were believed to be the proprietor of a floristry business in Windermere. More than enough to identify you. The point is, the attacker knows you survived. We can't avoid the assumption that he'll try again.'

'No wonder the hospital's annoyed.'

'You'd rather be at home anyway, wouldn't you?'

'I won't *be* at home. I'll be at my parents' house, like a child. That won't be entirely wonderful.'

'It's Christmas. Wouldn't you have gone there in any case?'

'For the day, yes. Not for weeks and weeks.' She groaned, largely from the pains making themselves felt in all parts of her. 'I'm just like my father's wretched cat.'

He kinked an eyebrow at that.

'It's got a broken pelvis as well.'

The detective inspector laughed. He dipped his chin and put a hand to his face and abandoned himself to a long minute of the most musical chuckling Simmy had ever heard. When he finished, he looked up with damp eyes. 'Sorry,' he said. 'I don't suppose it's funny, really. It's just that I haven't had much sleep …' He held her gaze. 'And you, Ms Persimmon Brown, have a very strange effect on me.'

Before she could find a response to that, a small team of medical people materialised at her bedside, and made it clear that Moxon had to leave. She was almost sorry to see him go.

Chapter Fifteen

IT FELT LIKE wanton cruelty to make her start learning to use crutches, barely twenty-four hours after surgery on her pelvis. The crutches were full-length, and bulky, designed to be positioned in the armpit. The soreness in her chest flared as she tried to hold the pads under her arms and rest all her weight on them. A muscle somewhere had been wrenched, and gone unnoticed until then. She dangled pathetically between two nurses and the disconcerting crutches not knowing which part of her hurt most or what to do about it.

Respite came when she was lowered onto the side of the bed and the newly-discovered sore place examined. For good measure, the site of the pelvic fracture was also given a close scrutiny, and judged to be doing remarkably well. 'Hardly any swelling,' the junior doctor reported. 'Nice clean wound.'

Pills were administered, and soothing cream rubbed onto the bruises. Her green breasts were turning blue, which was marginally less horrifying. But it hurt to breathe, which they agreed was a result of the broken rib. Trying to use crutches with such an injury might not be entirely wise, somebody pointed out. 'But we need to get her ambulant,' somebody else replied.

'Elbow crutches,' came a suggestion which drew general agreement.

'Should have gone for them in the first place,' said the first somebody.

Simmy let them talk with no sense that she needed to participate. Probably she would have been ignored even if she had made a contribution.

Different equipment was produced and she was urged to try again. With all the weight on her forearms, she made much better progress. The leg on the unbroken side of her pelvis was to be used for minimal weight-bearing while she swung along·between the crutches. Balance was difficult, the whole business awkward, but she could glimpse a time when it might just work.

'We'll try again later today,' she was promised, before being permitted to go back to bed. Exhaustion sent her into an abrupt sleep that lasted for over an hour, and blotted out all activity in the room around her.

WHEN SHE AWOKE there were two women at the bedside, apparently only just arrived. 'It *is* you,' said one of them. 'We thought it must be.'

There were three nurses in the small ward; two of them doing something to the confused old lady in the next bed. The other was standing by the door, arms folded, as if the unseen police guard had somehow metamorphosed into a hospital employee. She was closely watching Simmy's visitors.

'They said you were only meant to have visits from relatives,' said Gwen, with a defiant toss of her finely shaped head. 'But we persuaded them we were harmless. Even so, we're under surveillance, look.'

At her side, Nicola coughed a brief laugh. 'Don't worry,' she said. 'We promise not to ask you any more questions.'

'Nicola and Gwen,' Simmy said aloud, to show she still had the use of her mental faculties. 'This is a surprise.' It was rather more than that, she discovered. The women hardly knew her. What in the world were they thinking of?

'It was my idea,' said Gwen. 'When we saw it on the news, about what had happened to you, I thought we should call in and see for ourselves how badly damaged you are.'

'Why?'

'We thought perhaps you'd been to visit Nic's mother and got in the way of some low-life mugger, really because of us.' Gwen's expression was fierce at the very idea of what could happen to a woman in the streets of Ambleside.

'Not *entirely* because of us,' Nicola tried to explain. 'I mean – we still haven't the slightest idea who sent those flowers, or why – or anything. But Gwen's always been very particular about responsibility and that sort of thing.' She sighed and shifted her chair slightly further from the bed. 'I hope you're not too badly hurt,' she finished.

'I am, quite,' said Simmy, aware of at least three separate sources of pain. 'But I can't see why you should feel the least bit responsible.'

'*Were* you going to see the old lady?' Gwen persisted.

'Actually, yes, I was. But she wasn't there.'

'No – she's staying with Davy until after Christmas. That's what I *mean*. If she'd been in, and given you a cup of tea, you'd never have been attacked.'

Simmy began to wonder exactly what the news report had said. 'I wasn't mugged,' she began. 'Nothing was taken. Although I did lose my bag, I suppose.' Another major implication only just got through to her. Phone, credit cards, driving licence, house keys, car keys, were all in that bag. Perhaps someone had fished it out of the ghyll and it was safely at the police station already. Perhaps some efficient person had dealt with all the bureaucracy such losses entailed, without worrying her about it.

'Well, we were coming to Barrow anyway,' said Nicola. 'And Gwen has a thing about hospital visiting. That's all it is, basically. Oh, and we thought we might see Davy. She's a radiographer here.'

'Steady on!' protested Gwen. 'It's rather more than a casual visit, my girl. We marched into this poor woman's shop and tried to bully her into betraying a professional confidence, and the next thing we hear, she's half dead in a freezing river. Think how we'd have felt if—'

'It wasn't in any way your fault,' Simmy insisted. 'And you weren't especially unpleasant to me. I really can't see the connection.'

'Neither can I,' muttered Nicola, rolling her eyes. 'Because there isn't one.'

'Good old-fashioned human kindness,' said Gwen. 'All girls together, sort of thing. For all we know, you've got nobody to visit you, and could do with a bit of cheering up. Look – we brought you some chocs.' She proffered a box of truffles that looked madly expensive. 'And I got you a pair of angora bedsocks. I discovered recently that the key to all happiness lies in warm bedsocks.' She brayed a startlingly loud laugh at her own remark.

Simmy thought of her distant feet, under the flimsy hospital bedcovers and decided the socks would probably be rather nice.

'But I can't get them on,' she said. 'My pelvis is broken. I'm hope-lessly immobile.'

'Let me do it for you,' said Gwen, jumping up.

'I don't think—' Simmy began, only to be cut off by the watch-ful nurse leaping forward.

'Don't touch her!' she ordered. 'You're not allowed to touch her.'

'My God!' Gwen fixed an imperious gaze on the buxom girl. 'Do you think I'm going to kill her? What with?'

'Probably some sort of poisoned dart,' said Nicola tightly. 'Leave her alone, you fool.'

'It's only a pair of bedsocks.' Gwen proffered the items. 'You do it, then. She said she'd like to have them on.'

'Hospital patients do not wear bedsocks,' argued the nurse. 'Or if they do, we provide them ourselves.'

'Not angora ones,' said Gwen. 'Just do it, there's a good girl. And stop being such a twit.'

Simmy was beginning to like Gwen quite a lot. Perhaps she was thwarted of her do-gooding intentions by small-town attitudes to her unorthodox lifestyle. Perhaps the Women's Institute had shunned her, or the Red Cross given her the cold shoulder. Beside her, Nicola seemed colourless and somehow secondary. Nicola was a reactor, Simmy decided. No initiative and entirely depen-dent on Gwen for everything.

The nurse made no attempt to obey Gwen's instruction, and the socks were left on the bed. Simmy looked from one visitor to another, trying to summon a degree of clarity. They still had no idea of the identity of Candida Hawkins, then. The girl had not made herself known to them, as Simmy had expected her to by this time. And that was confusing, because it left Simmy unsure of her own position. Was it all right now to name the girl to these putative relatives? Would she be doing good by finally bringing them together? On the face of it, she thought she might. But there was still a thread of caution keeping her silent. Gwen was a tough woman, she suspected, capable of real anger if thwarted or provoked. There was an uncompromising look in her eye, as if she never felt ambivalence about anything. Besides, Simmy thought weakly, how would she ever broach the subject, here in the ward where interruptions were so frequent?

A clattering trolley could be heard approaching and Simmy realised she was yet again painfully thirsty. 'What time is it?' she asked. 'How long was I asleep?'

'Half past three,' said Gwen, without consulting a watch or clock. 'We should go. You don't look so bad to me. Does she, Nic? Do give a shout if we can help with anything.' She handed Simmy a business card. 'Everything's on there. We can post Christmas cards or do some shopping, whatever. I've got to work the rest of this week, but Nicola's got time on her hands. Davy's got everything covered with the old girl – and it doesn't look as if we'll be bothered by any more nonsense from the phantom granddaughter.' She laughed easily. 'So it's all going to settle down nicely. Don't you think?' She looked around, not just at Simmy and her partner, but at everybody else in the room. All activity seemed to have been suspended from the moment the guardian nurse had shown her mettle. The tea trolley was coming closer.

Nicola stood up. 'Yes,' she said, as if needing to placate everyone. 'That's right.'

Simmy watched them go with some interest. There had been something pleasingly old-fashioned about the visitation. In Dickens's time, it would have been entirely unremarkable. Underoccupied middle-class women would pack a basket full of good things and call on the sick without a moment's hesitation. Gwen was a throwback, if not quite to Dickens's time, then to the 1930s, where spinsters abounded and formed sisterhoods of numerous sorts. Nicola had hinted that this was something of a habit, and that Simmy was not being especially singled out for attention. And the bedsocks really were lovely. She stroked them as they lay on her chest, and savoured the warm softness of them.

AFTER TEA THERE was another gruelling session on the crutches. The intensive training ran counter to the somewhat sporadic and inefficient service that Simmy had vaguely pictured as being the norm. Either she really was an unwanted inmate, with her aura of victimhood, and therefore to be bustled off the premises as soon as was humanly possible – or things were very much better than the general public perception believed.

But it still seemed unkindly early to be forcing her to walk so soon after her latest operation. In fact, as she began to take more notice of the people around her, there was a wholesale lack of kindness on all sides, now she was on an ordinary ward. Brisk, encouraging, patient – yes. But barely a smile, certainly no friendly touch or warm reassurance. Was it because of her circumstances, or were they like this with everybody, she wondered? Some hint of irritation just below the surface made her suspect the former. She had not suffered from a random accident – she had been deliberately attacked. And it was automatic to look for reasons why a victim could be blamed. Because, she understood dimly, otherwise anybody could become a victim at any moment. And that was an insupportable thought.

The next day, they promised, would have more of the same. By the end of Thursday she would be swinging along as if she'd been born to it. First thing Friday, all being well, she could be despatched to Windermere and left to her own devices.

'What about my head?' she asked. Then, 'What about my rib? And the bruises? Does the plate in my pelvis stay in for ever?'

'Ask the doctor tomorrow,' they told her. 'He'll run you through it all.'

Before she could ask if they'd heard any news about her bag or her car, they were gone, and two more visitors were peering through the door in search of her.

Chapter Sixteen

A MAN AND a woman came hesitantly towards the bed. Simmy had time to feel moved, intrigued, surprised – a jumble of emotions that brought a smile to her face. 'Hey!' she said. 'How nice of you to come.'

Julie bent down to kiss her. 'What are friends for?' she said. 'You'd do the same for me.'

'And Ninian.' She stared at him, as if seeing him for the first time. None of the questions she wanted to ask seemed quite polite. Such as *What gives you the right to show up like this?* She didn't mean anything quite so confrontational, anyway. She just wondered, and the wondering refused to go away.

'I saw the note on the shop door,' he explained. 'And wanted to find out what had happened to you. I knew Julie was your friend, so I called her and asked.'

'And I had no idea, so I called Melanie,' Julie contributed. 'And then we – me and Ninian – decided we should come and see you. Melanie wanted to come as well, but she's got a party to go to this evening, and we weren't sure we'd get her home in time.'

Simmy had to keep reminding herself that she was in Barrow-in-Furness, which was something like an hour and a half round trip from Windermere, and not a place people went to on a whim. 'You're ever so kind,' she said, trying not to whimper.

'Well, I must admit I wasn't too impressed at not being told about it.' Julie stared at a point across the ward, without a smile. 'Melanie said she assumed I would have seen it on the local news, but I hadn't.'

'I haven't told anyone,' Simmy defended. 'I haven't made any calls at all. And you *always* watch the news.' She looked again at Ninian, who seemed no more comprehensible than before. 'You two know each other, then?' She could recall scraps of a conversation with Julie, in which she had not claimed any real acquaintance.

'Sort of,' said Julie, with a smile. 'In a casual sort of way.'

'It took me a while to remember that you two were friends,' said Ninian. 'But I have seen you once or twice together.'

This only increased Simmy's confusion, turning it closer to suspicion. 'When?' she demanded.

'Come on, Sim,' Julie protested. 'We all know each other, don't we? There's nothing sinister about it. You're the talk of the town now. Everyone's trying to guess what really happened to you.'

'So you came to see for yourself.'

'Actually, *I* came because I owe you an apology,' said Ninian. 'I never showed up when I said I would. I haven't got much of an excuse – just distractions mainly connected to my kiln and its temperamental ways. I didn't dare leave it in case it decided to blow the roof off the house.'

'Sounds dramatic,' said Simmy, a trifle dryly. 'But you were in Kendal, according to my mother. You sent a message through her, remember?'

'So I did,' he agreed easily. 'That was the next day, though, wasn't it?' He frowned in puzzlement and Simmy could well believe he regularly forgot what day it was, as well as what he might have promised to do.

'So – how *are* you?' Julie interrupted. 'What happened to your head?'

'Cracked skull. They don't seem worried about it. I can think more or less normally, anyway. The worst thing is my pelvis. I won't be able to walk or drive for ages.' The words still failed to summon any kind of reality for her. 'They keep making me practise with crutches, which isn't much fun.'

'So you'll be at your mum's, then.' Julie spoke as if it was an obvious, and not very interesting, conclusion to draw.

'Not much choice, apparently.'

'What about the shop?'

'I don't know. It'll stay closed till the New Year, at least.'

'I could run it for you,' said Ninian, so carelessly that Simmy wasn't sure she'd heard him.

'Pardon?'

'I could open up, and take deliveries and arrange the stock, and sell things to customers. I've done it before. And the girl – Melanie – would be there as well, I imagine. Easy-peasy,' he finished with a boyish grin.

'What about orders that come in on the computer? Funerals, birthdays – all that stuff? You'd have to take flowers all over the place – or turn the orders away.'

'I'd manage,' he said bravely.

'You wouldn't, Nin,' Julie said. 'You haven't got a car.'

'But she's got a van – I could use that.'

'No car? So how were you planning to bring me your vases?' wondered Simmy.

'In a massive great rucksack on my back, all bundled up in bubblewrap. That's the way I always do it, if people won't come to collect. They generally do, actually.'

There *were* people like this, Simmy realised. People to whom everything came easily, who regarded life as little more than a wholesale joke. And yet Ninian had endured some sort of breakdown, according to Julie. That could hardly have been amusing or particularly easy. Perhaps he was now on some medication that removed all anxieties or complications. Could such a person be trusted to conduct business on another person's behalf?

'It's weeks away yet,' she prevaricated. 'I don't have to decide about it now.'

'It's hot in here,' Julie observed, apparently at random. 'And those two don't look like very exciting room-mates.' She eyed the old ladies consideringly.

'They don't talk to me,' Simmy agreed. 'I'm not sure they've properly noticed I'm here.' Simmy's bed was closest to the door, at a different angle from the others. 'There was a policeman outside guarding me – did you see him?'

'Oh yes,' nodded Julie. 'Scary or what? We had to give him about fifty personal details before he'd let us in.'

'But you're not being watched,' Simmy noted. 'Not like the last people. I wonder why?'

'I mentioned Melanie's Joe, which might have helped. And they seem a bit busy out there. Do they think somebody's going to have another bash at killing you, then?'

Simmy groaned. Everything her friend had said so far brought unwelcome and demanding new trains of thought. She wanted to forget her shop, her parents and above all the cause of her injuries. She resisted the sense of being dragged back into all the responsibilities of her life, where she would have to make decisions and answer questions. 'You're as bad as Officer Moxon,' she complained. 'You're making me feel tired.'

Julie's eyes sparkled. 'So it *was* attempted murder!' she crowed.

Simmy met Ninian's eyes, and read an unexpectedly warm sympathy in them. 'Shut up, Julie,' he said.

'You're worse than Melanie and Moxon put together,' Simmy told her. 'You all seem to *want* me to be scared.'

'No! But you have to admit it's a bit of a drama.'

Simmy laughed weakly. 'I admit that,' she said. Then she saw two more faces at the door. 'Oh, there're my parents. I think you'll have to go. They'll never let me have four visitors at once.'

'The car's going to expire soon, anyway,' said Julie. 'It took us ages to find which room you were in.'

Simmy had no notion of conditions outside the walls of her ward. How her visitors found somewhere to park was far beyond her sphere of interest. Even the weather had ceased to concern her. The room had no window – for all she knew there was a blizzard blowing outside. She was institutionalised, she thought, with no sense that this was a bad thing. She waved to her parents, wondering how much of the wider world they were going to force onto her attention.

Her mother handed her a sheaf of folded paper even before she sat down. 'Letter from Ben,' she said. 'He doesn't appear to understand about envelopes.'

Simmy unfolded the papers and began to read. There were four printed pages, containing lists, observations, cross-references and lengthy explanations. Names were underlined and asterisks indicated 'Hard Evidence', which was listed on a separate page. It was a disappointingly short list. 'Heavens!' she said weakly. 'It's a dossier.'

'We didn't like to look at it,' said her father, with a glance at his wife. 'But we're not sure it's a good idea to give it to you, while you're still not right.'

'I think he's given a copy to the police,' said Angie. 'Which means you don't need to do anything. It's just for information.'

'It's amazing,' said Simmy, unable to take her eyes off it. 'He's got *everything* here.' She flipped from one sheet to another, looking in vain for a paragraph headed 'Conclusion'. 'But he doesn't seem to have actually solved the case.'

'He's got more sense,' said Russell, admiringly. 'They're more likely to take notice if he just puts the facts.'

'He's done more than that, look.' Simmy waved a sheet under his nose. 'He's quoted everything Melanie's gran told us, almost word for word.'

'Melanie's gran?' echoed Angie, and Simmy remembered how little she had conveyed to her parents about the killing of Nancy Clark and her summons to give the Kitchener man an alibi.

'Never mind. Listen – you don't need to come in tomorrow. It must be an awful hassle. They say I can go home on Friday, and I presume they'll want you to collect me.'

Angie rolled her eyes. 'Oh yes, I remember how that goes. I had to fetch my friend Hilda after her hip replacement. They told me she'd be ready at nine-thirty, and we finally got out two hours later. They'd forgotten to do the final x-ray or something. They think nothing of keeping people hanging about in these places.'

'Well, we won't let that happen,' said Russell stoutly. 'We won't set out until we know Simmy's all ready for us.'

'Hilda?' Simmy asked. 'Who's Hilda?'

'It was about nine years ago,' her father explained. 'She lives in St Albans now. I expect hospital procedures have changed since then.'

'Don't rely on it,' said Angie darkly.

The conversation drifted into plans for Christmas, the weather – which was gathering itself for something ominous, apparently – the progress of the injured cat and other minor domestic matters. Simmy found it blissfully restful to let them prattle on, nodding and smiling and making minimal comments.

They stayed for fifty minutes, having paid for an hour in the car park. It was more than long enough. Simmy had exhibited her new bedsocks and offered the chocolates – twice. They had all watched in fascination when a bent old man stumbled in to visit the old lady who snored all night, and who had still said nothing at all to Simmy. He sat beside her and held her hand and they murmured quietly together like a pair of doves. Simmy felt suddenly and hopelessly sad. A small tragedy was taking place right there in the room with her, and everybody was pretending it was all right. Was this how it always ended, then? Would one of her parents miserably attend the slow demise of the other in a hospital ward where nobody could be expected to genuinely care? It was the plain fact of abandonment that brought tears to Simmy's eyes. The old man could not fully trust that his wife would be reassured and comfortable, here in hospital. Whatever acute problem had brought her here, it was unlikely to go away. She had to be close to ninety. A broken hip would never properly recover. A replacement joint at her age – which Simmy vaguely supposed was what had happened – would surely prove bewildering and painful. She was a large old lady, too. 'Isn't it sad?' she whispered to her parents.

'Don't despair,' urged her father, patting her hand. 'I've seen old birds at least her age get up and carry on for a good few years after they've had a new hip. It's miraculous sometimes.'

'Is that what she's had?' Simmy had dimly observed him, on his first visit, strolling over to the other two patients and reading the charts that still hung at the foot of the bed. He would know a lot more than she did about her room-mates and their medical condition.

He nodded. 'And the other one's got a new knee,' he said. 'I'm appalled that you need me to tell you.'

'They don't talk to me. It's quite busy in here most of the time. I've had non-stop visitors, as well as two horrible lessons on how to walk with crutches. Plus they take me to the loo, just like you with your cat.'

'Oh, God!' groaned her mother. 'Am I going to have to do that when you come home?'

'I'll try to get the hang of it,' Simmy assured her. 'But it does need two pairs of hands at the moment.'

Finally they were gone and Simmy heaved a long sigh. It was hard work having visitors, she was discovering. They brought whole new swathes of things to think about, just when she rather preferred not to think much at all. Ben's notes lay at her side, waiting for a careful perusal. And now here was supper on its way, with, she hoped, a good-sized cup of tea. Yet again, she was thirsty.

The meal was unprecedentedly good. It was *delicious*, and she wolfed it down voraciously, despite the awkward angle. Her shoulders were too low, her arms too bruised and stiff for proper movement. Nobody seemed to be available to make the desired adjustments. It was cottage pie, with plenty of meat and onion, the mashed potato nicely crisped on top. The broccoli and carrots with it were plentiful and not overcooked. The whole meal was hot. A fruit salad containing figs, cherries and mango, as well as the usual pineapple and tiny sections of baby satsumas, followed, adorned with a very decent cream.

'Has the cook just come back from holiday?' she asked the woman who came to collect her plate. The blank look made it clear that jokes were neither understood nor appreciated when it came to hospital food. It hadn't even really been a joke. She did want to know what had changed. After a brief meditation on the subject, the idea occurred that it might have been her own state that had improved. Until then, she had not been hungry. Now the trauma was at last receding, and she could eat with enjoyment again.

It was the end of the day. Lights were already being dimmed and an atmosphere of packing away and finishing off prevailed. Simmy was taken in a wheelchair on the laborious trip to the lavatory by two tired-looking nurses. 'Can't I just have a bedpan?' she whined, as she tried to manoeuvre onto the seat.

'It's good for you to be ambulant,' recited one of them. 'Tomorrow you can do it on the crutches. It's mainly just a matter of balance.' *Ambulant* seemed a funny word to use for being wheeled to and fro, but she understood that it had a wider meaning here than was normal. On the way, she had a chance for a proper look at the police guard on the door. Until then, she had glimpsed a shoulder when the door opened, but had not properly looked at him. It seemed impossibly dramatic to have him there all day – and perhaps all night as well – vetting all her visitors and poised to leap into action if anybody made a threatening move. Who, after all, would dare try and kill her in the Furness General? She threw him a look of apology and commiseration, which he did not seem to observe.

She was settling down with Ben's notes when another visitor came in. For a moment, she was too absorbed in her reading to look up, and when she did, Moxon was only a foot away. 'Are you allowed in at this time of night?' she asked.

He cocked his head. 'It's ten to seven,' he said. 'Hardly the middle of the night.'

She was amazed. She'd been sure it had to be well past nine. 'But they're putting us to bed!'

'They do that in these places. I think you can ask for a TV, if you want one.'

'It'd disturb the others.' The two old ladies appeared to be dozing, as they so often did. Neither of them had been taken to the toilet, which raised uncomfortable questions about what happened instead.

Moxon seated himself close to her shoulder, and said, 'I see you have young Mr Harkness's spreadsheet as well.'

'It's not a spreadsheet,' she argued. 'It's a *dossier*.'

'Comprehensive, anyway. Very helpful. That boy will go far.'

'Yes.'

'Have you got to the end?'

She shook her head, reminded as she did so that there was still a bulky dressing above her ear that pressed unpleasantly when she made the gesture.

'He recommends a comprehensive follow-up to our questions of the townspeople in Compston Road, exactly a week after the killing of Miss Clark.'

'That was today,' she said uncertainly. 'Wasn't it?'

'Indeed. We would, actually, have done it without the boy's input. But it did turn out to be reasonably productive.'

'Oh yes?'

'A man in a shop opposite her house says he saw a person going in, without knocking or ringing the bell.'

Simmy waited expectantly. Suddenly it seemed to matter tremendously what was said next.

'A woman wearing a hat and black boots, carrying a bag on her shoulder. We think we know who it must have been.'

Chapter Seventeen

'Candida Hawkins!' Simmy supplied, before he could say anything more.

'That's one rather remote possibility,' he agreed carefully, with a glance around the room. 'But we can't make assumptions based on such a vague description, especially when we have you as an alibi for the Hawkins girl. This is one witness, a week after the event, who can't be totally sure he's got the right house. It's a long way from a convincing case.'

'Yes, but ...'

'And we can't find her, anyway,' he said, as if making a confession. He shifted on the chair, scratched an ear and sighed. 'We've been trying to trace her credit card, and it looks as if she's got into some trouble with the bank. Probably not her fault, just one of those glitches that take ages to iron out. I'm very sorry to tell you I don't think you'll be getting any money from that order.'

'But the card *worked*. It was confirmed by the whatsit thing on the computer.'

Moxon simply shook his head. 'I can't tell you exactly what happened, but it's possible you've been scammed. There are a lot of serious questions hanging over that young lady.'

'But I *met* her! When her car skidded. I *spoke* to her. She was natural and sincere. She told me personal things that she didn't have to. I *liked* her.'

'Her car skidded?'

'Outside my house. In the snow. I helped to push it free. All that seems a long time ago now.'

'What day was that?'

'Sunday. Yes, definitely Sunday.'

He gave this some thought, cocking his head as various hypotheses came and went. Simmy could almost see the workings. 'Do you think she could have been there with malicious intent?' he said. 'It seems highly unlikely she'd have been there by coincidence.'

'What? You think she meant to kill me in my own home on a Sunday morning?'

'It would be logical, if she was your attacker later the same day.'

It made very little sense to Simmy, the way her thoughts were swirling. 'You mean, if she was the one who killed Nancy Clark as well? But *why*? And how, if the Giggling Goose alibi counts for anything.'

'Exactly the question we're stuck on,' he nodded. 'Why indeed.' He stretched his legs as far as they would go, in an unselfconscious move that revealed his weariness. He looked at her for a long moment. 'How are you now? I should have asked before. Does it still hurt?'

'Not much. It all seems to be progressing very quickly. They're sending me home on Friday.'

'Amazing what they can do. I'm very glad to hear it. You were in a bad way on Monday.'

'There's a lot I still haven't thought about. I feel as if I'm hiding away here, evading all my responsibilities. Although you're my seventh visitor of the day, so I suppose you could say I have been keeping in touch.'

'Who came?'

She listed them, and showed him the bedsocks from Gwen. 'She's nice. Nicola says she's a compulsive hospital visitor. Sounds rather a sweet thing to do, to me, but her partner doesn't appear to think so.'

'I'm with the partner,' he admitted. 'I can't pretend to like these places. Tell me more about this Ninian bloke. Sounds as if he's got some kind of hidden agenda.'

She made an expression of mock outrage. 'Can't he just fancy me?' The idea hadn't formed itself until that moment.

Moxon was wrong-footed and had no idea what to do about it. He shrugged, and his colour heightened. 'Of course,' he muttered. 'But that's not really my line of enquiry, is it?'

'Your guard dog let him in, so he can't be on your list of assassins.'

'We're taking him off duty, from tonight. The hospital people have promised not to let anyone see you without supervision. We managed to persuade them it's in their interests – they keep everything secure in the baby unit, so they can probably manage it over here.'

Simmy remembered the locked doors and tedious systems for getting in and out, in Worcester, when she delivered her own baby. Tony had complained loudly about it. 'All because somebody stole a baby, back in 1981, or whenever,' he fumed. Simmy had noticed, even through the fog of misery, how like her mother he was. In some ways, at least.

'I'm not expecting anybody tomorrow,' she said. 'I'll be busy practising how to walk with the crutches. What about my bag? Has anybody found it? It's got my phone in, and a whole lot of other things.'

He turned his gaze to the ceiling in an effort to remember such a trivial detail. 'I'll ask,' he said. 'It'll be very wet.'

'I imagine it will,' she said solemnly, meeting his eye. Once again, she reduced him to giggles. His melodic chuckles burst out, with no warning. What a strange man he was! Every time she saw him, she changed her mind about him. He was astute, careful, committed – but also slightly sleazy, unshaven, almost unwashed. And he laughed. She had never heard of a laughing detective.

'Oh, God,' he sighed. 'There I go again. Listen – that car. The one in the snow. We need to find it. What can you remember about it?'

'A big thing, silvery colour. Wait a minute – it was a Mondeo. I can't remember any more than that. But the men who pushed it out probably do. You should ask them.'

'Men?'

'I told you, just now. There were four of us pushing it back onto the road. Two local men were helping.'

'I thought it was just you and the young woman.' He smacked himself lightly on the forehead. 'That's what comes of relying too much on the Harkness boy. There's nothing about two men in his … dossier.'

'Isn't there?' Simmy reached for the papers on her bedside table and shuffled through them. 'You're right. Perhaps I forgot to tell him, as well.'

'So who were they?'

She grimaced. 'One of them lives at Town Head – the top end of Troutbeck. I don't know his name, although he knew mine. The other one's from somewhere in the village as well. I knew him by sight.'

'Who else was there? Somebody must have seen the whole thing.'

'It was quite early on Sunday morning. One or two cars went past, but I've no idea who they were. You could try asking at the shop. The Town Head man is about forty, good-looking. He's got a wife and two or three children. He works somewhere. I mean, he's not a farmer. He reads *The Independent*.'

'How do you know that?'

'I heard him complaining when it didn't get delivered one day. In the shop.'

Moxon blew out his cheeks. 'Perfect job for a detective, then.'

'Candida said it wasn't hers. She borrowed it from someone.'

'What did you think of her? As a gut reaction?'

Simmy closed her eyes. 'She was confident, a bit self-mocking. She'd seen my shop window. She didn't know it was me.' Her eyes flew open. 'She only made the connection when I told her my name. So she can't have been *planning* to kill me, can she?'

'She could have been lying.'

'Oh. No – I don't think so. It was too *natural*. Nobody could pretend like that. Could they?'

'People are clever. And devious. Have you never been lied to before?'

'I don't know.' She tried to think of instances. 'Not really. My mother used to say she hadn't put mustard in the Welsh rarebit, when she had. I could taste it.'

Moxon visibly suppressed another chuckle. 'Lucky you, then,' he said. 'If that's all you can come up with.'

'And what about Mr Kitchener?'

'What about him?'

'Well – it was in the Giggling Goose that I saw him, last week, and then it was right beside the same place that I got pushed into the water. That seems like rather a coincidence.'

'He lives up there. It's not so surprising.'

'Does he?' This was a piece of news she wished she'd had before. 'I had no idea.'

He shrugged uncomprehendingly. 'Why would he attack you? You're his friend.'

She closed her eyes again, thinking it felt very much like bed-time, even if it was only seven-fifteen. 'Something Mrs Ellis said. Some falling out between his mother and Nancy Clark. It'll be in Ben's notes.'

'Yes,' he said impatiently. 'So what?'

'Because the Hawkins girl was there as well, in the café. He kicked her chair and she looked at him. Didn't I tell you that already?'

'I fear not.'

'I told *someone*. I'm sorry. I'm dreadfully tired. I think they want to give me more painkillers and put me to sleep for the night. Why did you come?' she mumbled, unable to grasp any convincing reason he might have had. His questions had felt almost casual, his attention not entirely on them.

'I wanted to see how you were getting on. The first time I was here, you were howling in agony. It left a very unpleasant impression on me. I'm very relieved to find everything so much better now.'

'Thanks. I get better every day, in every way.'

'Good. I should go, then. Thanks for your help.'

'Did I help?'

'I think so. Do you realise you're the only person who's seen this girl, whoever she is? Apart from two nameless men in Trout-beck, of course. And Mr Kitchener in the café. It's obvious that she's playing some game.'

'Murder's not a game.'

'No, I know that. But sending flowers to an unsuspecting old lady *is*. Mischief, I call that.'

'I should have refused to take the order. The whole thing's my fault.'

'Don't be ridiculous,' he said softly. She was more than half asleep before he reached the door.

SHE SLEPT QUITE well and dreamt of Melanie, who was organis-ing a big Christmas party with a lot of flowers everywhere, and a lot of bad temper. She blamed Simmy for everything that went wrong, stamping her foot and shouting. Ben was somewhere on the sidelines, dressed as a court jester and declaiming gibber-ish. When she woke, she looked around in blank bewilderment, unable to think where she was. Melanie was still reproaching her, somewhere inside her brain.

It was early morning, but the lights were being turned on, and a nurse was beside the bed of the old woman with the new hip. She was speaking in a loud urgent tone, first to the inert patient, then to the world in general. 'She's gone! Mrs Savage – she's gone.'

Simmy was fairly sure that this was not in the rules about how to proceed. There should be calm discretion, the curtains drawn around the bed and orderlies summoned. 'Do you mean she's dead?' she called across the room.

She received no reply. The nurse fled, returning seconds later with two colleagues. They huddled inside the quickly pulled curtain, before emerging with surprisingly pale faces. Surely they must be used to this happening? The woman was very old and had endured major surgery. Anyone could see she had been barely alive for days. Simmy felt no grief for a room-mate who she had never got to know at all. It seemed, if anything, quite a positive outcome.

Except for the poor old husband, of course. He would have to be told. He would crumple and weep, and grope blindly for some comfort. She hoped he had attentive children who would guide him through the funeral and perhaps even take him to live with them, where grandchildren would cheer his final years.

'Is Maisie dead?' called the occupant of the other bed. 'I do hope not. I *want* Maisie.'

Nobody had visited her and she received minimal attention from the nursing staff. Abandoned and forgotten, it seemed to Simmy that the kindest wish for her was that she too would slide quietly into death during the night; it was beyond Simmy to understand. Why anybody should think it worthwhile to replace the knee joint of a person who showed no sign of animation for large parts of the day, and when she did, it was to call for an invisible unknown daughter, sister, friend – who never came. It was an insight into a melancholy twilight world that Simmy would very much rather not know about. If she thought about it too much, she would end up like Gwen, visiting virtual strangers in hospital, in some inchoate attempt to make things just a little bit better.

She only had one more night here, she reminded herself. She was the lucky one in this trinity of medical dependency. She was young, her bones healed miraculously fast, and she had all her wits intact. If somebody had tried to kill her, then the fact that they had failed ought to boost her spirits. If she still had no notion as to what she might have done to warrant such violence and antipathy, then she trusted that one day it would all become clear. There were people working hard to achieve this end. Ben and DI Moxon stood shoulder to shoulder in her mind's eye, doggedly pursuing clues and making deductions that would identify the aggressor.

And Melanie. Her dream returned to her, with its very obvious message that she must not neglect Melanie.

Chapter Eighteen

By breakfast time, Mrs Savage had been tidied away, and a crisp new bed awaited the next inmate of the little ward. Simmy asked no further questions. She was preoccupied by the difficulty of contacting her assistant, with no mobile phone, and no memory of Melanie's number.

'Is there a phone I can use?' she asked the girl who brought her cereal. 'I've lost mine.' She remembered the call from Ben, on something that she had at the time assumed to be a mobile. 'What about the one I had a call on the other day?'

'Sorry. We only use it for incoming calls.'

She remembered a time, nearly twenty years earlier, when a college friend had her appendix out and Simmy visited. There had been a trolley arrangement, on which a coin-operated telephone sat. It could be moved from bed to bed, cumbersome but efficient. Gone were those days, she thought gloomily.

'How am I meant to contact people, then?'

The girl spread her hands helplessly. 'Everyone has mobiles. You could borrow one, maybe.' They both looked at the old lady in the bed by the window, and grimaced ruefully. 'Bad luck. I'll see if I can find someone who'll let you make a call.'

'Thanks.' It would be *two* calls, at least. The only number lodged in her head was the landline at her parents' house. She'd have to ask them to track down Melanie's number, or at least pass on a message. Plus, she found herself wanting to speak again to Julie, her hairdresser friend. But she couldn't remember her number, either.

The need to contact Melanie took greater priority, having a higher moral urgency to it. Her assistant would be feeling neglected, unsure of her role regarding the shop, if any. She would be jealous if she learnt that Simmy had spoken to Ben, and not her. Melanie had a knack, Simmy was discovering, of not being in the right place at the right time. And with her encyclopaedic knowledge of the community, this was a waste.

But the nurse did not come back with a borrowed mobile. Instead, there was an atmosphere of bustle. After her charts had been inspected and annotated, there followed an alarmingly prompt exercise session, which covered a substantial panoply of movements designed to cope with the demands of daily living. She was told how to sit, and how to stand up again without putting strain on her pelvis. How to manage steps – terrifyingly difficult – and how to get in and out of a car. 'I'll never remember it all,' she complained.

'We'll do it all again this afternoon. Meanwhile, you can stay out of bed for the rest of the day, and take yourself to the loo and back when necessary.'

'Gosh!' said Simmy, with a flash of apprehension. 'Am I ready for that?'

'You'd better be. There's a review of discharges in a little while. Don't want anybody to be stranded if we can help it.'

'Stranded? What do you mean?'

'Weather, pet. We're due a whole lot of snow tonight. Haven't you heard?'

'How would I?' Had her parents not seen the forecast, either? Had it changed since the previous afternoon? 'Are you saying I might go home *today*?'

'It's possible. You're doing well. No sign of infection, reduced pain, bruising fading. Not much we can do for you here that can't be done at home. Someone will pop in and see you over the weekend, I expect, to check you over.'

'Weather permitting,' added Simmy, her old forebodings about snow returning with a rush.

'It's never as bad as they say it'll be,' chirped the woman. 'And you'll be snug indoors. Still, it's a pain, I know. Everything grinds to a halt when it snows.'

Back in the ward, she sat in a hospital chair with a soft seat and adjustable back, trying to read a book that a woman had given her from a mobile library trolley. The words on the pages entirely failed to hold her attention. She could not have recounted the story or named the characters, two minutes after putting it down in despair. She found she was shivering, despite the overheated room. Her teeth were chattering. There was a sour taste in her mouth. Sweat was trickling down from her armpits and her chest started to constrict. *I'm having a heart attack*, she thought wildly, and tried to find the button they'd told her to press if she wanted anything.

'Nurse!' she called, her voice thin and breathless, as she fumbled blindly for the alarm. People were passing in the corridor outside, but none of them glanced in through the glass panel in the door.

'Maisie?' came the quavering tones of the old woman on the other side of the room. 'Is that you?' She reared up suddenly, her eyes sharply focused on Simmy for the first time.

'No!' croaked Simmy. 'For God's sake.'

At last she got hold of the button and pushed down with her thumb. As far as she could tell, nothing happened. But two long minutes later, during which she shook so much that the book fell on the floor, a nurse came into the room. 'What's up?' she asked.

'Something's wrong with me. Look!' She held out her quivering hands. 'I can't breathe.'

The nurse approached, and gave her a close appraisal, feeling her brow and clucking like a soothing mother hen. 'Shock,' she diagnosed. 'Delayed shock.'

'What?' *Delayed* seemed like a major understatement.

'It does this. Sometimes it's a week or more after the original injury. We've kept you busy with other things, plus the medication. Now it's catching up with you. We'll just pop you back into bed and you'll be fine.'

'Are you sh-sh-sure?' Her chattering teeth made speech difficult. 'I feel s-s-sick.'

'We'll give you a quick once-over to make sure there's nothing else, but I'm pretty sure, yes.' She attached the blood pressure monitor, fixing her gaze on the screen behind Simmy's head for a few moments. 'Yes, that's all good. No internal bleeding. It's your system finally realising something big happened to you. It'll all be over soon, you'll see.'

She summoned assistance to get Simmy back into bed, her sore pelvis and ribs making their presence felt in the process. 'It's worse for victims,' said the second nurse, who was older than most of the others. 'The sense of vulnerability throws you all out of balance.

Changes the way you see the world.' Her colleague gave her a star-
tled look at this non-medical observation.

Before she knew it, Simmy was weeping. Warm tears gushed
from her eyes and down her cheeks. Her nose was running. 'Now
look what you've done,' said the younger nurse, more amused
than annoyed. She plucked a bunch of tissues from a bedside box
and helped mop up the flow.

'Best thing,' said the philosopher. 'Very therapeutic.'

Simmy felt herself adrift on a dark sea of helplessness and
humiliation. She was pathetic, useless. What would her mother
say if she could see her? She took the tissues and blew her nose.
'Sorry,' she said wetly.

'That's better. You should try to talk to someone about it, before
long. Get it into perspective. And not that scruffy detective bloke.
He's only going to make it worse.'

That wasn't fair, Simmy thought. He'd had her best interests in
mind. He'd been worried about her. He'd sent a minion to guard
her, hadn't he? 'He's quite kind, really,' she protested.

'Everybody's talking about you,' said the younger one, recklessly. 'How you were nearly murdered. There's no sign of them
catching the swine who did it, either.'

'Hush, Maxwell,' chided her colleague. 'That's not going to
help, is it?'

'I expect they will,' said Simmy, noticing that her shaking had
abated. 'They're trying hard.'

'He certainly comes to see you often enough. Every day, isn't it?'

Simmy couldn't remember. It had not crossed her mind to
wonder how the hospital staff regarded her, except to assume she
was a nuisance, with her police guard and regular visits from a
senior detective. Were they gossiping and speculating about all

her visitors? Was there an amateur detective in their midst who was trying to make sense of it all?

'I don't think it was being attacked that set me off,' she said slowly, ignoring the immediate question. 'It was something else.' She looked around the ward with its crisp lines and clean floor. There were no patterns, no focal points – just a jumble of pastel colours and artificial lights. Her eye fell on the chair she had been sitting in. 'The chair!'

The memory returned, complete in every detail. She had waited in just such a chair for Tony to come and collect her after she had delivered the stillborn baby Edith. She had felt its yielding seat as she shifted her sore posterior. Then, as now, there had been padding around a bruised pelvic area, making it difficult to sit comfortably, delicate skin chafed and raw. Tony had promised to be there by five o'clock – ten hours after the baby had been born. He was late, and she waited, numb, hollow, content for him never to appear, if that's the way it was going to be. Life had seemed arbitrary, pointless and entirely conditional. She had not wanted to live without a baby. A husband was neither here nor there, utterly irrelevant.

Her brain had seized up then, as now. People had pushed and pulled her, faces had loomed smilingly at her, giving inane reassurances that were patently unreliable.

'It was the chair,' she said again. 'It brought back memories.'

'O-o-kay,' said the older nurse, doubtfully. 'That can happen. But you're all right again now, very nearly. If it happens again, you'll know what it is. You'll know not to panic.'

That sounded unduly optimistic to Simmy. If it was as easy as that, there wouldn't be ex-soldiers cringing in terror every time a car backfired. Her own trauma and loss seemed as bad to her, at that moment, as the experiences of a man on a battlefield must be to him.

'My baby died,' she said starkly.

Both women looked at her with wide eyes. Neither said a word, but a glance was exchanged. Something accusing, with a dash of defiance. A *Well, you can't expect us to have known that* sort of message passed silently between them. They were not good at death, Simmy understood. Who was, when it came right down to it?

SOMEHOW THE MORNING struggled on, and the lunch, when it came, was good. Breast of chicken in a bold sauce that did not skimp on the garlic. Sautéed potatoes and cauliflower came with it. Simmy made a clean plate, and tried to persuade herself that she was all right. How could she not be, if she could eat with such healthy appetite? In the bathroom, she manoeuvred unaided on and off the lavatory, and then undressed far enough to inspect her wounds.

Her bruises had faded even more, to bluish-grey in most places. The flesh was painful when pressed, and the prospect of wearing a bra made her wince, but she could see a possibility of a return to her former shape and colour. Painful breasts, too, were a reminder of the loss of little Edith, she suddenly remembered. Somehow, nobody had thought to give her the pills that dried up breast milk, so she became engorged and hot in that first day or two. It had been one of the most cruel aspects of an unbearable time. She had entertained mad ideas of offering herself to someone else's baby – even a puppy or kitten might succeed in alleviating the agony. Tony had laughed at this, before informing her that, in earlier times, precisely that had been tried as a remedy for the problem. Tony had a liking for odd facts of history, whether or not they held any relevance for modern times.

It had been the laughter that sliced through her, making her hate him for a few seconds, before she reminded herself that he had every right to laugh if he felt like it. At least nobody was laughing at her now, she thought, returning to the present. Nobody thought it funny that she'd been thrown into a freezing beck and battered half to death on the rocks a few inches beneath the hostile water.

And so she began again on the familiar round of questions. There had to be an answer hiding somewhere – some suspicion that if grabbed and articulated would incriminate the killer of Nancy Clark. She, Simmy, must know something without realising she knew it. She must have heard or seen some snippet of evidence, which somebody could not afford to let her pass on. And it could only have to do with Mrs Joseph's flowers, or the people in the café, or the car on the ice in Troutbeck. And all those instances included one person, and only one: the girl who called herself Candida Hawkins.

She thought again of Melanie, who was much the same age as the suspicious individual, and who might have insights into her character. She would be more likely to spot signs of dishonesty and subterfuge, knowing the sort of language to employ and the minutiae of daily experience. Or would she? Melanie had a street-wise manner, but had seldom been beyond the borders of Cumbria. If Candida really did live in Liverpool, she would be far more sophisticated, with a very different set of skills and assumptions. She, Simmy, was probably being deplorably ageist, just to think there might be invisible similarities.

A nurse came in quickly, distractedly, holding a clipboard. 'It's started!' she announced. 'Hours before they said it would.'

'What has?'

'The snow. We'll have to try and contact your people and get them to come for you. We've got staff who live up on the fells – they'll be wanting to go home early.' She was frowning, doing mental calculations, eyeing the still-empty bed in the ward.

'Is that allowed?'

'Not really, but we've got a system, based on where people live. Quite a few stay in Barrow overnight, instead of going home.'

'How bad is it?'

'Not much so far. It's supposed to really get going this evening.'

'Phone them, then. They won't want to be out in the dark if there's a blizzard.'

'It won't be dark for a while yet. And nobody said anything about a blizzard. It's not windy. But yes, I will. Remind me where they live.'

'Windermere. Forty minutes away, at least.'

The woman made a mark on her clipboard and went away. Simmy carefully pulled herself into a sitting position, mindful of the anguish this had caused a few days before. Now it was almost easy. She almost felt a fraud. Had her bones knitted together already? Had they ever been actually broken – or just cracked? Her crutches were tucked out of sight somewhere, rendering her helplessly stranded. She would presumably have to get dressed, in order to go out into a sub-zero world, in a car that might end up in a snowdrift. It seemed criminally reckless to eject her from the nice warm hospital. She realised that she really didn't want to go. Perhaps if she claimed a violent headache, or acute nausea, or a new pain in her ribs or back, they would relent and let her stay.

Chapter Nineteen

IT WAS HALF past two when her father came in, jangling his car keys on the monstrous key ring in the shape of Mickey Mouse that he hoped would ensure he could always find them. It didn't work, because it was uncomfortably large for a pocket, and so got plonked on any convenient surface, which might be hard to locate again.

'Taxi, madam?' he said. 'If you're ready.'

She was not wearing outdoor clothes, but the fleecy pyjamas her mother had brought in on Monday. They had been too warm for the hospital temperatures, but now they seemed the only option. Her father was holding a large carrier bag, which he opened. 'Dressing gown,' he announced. 'As good as any coat.'

She tried not to visualise the figure she would cut, struggling across the car park on crutches, wearing a long red garment that would come close to dragging on the ground. The hospital people had produced her boots, that she had been wearing on Sunday, and which had remained on her feet until she was fished from the ghyll. They had been soaked inside, but somebody had dried them out for her. They looked alien and misshapen and she had no wish to pull them on.

'We'll take you in a wheelchair,' said one of the nurses, and a young man appeared with the empty chair. 'You remember what we taught you about getting in and out of a car?'

She was handed a bag containing her original clothes, which had not been treated as kindly as had her boots. They were damp and dirty. The jeans had been cut apart to get at her damaged body quickly. She missed her bag with a sudden violence. Without it, she was less than human – a bruised body adrift in a snowy world, with nothing to show for her existence.

Outside, there was a thin white frosting on many surfaces, and the daylight was a threatening grey murk. The long sweep of grassy bank below the hospital was already a uniform white. 'Shortest day on Monday,' said her father, looking at the sky. 'The roads are all right so far. It's not freezing. We'll be back before four and can batten down the hatches then.'

His calm was deceptive, she could tell. He was struggling to accomplish his task without mishap, his head full of instructions.

'Sorry about this, Dad,' she said. 'I'm more of a handful than the cat, aren't I?'

'At least I've had some practice,' he quipped. 'It'll be all right. You're well on the mend – I can tell.'

They got her into the car and he reversed delicately out of the parking space. 'You could have left it closer,' she observed. 'Look – there's a place over there for picking people up.'

'So there is. I never noticed that.'

The roads were uncomfortably thronged with traffic, all trying to beat the onset of serious snow. There were large lorries, vans, family cars and the occasional minibus. Russell kept a careful distance from the vehicles ahead, and tried to maintain a confident tone, as he gave his habitual running commentary on the places they were passing. He had a Fleetwood Mac CD playing. It was an album from 1974, which Russell always said had been his favourite year of all years for music. Alan Price, the Scaffold, Eric Clapton, Roberta Flack – they were all household names for the Straws. Stuck in a forty-year time warp, Russell played their music to destruction, and then replaced the worn-out discs with the newest format, his car always loud with nostalgia. As they passed the sign to Bouth, he gave a happy cry. 'This is where Christine McVie grew up,' he yodelled. 'I wanted to live there for years, so I could be close to her in spirit.'

'But Mum wouldn't let you,' Simmy recited. She had heard the story many times, and even gone with him on a little pilgrimage, that summer. Bouth was less than ten miles from Windermere. Up to their left the ground rose gently to the Furness Fells. Another small road was signed to Rusland – where Mrs Kitchener had been buried.

'Newby Bridge in a minute,' said her father. 'We've almost done it.'

The scenery was magical, an image from a Christmas card. Snow fell in light dancing flakes that had covered the hedges with half an inch of white blanket. Shapes were blurring, landmarks disappearing. 'I bet it's bad in Troutbeck,' said Simmy with a sigh.

'Lucky you're not up there, then. They say it'll be three or four inches by morning.'

'That doesn't sound much.'

'It doesn't, does it,' he agreed heartily. 'The first winter we were here, it was fifteen inches in some places. Kentmere was completely cut off, I remember.'

'I suppose they coped.'

'Oh, yes. I think they rather enjoyed it. Lots of people like snow.'

'I wish I did.' It was true. What sense was there in moving to the snowy north, otherwise? 'I think I just sort of forgot about it. I don't remember much snow when I was little. It always seemed to happen somewhere else.'

The Straws had lived in Staffordshire for Simmy's first ten years, then Gloucestershire. She remembered the winters as being almost balmy compared to those of recent years. Something had obviously changed, and she was still trying to keep up with it.

'It's very character-forming,' Russell said, not for the first time. 'Pulls you back to the basics, teaches you the value of things. Besides, Windermere's going to be all right, whatever happens. The lake keeps things from getting too bad – especially this early in the winter.'

Simmy felt her character had taken more than enough moulding in the past week, and that snow could hardly effect any further battering. An image appeared of Ninian Tripp working with his clay, making shapes out of random lumps, like God making Adam. Was her character like that – waiting to be formed by a cosmic hand? Was there some inscrutable Plan at work somewhere? She hoped not – that would only increase her sense of victimhood.

'Is anything hurting?' Russell asked, hearing her sigh.

'Not really. Just an ache, all around here.' She indicated her hips and front pelvic bone. 'It's not very bad.'

'Fifteen more minutes at most,' he promised. 'We've made good time.'

Simmy was taken back to the hurried trip she had made down to Newby Bridge on Friday, before any snow had fallen, before she had been violently attacked, when the world had been a lot more dependable. It was an unremarkable little road, at the less scenic southern end of Lake Windermere. The water was visible, where it was hardly wider than a large river, with the tree-lined slopes on the further side of the lake now a pattern of black and white, light and shade. The surface was dark grey, absorbing the falling snow as if nothing were happening. As always, its presence seemed unreal to Simmy – the great body of water quietly lying there, watching the goings-on of the land creatures on its eastern flank. It was as if some other realm had been superimposed on the fells and ghylls, filling the crevices between them with a whole new element. Simmy was no swimmer and boats made her nervous. She saw very little connection between herself and the lake, other than an aesthetic one. She loved to pause and look at it, marvelling at the reflections and shifting colours. But with every passing week, it was creeping a little further beneath her skin, and now she felt a lift of her spirits at the sight of it. Lake Windermere was home, now; perhaps the only home she would know for the rest of her life.

The snowfall seemed lighter by the time they reached Bowness, with almost none sticking to the pavements and buildings. Lake Road, with the woods to the west, and the handsome Victorian villas set back from the road, was much as usual. But it was almost dark, and Simmy was tired and relieved to reach sanctuary. Just so long as her father managed to get the car in through the gate and safely parked close to the house, she didn't care what the weather might do. She would stay indoors for a week and let everything just wash over her.

But her mother evidently had other ideas. From the first moment, she fired questions at the invalid, demanding decisions and preferences. 'Are you hungry? Do you want a duvet or blankets? Is it warm enough? Have they given you painkillers? Is there a district nurse coming? Was it snowing much in Barrow? Did you hear the news about that earthquake in Syria? Do you need us to go to Troutbeck for anything? Are you going to want visitors here?' On and on they went, with pauses for replies that only seemed to spawn further enquiries.

'Stop it, Ange,' begged Russell. 'All this can wait for tomorrow. She's tired.'

'Yes. All right. Is the light all right for you in here? Will you want to read? Should I put a chamber pot under the bed?'

This last brought exasperation to the fore. 'How do you think I'd manage that?' Simmy snapped. 'That's a ludicrous idea.'

Angie blinked. 'I have very little experience of crutches,' she said tightly. 'I don't know what's possible.'

'Sorry, Mum. Neither do I. But it's not too bad, actually. I can swing along quite well on the level. The downstairs loo's going to be fine.' She took a deep breath. 'Look – I can sit in the kitchen or the living room, and keep out of your way, until bedtime. You don't have to fuss round me. I might get visitors, I suppose. I didn't finish doing my Christmas cards, and all my presents are at the house.'

All was an exaggeration. Being part of such a small family meant that she only bought gifts for her parents and Melanie. She had intended to get something for Ben, too, but could not think what he'd want, apart from computer games.

'If it snows in the night, they'll have to stay there, won't they. Lucky I don't have a pet to worry about,' she added.

She felt jangled and cross. Far from making her feel like a cossetted child, her mother was relying on her for direction and information. And the worst of it was that she knew she was being unreasonable in her expectations. Angie really did have no idea what she should do. Russell was no better. Having performed his duty as a taxi driver, he appeared to think his work was done. He threw sympathetic looks at her and then disappeared into the kitchen.

Eventually, they settled down. Simmy lowered herself into a big comfortable chair that was always well supplied with cushions, and mainly used by the cat. Her fellow invalid was still in his nest in the hall, but had progressed to taking himself outside without an escort. His gait was wobbly and he'd got thinner, but there was no suggestion that he was in any pain.

Angie made a pot of tea and then dug a large container of frozen soup out of the freezer. 'Beef and vegetable,' she announced. 'I made it months ago. It's more like a stew, really. My mother always did it for winter evenings.'

'Yes, I know.' Simmy had cheerful memories of her grandmother's soup-making skills. She had a variety for every occasion, ranging from crab and sweetcorn to an amazing minestrone. Angie's talents were unfortunately very inferior, despite her best efforts to maintain the tradition. Her beef stew somehow never worked, for reasons nobody could identify.

They were still eating it when the doorbell rang. Russell went to answer it, and came back followed by two young people. 'Visitors!' he announced, as if it was the best thing that could possibly happen.

'Hi, Simmy,' said Melanie. 'We had no idea you'd be home already. We came to see if we could do anything to help get ready for you.'

Ben stared at her, making no effort to hide his curiosity. 'You look okay,' he concluded.

'You should see the bruises,' she laughed, feeling suddenly buoyant. His eager step forward made her laugh even more. 'No, no. I'm not going to show you. It wouldn't be ladylike, given the places where they're worst.'

'I wanted to visit you in Barrow,' he said urgently. 'But there was no way I could. I'm not meant to be here now. It's the dress rehearsal for the play tonight.'

'Good God! What time does it start?'

'Seven-thirty. It'll be okay if I'm there an hour ahead. Even a bit less than that. The costume isn't very complicated.'

'He wears a tunic,' Melanie told them. 'I thought it should be a toga, but got that all wrong – didn't I?'

'Togas were only for the top people. I'm a prisoner. The tunic ought to be torn and dirty, really, but it's okay.'

'I had a look at the play,' Melanie confided. 'It says Ferrovius is powerful with a big nose and a thick neck. Not sure they got the casting quite right.' She poked Ben's chest, and then waved a finger at his narrow adolescent neck.

'It'll be all in the acting,' said Simmy loyally.

'It's a rubbish play, actually. Totally anti-Christian. There'll be complaints.' Melanie rolled her eyes. 'I don't know what they're thinking of, putting that on at Christmas.'

'What?' Angie gave up trying to follow the thread. 'What play is it then?'

'Androcles and the Lion,' said Ben. 'It's not very PC – but it makes you think. Any proper Christian would find it easy to argue their case. It's pretty literal-minded. I think it was an inspired choice. And it's quite funny. I do a take-off of a smarmy vicar, talking about washing souls and being meek and gentle. It's all a joke, see. My character is really just a lump of brawn, trying to behave the way Jesus says he should.'

'And does it work?' asked Angie.

'You'll have to come along and see. There's still a few tickets for tomorrow.'

'I've got one for Saturday,' Simmy remembered. 'I was looking forward to it.'

'A thing happened today,' Melanie interrupted. 'I was going to get your mum and dad to tell you about it tomorrow.'

'What sort of a thing?'

'My gran had a visitor. Penny Clark – that was. Nancy's sister. What happened – Gran phoned her, just for a chat about old times. All that talk on Sunday stirred her up, and she thought she should get in touch with some old mates. So Penny decided to pay a visit. She got a taxi all the way, because she can't drive any more, and didn't want her husband hanging about. She's all in pieces because of the murder, and wanted to talk to someone about it. Her husband just keeps telling her not to think about it. Typical farmer. They never care much about death, do they?'

Nobody took her up on this observation, so she carried on. 'Penny knows the Joseph girls, a bit. *Knew* them, anyway. My gran had the sense to sound her out, after all our questions about them. She's not daft, my gran. She worked out that there's some sort of mystery about them. And she's no prude, either. Penny told her all about that Gwen woman, taking up with Nicola Joseph, years ago, and ruling her life ever since. She's seen them about – they live up her way, and everybody talks about them.'

'They came to see me yesterday,' Simmy said. 'I thought Gwen was nice. She brought me some bedsocks. Nicola says she often visits people in hospital.'

'What if she does?' Melanie dismissed. 'That's not the point.'

'Isn't it? What does she do for a job?'

'College lecturer,' said Melanie promptly. Unlike Simmy, Melanie always knew immediately what a person did for a living. The information seemed to arrive telepathically sometimes. 'Psychology, at Carlisle.'

'And Nicola?' Simmy felt ashamed that she still had no idea of the answer.

'Nothing much, as far as I know. She's on the board of governors at the primary school where she lives, and she volunteers for things. Samaritans or something. And they've got a real showpiece of a house, so I guess she does a lot of dusting.'

Something about her impression of Nicola Joseph made this all too credible to Simmy. Angie Straw laughed scornfully and Ben cleared his throat.

'This is third-hand material,' he said. 'It's not really very useful.'

'It's a bit weird that somebody wanting to talk about her murdered sister should end up talking about the Joseph family,' said Simmy slowly. 'Even if your gran did steer the conversation that way. What about *Nancy*? She's at the heart of all this. She's the victim.' The word tasted bitter in her mouth; bitter and spiky.

'I get the idea there wasn't actually much to say about her. Nasty Nancy has finally done something good by getting herself killed, according to Gran. Penny admits she didn't like her much after they were sent to different schools. Nancy was always boasting and throwing her weight about. So now Penny feels guilty. But Gran wasn't having any of that and told her she had nothing to feel bad about.'

'Did that do any good?' asked Russell, who had not appeared to be following the conversation very closely. 'It's bad when somebody you dislike dies. You can't help feeling you did it, somehow.'

'You and Gwen should get together,' said Simmy. 'You could talk psychology at each other.' She said it lightly, with a smile, but the others took it as a sign that she was not her usual self. For her, it came over as rather a sharp remark.

'Enough of this,' said Angie. 'You'll be late, Ben. To be honest, I'm surprised they're going ahead with the play, when there's all this snow about.'

'Too late to cancel,' he shrugged. 'And it's not going to be so bad, after all. Latest I heard, it's mostly to the east of here. Over the high ground, as usual.'

'What about tomorrow?'

'Tomorrow's going to be okay. Eight degrees and some sunshine. It'll all melt by lunchtime.'

Simmy stared at him. 'So I needn't have come home today after all?'

Angie gave a muffled yelp. 'Aren't you *glad* you came today?'

'Yes, of course. But all that panic and bustle for nothing. It seems stupid.'

Melanie fixed her single eye on her. 'You're in a funny mood,' she said. 'Does it hurt somewhere?'

'Actually, no, not much. It's not really very bad. Some of the bruises are sore, still. I suppose I've been lucky.'

'What about the shop?' Melanie asked. 'Are you really staying closed until the new year?'

'I'll have to, I think.' She paused, choosing her words slowly. 'You know that potter chap – Ninian?'

Melanie nodded. 'What about him?'

'He's offered to cover for me in the shop, if need be. Obviously I said I'd have to talk it over with you, and that you might be able to manage. I think I'll be almost better by then anyway.'

She could see Melanie wrestling with conflicting reactions. 'He'd have no *idea*,' she began. 'He'd be worse than useless.' Then she frowned. 'But I can't miss any college work. Term starts on the 10th. I can't be full-time after that.'

'That gives us more than three weeks,' said Simmy, with confidence. 'Plenty of time to work out what we'll do.'

'Well, I've coped so far, haven't I? Since Sunday I've done everything required, without you even asking. I put a sign up saying we're away until further notice. Told the delivery people, and put a stop on new orders. There's a lot of wastage,' she finished sadly. Melanie grieved for every flower they threw away. 'I should go again tomorrow, and tidy up some more.'

'Thanks, Mel. You've been really good.'

Melanie wriggled self-consciously. 'No problem,' she mumbled.

'Tell the Moxo man, then – about Nancy Clark's sister,' Ben urged her. 'He's sure to come and see you sometime soon.'

'I thought you had a direct line to him yourself,' she said. 'Why do I have to do it?'

'Because you're the adult. He takes more notice of you.'

'No, Ben. That's not true. He was hugely impressed by your dossier thing. He said so.'

'Well he never told me.'

'He will. He's not too good at that sort of thing, probably.'

'It's all daughters and sisters, isn't it,' Ben changed the subject. 'Have you noticed? People who know a whole lot about each other – or ought to. All those women, with barely a man in the story at all.'

'Except Mr Kitchener. He's about the only one I haven't seen in the past week.' She thought about the sad little man and the police suspicions around him. 'I wonder if he's all right.'

Ben snorted. 'Lying low, if you ask me.'

Russell gave a soft clap. 'Well done, my boy!'

They all looked at him in confusion. 'What did I do?' asked Ben.

'Used the right word. I always want to scream whenever I hear someone say "laying low" or "lay of the land". You got it right. Hallelujah!'

'You're just a pedant,' Simmy told him fondly. Her spirits lifted like someone removing a damp smelly blanket and letting in the light and fresh air. 'And I'm so pleased to be here with you.'

Ben was considering the grammatical point. 'If you say "lay of the land", does that suggest a creator – someone who laid it out? Is that why Americans use it, because they're so religious?'

Russell responded with delight. 'I think not. I think it's wrong, even then. But it's a most intriguing point you raise.'

'Oh, you two,' sighed Simmy with a smile. But she still retained a picture of Mr Kitchener, who had seemed so grateful to her for the alibi, but who then might have pitched her into the beck and tried to kill her.

Chapter Twenty

THE EVENING PASSED slowly, with a low-level tension affecting all three of them in different ways. Angie continued to ask questions sporadically. 'When do you think you'll be able to go outside? Should we tell the police that you're home? Does anybody *really* think there's a connection between the murder of that Clark woman and you being assaulted?' Simmy did her best to answer, even though she and her father were trying to settle down with an old DVD of *On Golden Pond*. It always made them both cry, which was something they enjoyed. The scratchy father-daughter relationship in the film made them feel complacent. Angie always made some comment about not being in the least like Katharine Hepburn, despite what people might think. She had lost count of the times, throughout her life, in which she had been compared to the film star. Russell made no secret of the fact that the likeness had been one of her major attractions for him, back in the 1970s.

'I'd much rather remind you of Lauren Bacall,' she would insist. 'Or Faye Dunaway, even better.'

'They're all tall and wisecracking,' he would concede. 'You're just a glorious mixture of all three.'

And all considerably older than Angie, Simmy would think. Stars from a time long gone, just as her father's favourite music groups had either died or withered into unrecognisable old age. Christine McVie was over seventy, for heaven's sake. It was becoming more apparent with every year that her father essentially lived in the past. His contributions to the running of the B&B centred largely on lengthy breakfast homilies about the history of the southern Lake District, and quite a lot of the shopping.

Which meant he took an oddly peripheral interest in Simmy and her activities. He almost never visited her shop. He had dodged the darker implications of her current injuries, and only listened to conversations for their accurate use of grammar. She thought about all this as they watched the movie, and realised how restful it made him. Russell Straw seldom asked questions. He let most things flow quietly past him without feeling that anything was being demanded of him. The kind of man that many women despaired of as a husband, but which made a surprisingly good father.

Bedtime involved some complications which did little for anybody's temper. Russell made himself scarce, fussing over his cat and making milky drinks. Angie hovered irritatingly while Simmy went to the downstairs loo, washing minimally and cleaning her teeth in the small handbasin. The bed was a narrow fold-up affair, kept for emergencies in a cupboard. It sagged under Simmy's modest weight, and squealed every time she moved.

But in the end she slept soundly, worn out by the trials of the day. The padding around her pelvis sank into a hollow part of the ancient mattress as if it had been specially made to fit. Her damaged head was similarly cradled by a feather-filled pillow that

Angie said had belonged to her grandmother – which made it well over a century old. Few things ever got thrown away in the Straw household.

IN THE MORNING, Angie brought her a substantial breakfast, with no prior consultation. The relief of this gave Simmy considerable optimism for the day to come. December 18th, a week before Christmas Day, was going to be lazy, warm, and full of simple tasks like helping to make mince pies or stringing up cards that had come in their dozens from friends and one-time B&B guests. 'It's amazing, the number of people who remember the address and send a card,' said Angie. 'I never know where to put them all.'

'I'll get up at ten,' said Simmy, feeling virtuous. Some people in her situation would stay in bed all day. Except it wasn't the sort of bed you could stay in, once you were awake. It had no headboard, for a start, so sitting up was impossible. And it was narrow, so you couldn't spread sideways and strew newspapers across it. When her bladder demanded a trip to the lavatory at nine, with all the effort involved with the crutches, she realised she'd be better in the kitchen, rather than wallowing in the rickety old bed.

And that meant putting some clothes on. She didn't want a repeat of the previous day, when she had entertained visitors in her pyjamas. For the first time in many days, she had to think properly about clothes. Only the baggiest of garments would be possible. Her usual jeans wouldn't fasten around the dressings and any sort of tight top would hurt her bruises. 'Have you got a tracksuit or something that I could borrow?' she asked her mother.

Angie considered. Accustomed to finding spare clothes for children, it was much less usual to have to provide them for adults.

People did return from their fell walks covered in mud, from time to time, but they generally had something with them to change into. And if they didn't, they were too self-conscious and fussy to accept anything Angie might have to offer. 'I might find something,' she said. 'I'll go and look.'

She came back with a shapeless jersey two-piece outfit, in a colour between grey and lilac. 'I thought a skirt would be easier than trousers,' she said. 'It's got a stretchy waistband.'

Simmy grimaced, before putting it on. 'Where did it come from?' she wondered. 'I've never seen it before.'

'I think I got it in a jumble sale ages ago. I quite like the top.'

The top was long and spacious, with full sleeves and a high neck. 'It's silk!' Simmy realised. 'Silk and wool, look.' She showed Angie the label. 'It must have cost a fortune when it was new.'

The skirt was full and reached almost to her ankles. 'It'll trip me up,' she worried. But when she swung her way down the passage to the kitchen, the skirt simply adapted itself to her movements as if it knew what was required. It was a strangely feminine sensation that she had almost forgotten. 'It must be a year or more since I last wore a skirt,' she laughed.

'You look fantastic in it,' said Angie.

'Don't sound so surprised. Look at me, Dad.'

Russell was in the kitchen with the local paper, a mug of coffee at his elbow. He looked up, cocking an eyebrow. 'Very nice,' he said. 'Are you going somewhere?'

'Of course not.' Only then did she remember the snow. 'How's the weather?'

'Just as your young friend predicted. Sunny spells. No more snow. All a flash in the pan.'

'Good,' said Simmy. 'I might get you to take me up to Trout-beck later on, then. I need to get some clothes and things.'

'How do you feel?' he asked.

'Much better than I should. I feel a real fraud. I'm going to take this stuff off my head, I think. It's been on for ages.'

Angie gulped audibly. 'Do you think you should? What's underneath?'

'A few stitches, and a big bald spot. How long does hair take to grow again?'

'Better ask the cat,' said Russell. 'His is coming through a whole different colour.'

'He's got stripes. It's not the same. Isn't there something called "underfur"?'

'Don't ask me. I suppose yours will take a while. You could have it cut all over, to match. The Sinéad O'Connor look.'

'Careful, Dad. She's a bit recent for you. Can't be much more than twenty-five years ago she first had a hit.'

'I don't care for the music, but I can recognise her by her head.' He ran a hand over his own luxuriant grey covering. 'I've often wondered what mine would look like if I went bald. We don't know the shape of our own heads, do we?'

It *was* going to be a good day. She could feel it. Her injuries were healing, her brief but dramatic collapse the day before almost forgotten. Ambleside seemed a long way off, and entirely different from the gentle lowlands of Windermere. 'I think I'll just wear a woolly hat for a few months,' she decided.

'Good idea,' said Angie. 'And don't pull the dressing off, there's a good girl. You might damage something.'

'Somebody said there might be a nurse calling in to look at me,' she remembered. 'Will they phone first, I wonder?'

'Shouldn't think so. They'll expect you to be here, won't they?'

Conversation continued in a desultory way, Angie unnaturally idle, in the absence of any B&B people. Only gradually did Simmy grasp the reason for the difference in atmosphere. 'Where are they?' she asked. 'Didn't you have people coming?'

'We put them off,' said her mother easily. 'It was only a few, and we'd intended to be closed for the next two weeks, anyway.'

'But you had bookings for this weekend.' Her own self-absorption seemed shameful to her. 'I never even *thought* about it.'

'No problem,' said Russell emphatically. 'We needed the break. It's only brought it forward by a few days. You're the priority now. And the cat,' he added. 'He's much happier with all this peace and quiet.'

A quiet that was abruptly shattered by the pealing of the doorbell. 'Damn!' said Russell. 'When will I learn not to tempt fate like that?'

He slapped his paper down, and made a big production of hauling himself to his feet and shambling down the passage like a much older man. 'Maybe it's my nurse,' Simmy called after him.

It wasn't a nurse. It was Detective Inspector Moxon, freshly shaven, but not very thoroughly brushed. Her father escorted him into the kitchen, with eyes wide. 'It's the cops,' he said.

'I've only just heard about you being discharged,' Moxon began accusingly. 'It's a wonder I didn't waste half the morning driving down to Barrow. Luckily I called them first.'

She bit back an apology. Since when had she been expected to inform the police of her movements? She could feel her mother bristling with these and similar thoughts, as she leant back against the worktop by the sink and gave the detective a hostile stare. Simmy remembered that they had never met before. 'So what now?' she asked.

Her father indicated a wooden chair tucked under the big pine table; Moxon pulled it out and sat down. 'We're still trying to find that girl,' he explained. 'But we have far too little to go on.'

'Didn't the Troutbeck men help?'

'Nobody knows who they are. It's as if that whole incident never happened.'

'Well, it did.'

'I believe you. But we need more help.'

'From me?'

'I'm afraid so. How are you now? You look … fine.' He smiled stiffly. 'You look like a whole new person.'

'I think it's just that I'm forty years younger than most people the hospital has to deal with. My bones mend more quickly.'

'So …' He gave Angie and Russell a look that mixed authority with polite placation. 'Would there be a chance of you riding with me up to Troutbeck to try and sort this out?'

Simmy was amazed at the leap of excitement the suggestion produced. She had believed herself to be quite content to spend a week reading and doing puzzles and watching old films. Now, it seemed, she was every bit as keen as Ben Harkness to get on the trail of a murderer. But she needed to think logically before responding.

'Can't you just ask at the shop for the name of a man who takes *The Independent* and lives at Town Head?'

Moxon grimaced. 'We *could*, yes. But it's not always a good idea to jump in like that, in a small community. What if the chap's already got gossip going about him, over something else? It would unbalance things if word got out that the police were interested in him. And …' he held up a silencing finger 'don't say we could do it under cover, anonymously. There's no such thing as an under-cover detective out here. We're all much too well known. Especially in a place like Troutbeck, where there's such a tight network of old friends and relations.'

'You sound like Melanie,' she said.

'Miss Todd understands how it works, as well as anybody does.' He smiled ruefully. 'You were ahead of us on that – getting her granny to talk like that was an inspiration.'

'She wouldn't have done it with you, though. She doesn't really like the police.'

A quiet snort from Angie made it plain that Mrs Ellis wasn't the only one.

'Come on, then,' said Simmy decisively. 'You can take me to my house at the same time. Can I go like this?' She looked down at herself, in the elegant suit that had settled itself around her as if finally finding the exact right person to wear it. In Angie's hands it had seemed baggy and old, to the point of embarrassment. Now it was rapidly establishing itself as the best thing she'd ever worn. 'I don't think there is anything else here, actually.'

'You look splendid. But you'll need a coat as well.'

Her mother made no difficulty about finding a fleecy jacket and a pair of gloves for good measure. 'And a hat,' Simmy reminded her. The hat turned out to be a floppy blue beret that hid the damaged area without pressing uncomfortably.

She made much of showing off her proficiency with the crutches, out on the pavement. Moxon's car was thirty yards distant, and she swung along confidently, enjoying the chance of a clear straight course. The trick was not to think about it, she realised. Once problems of balance and weight distribution became conscious, the whole thing collapsed into wobbles and panics and a bent back. Elbow crutches only worked if they were long enough for the person to stand up straight. Simmy's were extended to their maximum length, making her wonder how anybody taller than her might manage.

'Your parents seem a bit thunderstruck,' Moxon commented, once they were comfortably in the car.

'No wonder. They expected to have to cosset and entertain me all day, not wave me off with a detective. They'll think I've been malingering all along.'

'They didn't see you screaming, the way I did.'

'True. I was much better by the time they turned up.'

The road northwards was bordered on both sides by a monochrome wintry landscape. The lake on the left reflected a looming mass of grey clouds, like a leaden mirror, Russell's sunny periods proving to be very short-lived. On the right, the bare trees had a sprinkling of snow on the boughs, and the spaces between them were splotched with white patches. The road was clear, but a grubby few inches of splashed grit and old snow had banked up on either side. When they turned up towards Troutbeck, these edgings grew cleaner and deeper. Before long, a strip of snow remained down the middle of the road. Ahead of them, the fells were shapeless white mounds, merging into cloud with no discernible differentiation.

'Why did I choose to live up here?' Simmy moaned. 'What was I thinking of?'

'Don't be daft. It's lovely. Best of all worlds. I wish I'd had the sense to do the same.'

'Where do you live, then?'

'Bowness,' he said shortly, and she realised it was a taboo question. Bowness, she supposed, was the *worst* of all worlds, if you liked solitude and wildness and unspoilt landscape.

'We should swop,' she said. At that particular moment, she would cheerfully have signed the papers without a second thought.

'Gladly,' he agreed.

'So what exactly are we going to do?' she asked. 'How will we find these men? And what are we going to say to them?'

'We'll drive up to Town Head, and see how it goes.'

She stared at his profile as he drove slowly up the winding little road. 'What? You think they'll just be standing out in full view, and I just have to point them out?'

'I think we might get lucky.'

She knew he was teasing her; that there was some convoluted scheme afoot that she wasn't privy to. He turned left at the church, and headed up the narrow lane towards the centre of the village. 'I hope it's not icy at the top,' she said. It was a manoeuvre she habitually avoided. The final few yards involved a narrow steep turn which was a disaster in any weather if you met something coming down. In treacherous weather, it didn't bear thinking about.

But it was not only easily accomplished, but Moxon began a wholly unexpected conversation in the process. 'Ninian Tripp visited you in hospital – is that right?'

'Er ... yes, he did. Julie brought him. He said he'd run the shop for me if I needed him to.'

'Did he indeed? How well do you know him?'

'I've seen him three or four times. I've heard a bit about his background.' She was stiff with defensiveness, her injured bones suddenly protesting. Dimly she imagined the official police impression of Ninian, with his peripheral lifestyle. They would automatically hold him to be a suspicious character, simply because he failed to adhere to the normal conventions.

'He told you about his criminal record, then?'

She wanted to lie and say of course she knew the whole story. She refused to take the bait, feeling a sudden scorn for the transparency of Moxon's thinking. 'I don't think I'd be very interested,' she said coldly. 'I take people as I find them, and I must say I liked him a lot.'

'And Julie – what does she make of him?'

'She likes him as well. And she's much more selective about people than I am.'

'Oh, he's a charmer, all right. And you'll let him loose on your shop, then, will you?'

'I might, if it makes the difference between surviving and going out of business.'

'Which it won't. Don't give me that.'

'Well don't you try to blacken a man's character for no reason!' she flashed back. 'You're lucky my mother isn't here.' She was overflowing with the many critical remarks she might make on behalf of her mother. They ranged from the way police officers assumed they could make judgements on people's lives to the everlasting surveillance that amounted to outrageous intrusion on everybody's privacy.

He sighed, and Simmy remembered how she had made him laugh when he visited her in hospital. *He likes me,* she thought. *And he wants me to like him.* It was a pity, she supposed, that she could only manage it about half the time.

'Let's stop at your house first,' he suggested. They were almost at her door as he spoke. Her whitewashed cottage looked chilly and neglected, and she felt a pang of guilt at how little she had thought of it. There were modest drifts of snow on the flowerbeds and the front step had an unspoilt inch or so of white topping like the icing on a cake. Evidently the postman hadn't been that day. Moxon turned off the ignition and opened his door. 'Come on, then. I should come in with you and check there's been no burst pipes or anything.'

Burst pipes were the very least of her worries. Lakeland plumbing took freezing temperatures for granted and she knew there was barely any risk. There was more likelihood of a fire, given that she had left most of her appliances switched on, assuming she would be back on Sunday evening, rather than five eventful days later.

She had almost certainly left the back door unlocked, despite a previous experience of somebody simply walking in and making themselves at home. Given what had happened on Sunday, this might not have been too good an idea.

'Yes, all right,' she said. 'But you'll have to help me out.'

Nobody had been in; the house was just as she left it. But her clothes were all upstairs and she had not yet tackled stairs. She looked at them dubiously. 'I suppose it's not so difficult,' she said. 'Just a matter of keeping my balance.'

'Right,' he agreed. 'Did they really say you mustn't put *any* weight on your feet? That doesn't seem possible.'

'Just use them for balance, they said. It's not so bad when you get used to it. But *stairs* ...'

They both knew he should offer to go up and make a selection of pants, jumpers, socks, enough to last a week or more. And they both found the fact that he was a professional male police detective came as a block to such assistance.

They were saved – or so it felt – by his phone going off. He answered it on the second beat and after twenty seconds thanked the caller with a tightness that Simmy interpreted as urgent excitement.

'We have to go back to Windermere,' he told her, looking at her with something like frustration. 'They think they might have found her.'

'Who?'

'Your granddaughter person. In that same pub we were in last week, as it happens. The Elleray. She's staying there with another woman.'

'She told me on Sunday that she was going home,' Simmy protested.

'It might not be her. We don't have a picture of her, remember. More likely, she lied to you. But we've got forty officers watching out for a young woman in a Mondeo, possibly acting strangely. Now they've found one, okay? And I've got you with me to identify her. We need to go.'

'Isn't it rather early to be in the pub? What time do they open? She must be very conspicuous.'

'Precisely. That's why they called me.'

'Who did? The pub people?'

'No more questions.' He made as if to grab her arm, but did not make actual contact. Instead he flapped a hand at her. 'Please come on.'

She looked around her house, disliking being rushed. 'I should turn the heating down, at least. And switch the telly off on the wall. I don't know when I'll be back, do I?' The clothes, so near and yet so far, nagged at her. 'And I really do need some clean pants. My mother's feel all wrong.'

Without a word, he ran upstairs, not asking her for any instructions. Less than a minute later he was back holding a canvas bag that had been in a cupboard, stuffed full of random clothes. Then he went into the sitting room and disconnected the TV. 'The heating can stay as it is. Are you on gas or oil?'

'Oil,' she said, with a wince. 'What a waste!'

'You won't want to come back to a freezing cold house. It's best to leave it. Now can we go?'

It had only been five minutes since the phone call. She had no reason to reproach herself for delaying him – especially as it had been his idea to come to Troutbeck in the first place. She thought wistfully of the odd little piece of detective work he apparently had in mind, now no longer required, if it was indeed Candida at the Elleray. For the first time, her heart began to thump with anxiety.

It took two more minutes to get her back into the car, during which she said nothing. But once they were moving, she asked, 'What if it was Candida who pushed me into the water? What'll she think when she sees me?'

'Well … she'll know from the news that you're still alive, so it won't be a complete shock. Beyond that, I have no idea. That is rather the point of the exercise. Or part of it.'

'Isn't there some evidence at Miss Clark's house? Fingerprints or something?'

'A few, of course. Three or four sets from people we can't identify, which might include your Hawkins girl. We haven't got hers to match anything against. And there's the usual collection of hairs and fibres and footprints, which may or may not have anything to do with her killer.'

Simmy sighed, wishing she'd watched the same forensic programmes as Ben and understood at least something of the way it all worked. She had a suspicion that she was in a very small, very ignorant minority, with virtually no working knowledge of how – for example – a DNA test was done, or what the vital signs of strangling might be. Even the garbled story of how Miss Clark had been killed by a hypodermic made very little sense to her. Moxon had told her almost nothing about how the murder had been committed, leaving her to wonder about the accuracy of the rumours. Besides, there was still the major question of the alibi.

Unless something new had been discovered about the time of death, Candida Hawkins was still in the clear.

Moxon sighed in unison. 'The whole business has been frustrating,' he confessed. 'We might have come up with a whole lot of useful information, if we'd been cleared to do a deeper forensic exploration. But that's expensive, and the powers that be wanted it done in the old-fashioned way, if possible. Asking questions and watching certain individuals can very often work better than sifting through a hundred evidence bags – which can have a very annoying habit of losing their labels.'

'That must be expensive as well – in manpower?'

'Less so. They'd mostly be working anyway. We've just diverted people from other jobs for a few days.'

'It's crazy, though, isn't it, to think Candida killed the old lady? What about the timing? How come you were so sure about that, when you wanted me to give Mr Kitchener the alibi?'

'Miss Clark's neighbour spoke to her at ten-thirty that morning. A man delivering a parcel found her body at eleven-thirty, still warm. *Very* warm. And there were clear signs that her death was not natural.'

Simmy wished she hadn't asked. But there was no retreating now. 'How did the parcel man find her?'

'He said he knew her slightly – well enough to try her door and open it when he found it wasn't locked. She was lying in the hallway. But there is that hour, you see, when it was done. With some very clever footwork, it could just possibly still be either of the people you saw in the café.'

'And you've opted for the girl, because she can move faster and there's a mystery around her? Seems to me you're clutching at straws.'

'When there's only one or two straws available to clutch at, it might turn out to be a lot better than nothing.'

'I don't see how. You'll drown in any case.' Her mind filled with pictures of cold swirling water and a flimsy stalk offering no prospect whatever of rescue.

'You're forgetting Ben Harkness's spreadsheets. He makes a credible case for there being a connection between the Josephs and the Clarks, even if it goes back to before this granddaughter was even born.'

'And her being born seems to be a key factor,' Simmy offered, feeling rather clever.

'If she is what she says – which some people seem to doubt. We've gone into it thoroughly, and there's no indication at all that either of the Joseph daughters ever gave birth to a child that could be her. Davida gave her child up for adoption, decades ago – I've lost track of how long it must be – something over forty years, I think – and then had a son who lives with her and her husband. The other one's gay, and never had a child. In fact – and this is very weird – she produced an affidavit she signed when she and her partner first set up home together. It's a sworn statement to the effect that she has never slept with a man. They produced it as final proof that the granddaughter couldn't possibly be hers.'

'That *is* weird. Who would ever go to so much trouble? I mean – whatever *for*?'

'Something between the two of them, obviously. I didn't think we needed to go any more deeply into it.'

'Wait a minute. When did this happen – the police questioning, I mean? Why would you do that? What did you say to them?' The realisation that the Joseph family now had plain proof that she,

Simmy Brown, had disclosed their personal business to the police was disturbing. 'I never imagined you'd do that,' she complained.

'Calm down. We had no choice when we knew what took you up Peggy Hill on Sunday. Somebody tried to *kill* you. We take that sort of thing extremely seriously. So we located Mrs Joseph and her daughters.'

'I see that, I suppose. But Mrs Joseph is staying with Davy. And why would you need to speak to Nicola anyway?' She looked at him. 'Were you there personally?'

'No I wasn't, as it happens. The three women were all there together at the older daughter's house. They seemed quite eager to tell the story. They expressed great concern for your welfare, and worried that they were somehow responsible. They volunteered the information about the granddaughter. At least, the old lady did.'

'And Nicola had that affidavit about her person?'

'In her bag.'

'That's bizarre.'

'Maybe not, given that the whole question of the granddaughter was so central for them. I think she'd been showing it to her mother, to convince her there was no way it was her child.'

'That makes sense,' Simmy agreed. 'So you didn't tell them Candida's name?'

'No, we didn't. But I don't see why it would matter if we did.'

She frowned thoughtfully. 'I suppose it wouldn't. I just feel it would be a bad idea, somehow. I'm not sure why.'

'Because you know there's a chance this girl is a killer,' he suggested.

'With no reason whatever to murder Miss Clark – or me. I'm sorry, but without some sort of motive, you're never going to persuade me.'

'I don't really want to,' he said, with a smile. 'It's not really about persuasion.'

But she was still immersed in the morass of questions that remained to be answered. 'That brings us back to Mr Kitchener, doesn't it? We know his mother and Nancy Clark were very far from being friends, for reasons even Mrs Ellis didn't seem to know. Maybe it's something really awful, and old Mrs K extracted a deathbed promise from her son to do the deed.'

'And that raises the exact same question again. What might he have against you, to tip you into the ghyll? Unless he was scared the alibi would fall apart once other facts emerged, and needed you to be unavailable for further questioning. I don't think that's much of a theory.'

'So you think it's someone else entirely? Ninian Tripp? Miss Clark's nephews? Who else?'

'Someone we haven't even thought of, probably. That would be unusual – but this whole case has been unusual from the very start.'

They were back on the main road, barely a mile away from the pub. She had run out of intelligent questions to ask. Her anxiety had abated somewhat, the reason for it still obscure to her. She was far from enjoying herself, even so. Some people – specifically Ben and Melanie – would have loved to be in her situation. She could see no possible good outcome from the next development, and she was worried about her cracked bones. 'I should never have come with you,' she complained.

'I didn't give you much option,' he reminded her. 'Don't worry – I'll make sure you're safe.'

'I didn't think I'd be in any actual danger. It's more ...'

'I know,' he said, surprising her. 'It's the unpredictability, the strangeness. It's not your world, I understand that. It does seem like a perverse fate that brings you face to face with violence a second time in a few months.'

'Thank you. It's nice that you can see that. Reassuring.'

'Don't be too reassured. Somebody wanted you dead. Presumably that hasn't changed.'

He parked in a narrow street adjacent to the pub, on double yellow lines. 'Sorry – but I'm going to ask you to come with me,' he said. 'We need to do it quickly, without warning. Just walk in and see if she's still there.'

It had been fifteen or twenty minutes since he got the phone call. 'Okay,' she agreed.

'And if she's not there, I'll buy you a drink,' he said lightly.

'Where are your people?' She looked round at the quiet streets. Traffic was passing thinly, and a man walked past carrying a Christmas tree over his shoulder.

'Dotted about. They know we're here.'

'I thought you said undercover didn't work round here.'

'They're not pretending to be anyone else. They're just quietly minding their own business. Not asking any questions, not bothering anybody. They won't have been noticed.'

She scanned the area. A couple were chatting quietly on the next corner; a young man sat in a car in a legal parking spot fifty yards away; a middle-aged woman was cleaning the window of a house further down the street. Ben would instantly spot the cops, she thought. She resolved to develop the habit of watching *Spooks, CSI* and *Silent Witness* as a matter of urgency.

She struggled out of the car, feeling a flash of pain as part of the dressing on her pelvis pulled loose. The delicate skin protested grievously. 'Ow!' she yelped.

He was at her elbow, frowning worriedly. 'I'm all right. Sorry,' she panted.

He ushered her into the pub, and through to the single big bar, which took her back to the oddly intimate lunch they'd had there a week earlier. The same cheerful man was there, washing glasses and whistling. There was no sign of Candida Hawkins. Two women were at a far table, side by side. 'It's Gwen and Nicola!' said Simmy, loud enough to attract attention to herself. Except that their attention had already been engaged, and they were staring hard at her, eyes wide.

Chapter Twenty-one

NICOLA WAS THE first to speak. 'You're out of hospital already! That's amazing. What a wonderful surprise!'

'Hello,' Simmy called, across the uncomfortably long intervening gap. 'Fancy meeting you here.' She considered introducing Moxon to them, but some telepathic warning told her not to. They might just think he was a boyfriend, or brother, or volunteer carer, she supposed.

Gwen laughed. 'Drinking before lunch – disgraceful, I know. But Nicola had some urgent reason to get to the shops, and I decided to lend a hand, since I'm on vacation and have remarkably little to do. We've only been here five minutes.' She gave her partner a sharp look.

Moxon seemed at a loss, having immediately established that Candida Hawkins was not in the pub. After dithering for a few seconds, he left Simmy to her own devices and went to speak to the publican. He cocked his head to indicate a desire for a private word, and the two men moved to the opposite end of the long bar from where the two women sat. Simmy swung herself towards

Nicola and Gwen and addressed them in a voice that was just slightly too loud.

'Everyone's been admiring the bedsocks,' she said. 'I was sent home yesterday because of the snow. But it never really came to much, did it? Even up at Troutbeck, it's not really bad. We thought we'd stop in here for a coffee, actually. My … friend knows the staff here, and wanted a chat as well. He's been escorting me in his car, because I can't drive – obviously.' She forced a laugh. The prattle was exhausting, and she began to worry that she sounded insane. The women probably knew exactly who Moxon was, anyway.

'Coffee,' Nicola repeated. 'We should have asked for coffee,' she said to Gwen. There were two half pints of beer in front of them, barely touched. Simmy began to detect something of an atmosphere between them, as she closed the gap even further. Without conscious intention, she leant across the table towards them. 'Oof!' she gasped. 'I'm still not really up to this. Sorry. I'll go and sit somewhere else.' With an effort she got herself upright again and hopped down the big room to a table not far from the door.

It was increasingly evident to Simmy that the presence of Nicola Joseph in the very pub where a claimant to be either her niece or her daughter had been sighted was no coincidence. There was no way it could be. She wondered whether Moxon had worked out who they were, and if so, what he made of it. So why *were* they here? Had Candida made some sort of assignation with one of them, to be thwarted by the presence of the other? Or had she spotted the lurking detectives and made her escape? Was there some conspiracy going on, as Simmy had at one point suspected? She tried to recall what Ben had said about such a theory, in his dossier. But she wasn't able to summon up anything. It was difficult enough trying to remember all the complex relationships they'd heard about from Mrs Ellis – none of which made reference to Candida.

Moxon was suddenly at her side, smiling apologetically. 'Sorry, love. I've got to go, asap. Change of plan. You know how it is.' He was apparently adopting the persona of a sort of spiv, patronising his burdensome girlfriend, hoping Nicola and Gwen wouldn't realise who he was. 'I'll get our Mel to come and take you home. Just wait here ten minutes. Bye!' And he was gone. Simmy could not believe it. She met Gwen's interested gaze, and smiled helplessly. Somewhere, she knew there was a message, a meaning, in what had just happened. *Our Mel* repeated in her head. Somehow Moxon was going to arrange for Melanie to take her home – a distance that would normally be a ten-minute stroll at most.

He left and she waited, sitting awkwardly, not sure whether she should order a drink. She was aware of a reprieve. The detective would probably have harangued her about her stubborn wish to avoid further involvement. *Don't you care about justice and the rule of law?* he might have demanded. *Can't you provide a bit more help here?*

Or was she simply projecting her own uneasy sense of guilt at her selfishness? She had yet to shake off the idea of herself as a victim, essentially passive and traumatised. In some ways it suited her, providing an excuse for not becoming some sort of honorary policewoman. She imagined Moxon signing her up as an informer, passing on titbits of gossip heard in the shop, and what her mother would say if that happened.

Gwen and Nicola were leaving. Nicola had a thwarted expression, as if she'd hoped for a longer sit-down with her beer. Gwen looked stern, a schoolteacher marching a delinquent pupil to the head. But beneath these expressions there was a closeness, a basic solidity to them that marked them as a settled couple, readily cresting the occasional waves of disharmony.

Melanie must have seen them leave, because she arrived half a minute later. She walked in looking tall and young and reliable. There was a lot about Melanie that was dependable, Simmy had discovered. Physically solid and emotionally robust, she stood out from her family like a cuckoo chick. Even her grandmother with her total recall and plain speaking was a faded shadow compared to Mel. Simmy had only met the girl's parents and siblings once, as they all milled about on the lake shore in Bowness one Sunday afternoon, but they had been forgettably colourless beside Melanie. Even her clothes had more character than her spotty sisters and round-shouldered father.

'Your taxi awaits,' she said, with a little bow, echoing Russell the day before. 'What on earth are you wearing?'

'My mother found it. All my clothes are still in my cottage. It feels really nice, actually.'

'Cool,' said Melanie dubiously.

Simmy looked around and noticed that Moxon had left the canvas bag containing spare clothes on the floor by her chair. Melanie followed her gaze and picked it up for her.

'Gosh, Mel, this is embarrassing. How did they get hold of you? Were you busy?'

'They've got my phone number – duh!' laughed the girl. 'I was at my gran's, anyway. It's about a minute's drive from here.'

'Did you park on double yellows?'

'Certainly not. There's a space just round the corner. How far can you walk?'

'Far enough, on the level. What time is it?' She wasn't wearing a watch, and couldn't see a clock in the bar. It felt as if half the day at least was behind her.

'Ten to eleven. Why?'

'No reason. I just wanted to keep track. It's been a very funny day so far. Every time I think I know what's going to happen, it all changes. It's like being in a dodgem car.'

'It's a bit like that for me as well,' Melanie nodded. 'Do I need to hold on to you?'

'No. I'm better without that. Look.' She swung herself out onto the pavement, while Melanie held the door open for her. 'But I keep thinking I'm going to fall over. It makes me giddy after a bit.'

'Weird. You look okay. Much better than yesterday.'

'My head hurts,' Simmy noticed. 'Throbbing.'

Melanie made a sympathetic face, saying nothing. She led the way to the elderly car that she shared with an older brother, and Simmy lowered herself into it with a sense of having had rather too much practice at this manoeuvre in the past hour or so.

'Oh!'

'What? Did you hurt something?'

'No – see who's over there.' Simmy tipped her chin at a man on the pavement, who had plainly recognised them. 'Mr Kitchener, of all people.'

'Oh, yes,' said Melanie with no sign of surprise. 'He was at my gran's this morning, as well. He might want to talk to you, actually.'

Simmy felt tired. 'Do I have to?'

'He's in quite a state. The police have been at him again, thanks to Ben.' She tutted crossly. 'He doesn't consider anybody's feelings, you know. It's all just a puzzle to him.'

Simmy had a sense of numerous conversations and developments that had been going on without her, while she languished in
hospital. 'I've missed such a lot,' she complained. 'I'm never going
to catch up.'

'Do you *want* to?'

Good question, she thought. Ten minutes ago, she'd been glad
to escape any further time in Moxon's company. 'I want it all over
and done with.'

'I think people have been pretty good at keeping you in the
loop, actually. Just about everybody's been to see you since your ...
injury.'

She was going to say 'accident', Simmy realised. Even Melanie
shied away from the idea that somebody really seriously tried to
kill the most innocent and undeserving person in Windermere.

'Just give him a minute. He might have something important to
tell us. My phone went before he could get to the point, just now.'

The man came to Simmy's window, and she tried to open it.
'Sorry,' said Melanie. 'It doesn't work. You'll have to open the
door.'

It was no way to discuss delicate issues around murder and
suspicion and the apprehensions that came with them. 'He'll have
to get in the car,' said Simmy. 'And you can drive us down to Lake
Road, where it's quieter.'

'It's quiet enough here,' argued Melanie, only to be contra-
dicted by two large delivery vans trying to pass in the small street,
with a smart red BMW almost sandwiched between them. Horns
began to sound, and a man shouted.

Melanie's car only had two doors. With poor grace she stepped
aside and waved Mr Kitchener onto the back seat. 'Sorry about the
mess,' she muttered. 'It's my brother's stuff mostly.'

'It's good to see you up and about,' he told Simmy, his eyes moist. 'I was distraught when I heard what'd happened. Where's all this madness going to end?'

'You may well ask,' said Melanie.

'Nancy Clark,' he said, having taken a deep breath. 'It's all because of that woman. My mother could tell you some stories about her. I know we ought not to speak ill of the dead, but in her case … well, she probably had it coming.'

'Careful!' Melanie warned him. 'For God's sake don't make a confession to us. We won't know what to do if that happens.'

'I didn't kill her. I have no idea who did. I'm just saying there's a long list of candidates. People she worked with, mostly, seeing as how she never had any friends.'

'But that was *years* ago. Why bump her off now?' Melanie was still doing all the talking. Simmy found it impossible to twist round to address him, or meet his eye, until she found he was staring at her in the car's rear-view mirror.

'My mother always said she was a blackmailer. Sometimes that sort of thing takes a long time to catch up with a person. People just reach the end of their tether and decide it has to stop.'

'Blimey!' said Melanie. 'Blackmail!'

'She worked in a clinic,' said Simmy slowly. 'And was having an affair with a consultant for a long time. When did she retire? And what sort of clinic was it?'

'She retired at sixty-five, twelve years ago. There was a big party – they must have been delighted to see the back of her. It was in the local paper. It's a private clinic, quite exclusive. I always imagined it did abortions mainly, for rich women.'

'Great scope for blackmail,' whooped Melanie. 'But surely the police will have checked into all that by now?'

'Yes,' agreed Simmy. 'All they have to do is go through the records and see if anybody has been near Nancy Clark recently.' Already she could hear the naivety in her own words. 'Although … I suppose that might not be very easy.'

'They could start with people who've come to their notice lately,' insisted Melanie.

'I'm not sure—' Simmy began.

'You're talking rubbish,' Mr Kitchener told them both. 'That's not the way it'll work. The records won't be given up without a fight, for one thing. Probably they destroy them after seven years or thereabouts. Or use false names. People *pay* to go there, not like the NHS. They're paying for discretion and anonymity.'

Simmy thought back to the few times she had met this man. They had been overlaid with other people's comments on him and his continuing role as possible murderer, when all along she had liked him and felt sorry for him. 'Do you remember that girl in the café?' she asked, before she'd known she was going to speak. 'You accidentally kicked her chair, and she looked at you.'

He and Melanie both went silent with surprise. 'Girl?' he said, eventually. Something in his voice told Simmy that he did remember at least a shred or two.

'She was at a table by herself, looking thoughtful. You kicked her chair,' she repeated.

'Ah. She reminded me of somebody. Her eyes. Gave me a bit of a shock. Who was she, then?'

'You honestly don't know?'

He gave a kind of growl. 'Is nobody ever going to believe a word I say, ever again? Why the hell should I lie about it?'

'You might have been in cahoots with her,' said Melanie, catching on. 'The kick might have been a signal.'

'Cahoots,' he echoed scornfully. 'Just you be thankful my mother can't hear you. What sort of a word is that?'

Or my father, thought Simmy, with a faint smile. 'You know what it means,' snapped Melanie. 'Who did the girl remind you of?'

'It took me a minute to work that out. Then it came to me – Matt Joseph. I worked for him at one time, thanks to my mother. At the printworks. It was the best job I ever had,' he said wistfully. 'They all knew each other, back in those days.'

Melanie smacked a hand lightly on the dashboard. 'You don't need to tell *us* about it,' she said. 'We had all that from my gran, last weekend.'

Simmy's insides were surging with excitement. The puzzle was coming together like magic, pieces simply slotting into place by themselves. 'Matt Joseph's eyes? Matt Joseph who was married to Mrs Mary Joseph, with the two daughters? What about his eyes?'

'They were unusual. Dark grey, close together, full of character. Mesmeric, some people said.'

Matt Joseph had been every girl's heart-throb, according to Mrs Ellis. 'Charismatic,' Simmy added. She visualised Candida Hawkins, with her smooth young skin and energetic hair. Her eyes were much as Mr Kitchener had just described.

'That too,' sighed the man. 'Matt was lovely, right up to the day he died.' The emotion was undisguised. *Every boy's heart-throb, too*, thought Simmy.

'So – that does make the girl Mrs Joseph's granddaughter,' Melanie summarised. 'If she looks like *Mr* Joseph, that clinches it. We need to find her and get the cops to do a DNA test on her.'

'Wouldn't prove anything,' Mr Kitchener pointed out. 'Even if she is the granddaughter, that doesn't make her a murderer.'

'They're looking for her, don't worry,' said Simmy, thinking Melanie's lack of logic felt more persuasive than Ben's insistence on rational processes. 'She was here at the Elleray half an hour ago, but when we got here, she'd gone. But Nicola and Gwen were here. They probably saw her.' The puzzle came apart again. 'And that's weird, isn't it? I mean – do they *know* her at all?'

'What do you mean, she was here? Who says? Nobody else even knows what she looks like.'

'Except me,' Mr Kitchener reminded them. 'But I still don't know who she is, or why she matters. Because I am *not* in "cahoots" with her.'

'Moxon got a call from someone saying there was a girl in the pub who they thought might be her. They've had dozens of police people searching for her all week, apparently. We were in Troutbeck, looking for the men who helped her push her car back onto the road. Except we never got started, because the phone call came.'

'Dozens of police people?' Mr Kitchener seemed awestruck. 'All for horrible Nancy Clark who got what she deserved?'

'Nobody deserves to be murdered,' said Simmy angrily. The matter had become inescapably personal for her.

'Some people do,' he persisted. 'And I've met a few of them in my time.'

'She could be Matt Joseph's *daughter*,' Melanie interjected, with a note of triumph. 'That would be more likely, if she looks so like him. I know – she's the result of incest. He made one of his girls pregnant, and it was all hushed up, but Nancy Clark found out about it, and now somebody wants it kept quiet. The girl herself, most likely. I mean – you wouldn't want people to know that about you, would you?'

'Shut up,' Simmy begged her. 'That's horrible. And it can't be right, because the police have double-treble checked, and there are definitely no secret babies. You can't just hide the fact that you've had a baby, these days. Nicola's a virgin, anyway. She signed a legal thing to say she was.'

Mr Kitchener gave an embarrassed cough.

Melanie gave a sceptical sniff. 'She might have been lying. And I think you *can* hide a baby if you try hard enough. Besides, if Candida has come back to confront them, they didn't do a very good job of it, did they? She's tracked them down.'

'To kill them,' said Simmy dramatically.

'No – she sent the old lady flowers, remember?'

'And it's bloody old Nancy that got killed,' said Mr Kitchener.

'And nearly you,' added Melanie. 'But we're getting closer. This is brainstorming,' she informed them. 'That's what we're doing. It's a very useful tool.'

'And now we can stop. Please. I need to get home. Back to my parents', I mean.' Simmy thought of her abandoned little house with a painful stab of guilt. 'They'll be wondering whether I want lunch or not.'

'Thank you for talking to me,' said Mr Kitchener, a shade too humbly. 'I appreciate it.'

'Do you need a lift anywhere?' Melanie offered. 'I'm at your disposal once I've taken Simmy home.'

'No, no, thanks. I've got to get back to Ambleside. The bus goes any time now.'

'Bus?' Simmy queried. Surely he had a car of his own? 'Where's your car?'

He coughed, with renewed embarrassment. 'Lost my licence,' he mumbled. 'I thought you knew.'

'No, I didn't.' She had no idea why he might have been banned from driving, but it made him even more of a loser than she'd first realised. She sighed.

Melanie and Mr Kitchener both got out, while Simmy waited impatiently to get moving. She needed the loo and was cold from sitting in an unheated car for half an hour.

'Did that get anybody anywhere?' she asked Melanie, when they finally got started. 'Or have we just gone round in another circle?'

'We need to think. And where did Moxo dash off to, anyway? Is something going on?'

'He's very self-important today. With his dozens of officers prowling around Windermere and Ambleside. Why Windermere, anyway?' she wondered for the first time. 'Nobody's suggested anything bad's going to happen down here.'

'*You're* here now, that's why,' said Melanie with heavy emphasis. 'What did you think?'

'No – that's not it. He's not worried about me. He's looking for that girl. He must think she's the killer.'

'You saw her in Troutbeck, remember. She could be anywhere.'

They were outside Beck View in under three minutes. 'Thanks, Mel. At least you're all up to date now with everything that's been going on. You can't say you've been left out this time, can you?'

'Is that your dad's car?' Melanie was frowning at a black Volvo parked just ahead of them.

'No, of course not. His is in the drive, look.'

'Hmm. Well maybe you've got a visitor, then.'

'Or maybe somebody just bagged a handy space.'

But when she got herself inside the house, calling 'I'm back!' down the passage from the front door, she discovered that Melanie had been absolutely right.

Chapter Twenty-two

'AT LAST!' HER mother appeared from the living room, with a harassed expression. 'We wondered where on earth you'd got to. There's somebody here to see you.'

Her first thought, rather to her own surprise, was that it was Ninian Tripp. Or Julie. But her mother's tone implied somebody more unexpected than that. A childish notion flittered through her mind that it was Santa Claus, or a long-lost fairy godmother.

'I've got to go to the loo,' she said urgently. 'If that's okay.'

'Hurry up, then. We don't know what to say to her.'

The silky skirt was blessedly easy to manoeuvre, and she was quickly back in the living room doorway. The woman standing by the empty fireplace was familiar, but it took a few moments for Simmy to identify her. When she did, she wasn't sure how to address her. She could hardly say 'Davy!', as if to a friend, but she could not recall hearing a surname. 'Hello,' she managed. 'What a surprise.'

'We'll leave you to it, then,' said Angie, with a show of briskness. Russell was already disappearing towards the kitchen. 'Just give me a call if you want anything.'

'Thanks, Mum,' said Simmy, wondering whether the visitor had been sitting down at any stage, or remained stiffly standing as she waited. 'Well – here I am,' she added superfluously.

'I needed to see you,' said Mrs Joseph's elder daughter. 'I hope it's not a nuisance.' She didn't look as if this was any real concern to her.

'How did you know where I was?' It was a foolish question, but the feeling that she was fair game for a succession of people, wanted or not, was an unpleasant one.

'I asked around,' was the unsatisfactory reply. 'It didn't take long.'

'I saw your sister this morning.' That too was a silly thing to say, she supposed. It was probably axiomatic that you did not volunteer information during a murder enquiry. The complications of who knew what were all part of it. It was unwise to make any assumptions. But Simmy had lost patience with this sort of behaviour at some point in recent days. She could not begin to imagine why this woman should want to see her.

Davy seemed uninterested in her sister. 'I wanted to see you because of what happened to you at the weekend,' she said, speaking haltingly. 'I gather it happened close to my mother's house, and the police were informed that you were there in the hope of seeing her. They came to see us yesterday, with a whole lot of questions that I felt were entirely beside the point. I wanted to clarify in my own mind and more importantly yours that there is absolutely no connection between my family and your … mishap. I don't know the details, of course, but it's clear that the police have got hold of the idea that we as a family are involved. The assumption on all sides is that there's a link between the murder of the old lady in Ambleside and the attack on you a few days later. That's as maybe, but it appals me that some people have implicated my relatives in the business.' She stood there, one hand on the back of Angie's best sofa, her shoulders square and her jaw tight. 'I have no idea why such a link might be made,' she went on, 'because the only possible common factor must be you. And all you did was to deliver flowers from some troublemaker, on the day the old woman was murdered. Unless you can tell me differently.'

Simmy had been transfixed by this speech, still barely inside the room. Now she finally managed to sit down and draw breath. 'No, I can't tell you differently,' she said. 'I *agree* with you, more or less. At least I would have done a few days ago. Now it all seems very much more complicated than either of us would wish. I mean – there does seem to be a connection somewhere, but I don't really understand what it is. For a start, most of the people involved do actually know each other. Your father was at school with Nancy Clark and Mrs Kitchener. *Mr* Kitchener worked for him – your father.'

'Wait!' Davy ordered. 'Who are these Kitcheners? I don't know them.'

'He's called Malcolm. He was suspected of the murder, until I gave him an alibi. His mother died a month or so ago, and I did the flowers for the funeral. I've just been talking to him. And he's been to see Mrs Ellis – who knows absolutely *everybody*. Although your mother seems to have been on the outside. Nobody really knows her very well, as far as I can gather.'

'She minds her own business, that's why.'

'Anyway, it all keeps coming back to this girl – the one who sent the flowers. She's the key to it all, but nobody knows her, nobody's seen her – except me. Somehow she really does seem to be a relative of yours. Mr Kitchener says she looks like your father.'

'What? *What* did you say?' Fury turned her nose and cheeks deep pink. 'How many times do we have to tell you she is nothing whatever to do with us?'

Simmy sighed, refusing to be intimidated. 'I know. But why is she here? What's the point, if she's really not connected? Do you think she's just some madwoman who latched onto your family at random? That's not very plausible, is it?'

Davy backtracked. 'You gave the Kitchener man an alibi – is that what you said?'

'Yes. I saw him in the Giggling Goose, at the time of the murder. And the girl was there as well.' She conveyed this final fact with some reluctance. It still bothered her that the two people most likely to be killers were in the same place at the same time. The notion of a conspiracy refused to go away.

'I don't *care*. I just want all this to stop, and let my mother get back to normal. She keeps on about it. And Gwen's getting difficult again.'

Simmy did a double take. 'Pardon?'

'Oh, nothing. She's fine, really. But she's always been a bit … volatile. She's had a hard life, before she met Nicola. They've been very good for each other, on the whole. Nicola was always unsettled and dissatisfied, before Gwen came along. Now they've been together for ages and it's come as a big relief.'

'So what's her problem now? She seems all right to me. She gave me some bedsocks.'

Davy loosened slightly at this. 'Did she? There you are then,' as if a point had been proved.

'She's nice. I saw them – Gwen and Nicola – this morning.' Perhaps this would register better a second time.

'Did you? Where?'

'In the Elleray.'

'Good Lord! What were you doing there? What time was it?'

Discretion asserted itself. 'Oh, I was just tagging along with someone.'

Davy tipped her head like a disappointed teacher. 'Come on – your mother already told me you'd gone off with the policeman ... detective, whatever he is. He's not stalking my *sister* now, is he?'

The emphasis in this remark suggested that Moxon had been stalking one relative after another, which seemed unlikely. Unless she had inadvertently included Candida Hawkins as a relative – contradicting everything she'd been saying.

Simmy did not reply, and the conversation sank into a short silence. 'Well, I'd better go. I know none of this is your fault. You had a terrible experience, of course. I don't want you to think any of us wish you ill, in any way. My mother likes you, despite everything.'

Despite what, Simmy wondered? The flowers, she realised – the cheap bouquet that had started it all off. 'No, it wasn't my fault,' she said. 'I've done nothing at all wrong – except it was daft of me to go up to Ambleside on Sunday. I knew at the time, really.'

'So why did you?'

'I'm not sure now. Something about warning your mother. After talking to Mrs Ellis, it felt as if she might be at risk. And I was toying with the idea of telling her the name of the girl who sent the flowers, after all. But she wasn't there, so I needn't have bothered.'

'You have no reason to worry about my mother.' The stiffness was back. 'But I would be extremely grateful if you would tell me the person's name now. Then your part will be finished. You'll have no reason to concern yourself about any of us, for another second, but just get on with your own life. That's really what I came to say. Just concentrate on getting better, and stay out of it. You'll be doing everybody a favour, then. Including yourself.'

'I would if I could,' said Simmy. 'Believe me.'

'So ...?'

'What?'

'The name.'

Simmy tried, but found her tongue had frozen up. 'I can't,' she discovered. 'I daren't. I don't know where it might lead. I don't think I would have been able to tell your mother, either. It just seems wrong. Dangerous. I'm sorry. Perhaps you need to follow your own advice, and just forget it all. Leave everything to the police. You said yourself, there's no reason for your family to be involved. Go home and have a happy Christmas.'

Davy made no further attempt to persuade her. She muttered something about being on duty at the hospital for most of the Christmas holiday, and made her departure.

LUNCH WAS A frosty affair, with Angie making no attempt to conceal her feelings. Even Russell, normally so unflappable, was quiet and unsmiling. Simmy could hardly blame them. She had turned their lives upside down, losing them business, and then disappeared for half the morning without a backward glance. They had expected a helpless invalid, quietly recovering with a book or DVD – not an unpredictable figure at the centre of a murder investigation. *Whatever next?* was the question circling the dining table as they ate the carelessly assembled meal.

'Is that detective coming back?' Angie asked.

'I don't know.' It was Moxon who had done most to upset her mother, Simmy supposed. 'He's not a bad chap, you know. He's doing a difficult job, after all.'

'I understand that. I have nothing against him personally. He's not interested in me, thank goodness. I just wish ...' She gave a dramatic sigh and left the sentence unfinished.

'So do I,' said Simmy. 'None of this was my choosing.'

'You *say* that,' Angie burst out. 'But it's not entirely true, is it? I still don't have the slightest idea why you went back to Ambleside on Sunday. What were you thinking of? If it had nothing to do with you, why not just stay out of it altogether?'

'Because I'd met the granddaughter by then,' said Simmy. 'It's as simple as that. I couldn't just leave it there.'

'I don't see why not.'

'It's hard to explain. I never met Nancy Clark, so why should I care what happened to her? I think I cared more about Mr Kitchener. He seems so pathetic – he has done since I first met him. And vulnerable. You should have seen him sitting there in the police station. He's such a sad little man.'

'And you thought you could save him?' asked her father, with a frown. 'I don't think I'm following that train of thought very well.'

'No. It's not logical. I can't actually explain why I went up there on Sunday, except it seemed to be right, somehow. I wasn't even going to see Mr K. It was Mrs Joseph I was looking for. I felt bad about her, and wanted to put things straight. Or something.'

'You might have *died*,' Russell shivered. It was the first time this had been spoken aloud between them. 'Most people would have died.'

'I was lucky.'

'So why push your luck by going off again?' Angie demanded. 'Somebody out there intends to harm you. You should stay here out of the way.'

'I can't do that for ever, can I? I can't just put my life on hold indefinitely. I've got to open the shop, go back to Troutbeck, rescue my car, get on with things.'

'So you're confronting the faceless killer,' said Russell, smiling at last. 'Brave girl.'

Angie just tutted in frustration, but the air was clearer than it had been.

UNDENIABLY DRAINED BY the events of the day so far, Simmy agreed to stretch out on the sofa after lunch, and have a proper rest. She had actually fallen into a doze when the doorbell rang again, and she started awake with a great *thump* of her heart. Was Moxon back? What had he been doing, anyway, when he had rushed off leaving her with Melanie? His mysterious team and professional discretion made his activities deeply opaque to her.

Voices came through from the hallway, neither of them Moxon's. There seemed to be two callers, both female. Listening intently, Simmy recognised one of them and rolled herself awkwardly off the sofa to go and investigate.

Before she could find her crutches and get herself upright, a little group came into the room. Her father pushed the door wider, and admitted Candida Hawkins and another woman. They stood looking at her, without speaking. 'Hello,' said Simmy.

'You poor thing!' cried the girl. 'I was so *appalled* when I heard what had happened to you. I had to come and see how you were getting on.'

'You said you were going home on Sunday. Didn't you go?'

'I was going, but I changed my mind. Things got a bit difficult. This is my mother.'

'Jane Hawkins,' the woman introduced herself. She seemed to be around sixty, well dressed and expensively groomed. Her hair was cut like a helmet, a very natural-looking mid-brown colour. 'Candy and I have an apology to make to you. It appears that we might have got you into trouble with the Josephs. We wondered whether you'd be well enough to accept a little treat from us in recompense?'

Simmy's eyes stretched wide. She wondered whether she might be dreaming. 'Treat?' she repeated.

'Dinner at the Belsfield, perhaps? We can explain everything to you, as we eat. I always think that's the most civilised way of doing things.'

Her daughter laughed. 'That's definitely true. She always thinks people won't escape if they're sitting at the dinner table when she starts telling them what's what. Mind you, my father has been known to make a run for it, even then.'

The original alarm that Simmy had felt came back. Who *were* these people, anyway? The idea of going off with them into the dark night was not reassuring. 'I don't think I can,' she said. 'I don't think you owe me anything.' Then she had a thought. 'Except I gather your credit card doesn't work, so you probably do still owe me for those flowers.'

'Oh, my God!' squealed the girl. 'That's so embarrassing. I forgot it had been cancelled. Let me give you the cash instead.' She pulled a wallet from a shoulder bag and took out a twenty-pound note. 'Is this enough?'

Simmy took it awkwardly. 'Thanks,' she said, remembering the disappointing quality of the flowers.

'You really can trust us,' said Mrs Hawkins, with an amused smile. 'I promise you. We'll drive you home again afterwards, obviously.'

'Where are you staying?' Russell Straw asked, speaking for the first time. Simmy could see that he was trying to hide his bewilderment with a sensible pragmatic question.

'Not the Belsfield,' Jane laughed. 'But I gather they do a good dinner, and they still had a table to spare. Most places are completely booked.'

'We're staying at the Elleray,' Candida answered the question. 'We've been there two days already. We're going home tomorrow.'

Simmy visualised Gwen and Nicola sitting in the bar that morning. Had they known the Hawkins women were there? Had they already met and settled the mystery of Candy's birth? Was everything amicably resolved by now, with the injured florist the only remaining loose end?

'Think about it,' Jane urged her. 'The table's booked for seven. We'll come for you here at six-thirty. You can tell anyone you like, if you're worried about trusting us. There's no secrets, nothing sinister. I can understand you'd be nervous, after what happened to you, but we aim to convince you that it had nothing whatever to do with us.'

'Who said I thought it did?'

'We'll explain all that, as well. We've got something else to do this afternoon. Here's my phone number ...' She held out a card. 'Call us if you really won't come. Otherwise, we'll see you at six-thirty.'

Simmy took the card, knowing she would accept the invitation. Knowing that they knew she would, because what woman anywhere in the world could resist the lure of a mystery solved, an explanation made and a lavish free dinner into the bargain?

Chapter Twenty-three

THE AFTERNOON DRIFTED by slowly, with Simmy wondering what she ought to wear for her special treat. 'You can't hope to do better than that suit,' said Angie. 'You haven't got it dirty this morning, have you?'

'I don't think so.' Simmy looked down at herself. 'But it'll feel strange not changing into something else.'

'Add a scarf, earrings, smart shoes ...'

'All of which are up at Troutbeck,' Simmy reminded her.

'Dad can drive you there to fetch them.'

'I suppose so.' The prospect was unappealing. She felt instinctively that she should conserve her energy for the evening to come. Just getting in and out of a car was a challenge, and risked aggravating her fragile bones. 'And what about my head? I look terrible like this. My hair needs washing – what's left of it.'

'We can do that, at least.'

'Only if we take the dressing off. And what about the stitches? Are they allowed to get wet?'

'I don't see why not. We'll use that baby shampoo I've got for guests. It's been tested on rabbits' eyes, so your skull should cope with it.'

'Oh, hush, Angie,' scolded Russell. 'You know they don't do that any more.'

'I bet they do,' said Angie darkly.

'I don't think she ought to go, anyway.' Russell folded his arms and attempted a demeanour of authority. 'The idea's ridiculous.'

'You're right,' Simmy told him. 'But I'm going anyway. I can't resist it. And when you think about it, there's really no chance at all that they'll do anything to hurt me. Not now we know who they are and where they're staying. If I'm not back by half past nine, you just call the police.'

'Three hours after they've spirited you away and done their worst with you.'

'That sort of thing only happens in stories, Dad. I know – we can call the Elleray now and check that they really are staying there. Would that help?'

He mulled it over and shook his head. 'They could have used false names – to us as well. How would we ever find them if they just disappeared with you?'

'Take the registration number of their car when they come to fetch me. Even if it's a hired one, they'll have had to give ID to get it.'

'What if they come in a taxi?'

She had no reply to that.

'See?' he said, like a child.

'It'll be all right, Dad,' she insisted. They both recognised that the scene rightly belonged to a time in their lives over twenty years earlier, except that now there was a genuine reason to be anxious.

Something awful really had happened to Simmy, and her father was more than justified in reacting as he did. 'Mum's not worried, is she?' Simmy pointed out.

'She's confused, the same as me. Listen – I want you to send me a text message every hour, on the hour. Just put "OK" or something. What are these damned gadgets good for if not to set a parent's mind at rest?'

'All right, then,' she agreed, almost liking the idea. 'Should I start at seven or eight?'

'Seven, of course.'

ANGIE WASHED HER daughter's hair with extreme care, having picked away the hospital dressing and examined the wound. 'It's quite small, considering,' she remarked. 'And looks clean. No pus or angry red swelling.'

'It feels all right.' Simmy ran delicate exploratory fingers over the place, which was at the back of her head. 'Except for the shorn area.'

'If I remember rightly, that's the toughest part of your skull. Did you land on it, do you think?'

Together they described somersaults and arcs that Simmy might have performed as she flew off the bridge head first. It was both insensitive and therapeutic of her mother, she discovered. 'I don't suppose we'll ever know for sure, but I think it's more likely it got bashed on the way downstream. There's another sore area here.' She put her fingers to a spot above her left ear. 'And in plenty of other places.' The bruising on her chest still couldn't bear any pressure.

'I'm not at all sure you ought to go out,' said Angie. 'Didn't the hospital say anything?'

'I've already *been* out,' Simmy reminded her. 'And that was fine.'

The hair was dried, and an ordinary sticking plaster applied to the stitches on her scalp. It took the biggest one Angie could find. 'I thought you said the wound was small,' Simmy objected. 'That patch is enormous.'

'*Relatively* small. It's still a good two inches long. More than the average cut finger or grazed knee. Which is what these things are intended for. Besides, I need to allow plenty of margin, so the sticky bits don't pull at the stitches.'

They had tea and scones, and talked about nothing much until six. At that point, Simmy began to feel agitated. Her stomach was churning. She tried to analyse the reasons, prioritising her fears as methodically as she could without revealing a hint of the process to her parents. Angie was rummaging through her jumbled jewellery box in search of earrings or necklace, and Russell had returned to the kitchen to listen to the radio, leaving Simmy alone in the living room for a few minutes.

With no great certainty, she concluded that it was more a worry about going out into the cold, dark night, where there would be icy surfaces, than any apprehension of attack by Candida or Jane Hawkins. Or it could have been nothing more than a generalised loss of confidence in a reliable world. Unknown things might happen. Everything was a risk and there could be no guarantees.

THE CAR ARRIVED precisely at six-thirty. Jane Hawkins came to the door as Simmy made her way down the hall. Russell had announced a sighting from the living room window.

'Enjoy yourself,' he called from the doorway. 'At least it's not snowing!' On the contrary, it was a clear starry night, with every chance of a hard frost.

The car was small and appeared to be red, under the street lights. Jane opened the passenger door, and swung the seat forward so she could climb into the back next to Candida – which she promptly did. Simmy was left on the pavement to get in unaided. She bent down to look at the driver and was astonished to meet the gaze of Nicola Joseph. 'Oh!' she said.

'Hello again. Do you need any help?'

'Well – can you take the crutches?' She tried to hang onto the top of the car door while passing the metal poles to the woman. 'Sorry – no, I can't do it by myself. I need somebody to hold onto.'

'Oh, all right.' The tinge of impatience was uncalled for, Simmy thought. 'Wait a minute.' Nicola made a production of unclipping her seat belt and getting out of the car, walking round the back to Simmy's side. 'What do you need me to do?'

'Just keep me balanced. I need to lower myself gently, that's all.' She put a hand on Nicola's shoulder, and sank carefully onto the seat. 'It's more difficult in a small car,' she said, as if needing to justify herself.

'All set, then?' Nicola asked, once back in her own seat. Simmy looked round at the pair in the back.

'Okay,' Jane and Candida both muttered.

'You've met, then,' Simmy said fatuously.

'Eventually,' said Jane in a tight voice that suggested tribulation and possible ill feeling. 'I hope it's all right with you that we're a foursome? It seemed too good a chance to miss, when Nicola suggested we use this evening for a good long talk.'

'I'm honoured,' said Simmy, feeling that this was what she ought to say. The reality was something closer to trepidation. 'After all, it's none of my business, is it?'

'As we said earlier on, we feel guilty at the way you've suffered. Don't we, Candy?'

The girl murmured a wordless agreement.

The distance down to the Belsfield Hotel was less than a mile. In normal circumstances it would be a very easy walk, downhill all the way. Nicola drove quickly and they were in sight of the large floodlit building on the left before they knew it. Simmy was already wondering whether she would be willingly helped out of the car, when they suddenly veered to the right, and onto the hard area where people waited to board lake cruisers. A small green and white building loomed ahead, with a sign offering boat hire, and Simmy shouted, 'Where are we going?'

'This is where I always park,' said Nicola, sounding annoyed. She drove past two jetties where swans congregated during the daytime and rowing boats were generally waiting in rows for people to hire them. Now it was all quiet and deserted.

'But—' Something was terribly wrong. The strangeness of driving over an area intended for pedestrians was compounded by a horrified realisation that they had accelerated dramatically, then veered right again, careered down a shallow step and were now facing the black waters of Lake Windermere only four or five feet away. The abrupt swing to the right, accompanied by the increased speed, sent the car tilting onto two wheels, so that it began to slide sideways down the slope into the water.

Simmy watched uncomprehendingly as Nicola somehow opened her door and jumped out, leaving one foot to kick down on the accelerator. 'I can't help it,' she said wildly. 'I need this to happen. It'll look like an accident.'

She spun away with a small cry, leaving three trapped passengers to plunge over a low wooden platform and into the cold water. The door that Nicola had left open swung itself closed as if slammed by an invisible hand. 'We won't drown,' said Simmy to the others. 'It's not deep enough.' But the Hawkins women in the back were both squealing, and the car kept rolling onto its side and sinking down into water that was a lot deeper than might have been expected.

The heavy metal box that was the car embedded itself on its right side, tipping Simmy painfully onto the gear stick and then the steering wheel. The engine went on running for a moment, before dying with a gurgle. Cold water poured in over Simmy's feet and then knees. 'Don't panic!' she said. 'Candida – can you see if you can open the driver's door? It's on your side.'

There was no way they would drown, she kept telling herself. They'd be cold and wet, but not dead. But the car was sinking lower and Candida was making no progress getting the door open. She was having to reach over the driver's seat and could get no leverage on the door handle, and no weight behind it to shove it open. Lights from the nearby street cast a dull orange glow through the car windows. 'Somebody must have seen us,' cried Jane. 'Surely they must.'

It had all happened so quickly that Simmy could well imagine that the whole incident could have gone unobserved. There was no activity on the waterside on a cold December evening. Cars driving past would hardly notice movement amongst all the clutter of kiosk and uprights that bordered the jetties, even if they were barely twelve feet away. The roof of a car sticking out of the water might eventually attract attention, but there was no guarantee.

Candida was crying as she pushed ineffectually at the door. Her mother was making strange bleating sounds, at the same time as throwing her weight against Simmy's seat, as if hoping to dislodge it completely. 'Don't do that,' Simmy ordered her. 'It's making things worse.' Water had reached their waists, as they awkwardly strained to lift themselves away from it. Already Simmy's feet were numb. 'How deep is it here?' Candida asked hysterically.

'I have no idea,' Simmy gasped back. The car being on its side actually helped, in a way, she realised. It was, after all, wider than it was high. She guessed they had a foot or two to go, and the water really couldn't be deep enough to swallow the whole car.

'I'll try and open my door.' She pulled the handle set into the inside of the door, and exerted all the upwards pressure she could, clumsily trying to find something to brace against. Pain exploded in her pelvis and ribs. 'Aargghh!' she screamed. For the first time, stark fear gripped her. If she couldn't move, she would be in the car until she died. She waited for the pain to subside, aware that her scream had frozen the others into silence. She fought to prevent herself from collapsing into absolute panic. Pain, fear, confusion, shock – and many allied reactions – turned her flesh cold and her mind numb. Somewhere she understood that the situation was not entirely unprecedented, but unlike the earlier one, she was conscious this time and required to save herself if remotely possible. She was also not alone.

There were two people in there with her, neither of them handicapped by physical injury. They had to be able to open one of the doors. Dry land was only three or four steps away. The car was stuck in soft shingle and mud, so it was unlikely to sink any further. Simmy forced herself to think in simple factual bytes. 'Help the girl to push,' Simmy shouted at Jane. 'Don't just *sit* there.'

Wasn't panic meant to galvanise people into superhuman feats of strength? Didn't they rip the doors off planes to escape after a crash? Where was the survival instinct when you needed it?

'I can't undo my seat belt,' came a strangled reply. 'I've been trying and trying.'

'What?'

'It doesn't work properly. I had to force it in and now it won't release.'

'Shout,' ordered Simmy. 'Scream as loud as you can.'

The resulting noise couldn't fail to alert somebody, she was sure. The idea occurred to open the window beside her, for the sound to carry. But there was no handle – just an electric button, which was unlikely to work, now the car had died. But she tried it anyway, and the glass slid down a few obliging inches. 'Again!' she ordered.

'All right,' came a new voice, muffled but authoritative. Simmy had no idea where it came from, and for a second imagined it was a supernatural being of some sort. An angel, perhaps.

The door she was hoping to open was wrenched violently away from her, and she pushed her head up and out to see what was happening. Water flowed around her knees, swilling into her lap and completing the ruin of the lovely wool and silk skirt. 'Who's in here?' said the voice.

A woman was bending down to peer into the car. Simmy reidentified it from an angel to Gwen, partner of the treacherous Nicola. But the recognition brought no new fears with it. She was considerably beyond drawing any sort of rational conclusions from whatever might happen from here on.

Nobody answered the question. 'Just get us *out*,' shrilled Jane. 'For God's sake.'

Gwen appeared to pause, to assess the nature of the task. But before she could take action, another woman splashed up to the car, sobbingly distraught. 'Gwen!' she howled. 'Don't! Oh, Gwen! Why are you here?'

There was the sound of a sharp slap, and a high-pitched shriek. 'I'll speak to you when this is dealt with,' said Gwen. Her voice was at least as icy as the waters of Lake Windermere.

The commotion at last attracted attention from capable passers-by, and men materialised who levered the car valiantly back to a more normal angle, and then wrenched open the driver's door and hauled Candida out from the back with little ceremony. Jane's imprisoning seat belt was laboriously severed, once Simmy had been transported to dry ground. All three of them were escorted or carried up the tortuous winding path through the grounds to the Belsfield, as the closest building with heating and light still operating. Nobody, it seemed, had thought to call an ambulance.

With Gwen and Nicola, also in need of drying out, they made a group of five tear-stained, shivering, bewildered women. Wide-eyed hotel staff whispered in huddles, unsure of what might be expected of them. They had been put into a small room that looked as if it was normally used for discreet private lunches. A man who might have been the manager said the police had been informed, and were on their way.

Candida was the first to recover enough to speak. 'You tried to kill us,' she accused Nicola. 'Are you mad or what?'

Nicola was blindly clinging to Gwen, ignoring everyone else. She was still sobbing loudly, and appeared not to hear the accusation. But Gwen heard it. She gripped her partner by the upper arms and forced her away. 'What were you thinking of?' she shouted. 'Stop crying and tell me.'

'Oh, Gwen! I did it for you. For *us*.' The words were slurred, but quite audible. 'You said ... I promised you ... we promised there were no children.'

Gwen glanced at the others, then back at Nicola, who received a violent shake, like a dog in need of punishment. 'What do you mean? What are you saying?'

Nicola wailed out a garbled explanation that took no heed of the arrival of DI Moxon and two other detectives. Simmy caught his eye and waved at him not to interrupt.

'Gwen – you remember, when we first met. You made me swear I'd never been with a man, never had a child. You said that was the absolute most important thing for you. Remember?' Gwen nodded cautiously. 'Well, it was *true*. I never did. I did swear, and I do, still. I can't *bear* men. You *know* that. But I didn't understand that you never wanted there to be children for other reasons.' She wiped her face with her hand, and gave a bubbling sniff like a heartbroken child. 'It wasn't just jealousy about the … sex side of things, was it? You needed there to be no claims, nobody who might want something. I didn't see that until a few days ago. When those flowers came, you said that if you discovered I'd lied to you, it would all be over between us.' For the first time, Nicola looked at the others, fixing her gaze on Candida. 'Those flowers were what did it, finally. When I discovered you'd sent those flowers, I knew you must have been speaking to Nancy. She must have told you the whole story, despite all her promises. How else would you have known it was my mother's birthday? I couldn't let her get away with it, could I? What might she do to me next, otherwise? I flew straight down to her house, without even thinking what I was doing. I was so completely furious with her.' She wailed afresh, and pushed her head against Gwen's resisting shoulder. Then she kept on talking, mainly to Candida, who was cringing shivering on a handsome Victorian dining chair, and shaking her head hopelessly at the accusations.

'You did get it all from Nancy, didn't you? After all the trouble I went to to make sure there were no records, it was still all inside her head. And she was *such* a horrible woman. No kindness in her.' She turned her attention to Jane. 'Was she kind to you?'

'Not very,' said Jane tightly. 'But she told us everything we needed to know.'

'Not the birthday, though,' muttered Candida. 'I got that from the birth certificate.' She raised her head slightly. 'I got all the birth certificates, you see.'

'And Nancy did it all for money,' spat Nicola, unstoppable. 'She *sold* me to you, just as she did nineteen years ago.'

Assorted frowns and blinks greeted this. 'Sold?' said Gwen, dazedly. 'Did *you* kill Nancy Clark? Nic? Is that what you're saying?'

Nicola raised her head and gave a grotesquely proud smile. 'Davy told me how. It's quite easy really. And painless if you do it properly.'

Again, the room jolted at this new revelation. 'Davy *helped* you?'

'Oh, no. She had no idea. She was just rambling one day about the easiest way to kill someone. They do it with animals, apparently. You need a big syringe, full of air. Sometimes you have to do it twice. It must go directly into a blood vessel, of course. I'd got it in a little bag in my car, all ready, after the last time she threatened me. But I never really imagined I'd use it on her.' She moaned gently. 'It worked, though. I didn't think it would, when it came to the point.'

'Nicola, you must shut up. You're saying too much. You're hysterical.'

But the hysteria that had hovered five minutes earlier had subsided and Nicola was sounding all too horribly rational. Simmy's fuddled brain had grasped one or two significant elements in the outpouring, and was slowly making deductions. 'Did you throw me into the ghyll?' she asked.

'Sorry,' said the woman.

'She's mad,' said Candida. 'She's my biological mother and she's mad.'

'*Why?*' shouted Simmy, making her ribs hurt in the process.

'You brought those damned flowers and spoilt my mother's birthday. That's why I was at her house. I heard you ask her about grandchildren, and in just a few words sow the seeds of suspicion. She told you far too much. You were sure to work it out, especially as you could contact her whenever you liked. You'd got this girl's name and address from the order for the flowers. I thought you were nosy enough to follow it up.'

The irony made Simmy feel even weaker than before. 'Your mother didn't tell me anything. I had no wish to pry into your business. It was everybody else who kept it all going, not me.'

'I *had* to stop you,' Nicola insisted doggedly. 'You were a danger. I wish I'd had the syringe with me when I saw you, but instead I had to shove you over the bridge. Sorry,' she repeated.

'You're not sorry at all. You've just tried to kill me all over again.'

'And me. And Candy,' said Jane Hawkins. 'Who else did you think should be stopped?'

Nicola said nothing. Candida stood up and went to within an inch of her, bending down and looking her in the face. 'You're mad,' she said again. 'How would driving us into three feet of water kill us? We *saw* you do it. We already knew you were my mother. Whatever did you think you could do to hide that now?'

'I thought it was deeper. It made sense at the time,' Nicola mumbled. 'Nobody else knows but you three. Nobody at all.'

Simmy had been watching DI Moxon, standing quietly by the door with his two minions. How unusual it must be for them to hang back like this, with none of the noise and bustle and frightening shouts that one saw on documentaries. What would Ben have said about it? Shouldn't they issue the convoluted police caution, without which they couldn't quote anything they were hearing Nicola say?

'But *how*?' Gwen croaked, her face grey. 'How did you sell a baby, when everyone says there was no way you managed a secret pregnancy?'

'I sold an egg. *Five* eggs, to be exact. It was the first clinic to do egg donation. Only one of them worked, thank God.'

'And they *paid* you? Was that legal?' Everyone automatically looked at the police officers for an answer, but none came.

'They called it expenses. It was Brenda's idea, in the first place.'

'Who the bloody hell is Brenda?'

'Brenda Kitchener. She went to Australia, without me. She said she wanted a baby, but her ovaries didn't work, and we decided she could have one of mine. But then she changed her mind, while I was in the clinic.' Nicola's sobs returned louder than ever. 'She *betrayed* me.'

'Her loss must have been my gain,' said Jane Hawkins. 'They phoned me late at night and said if my cycle was at the right point, they could offer me an egg at short notice. My husband and I drove ninety miles at midnight to get there in time.' She smiled at Candida. 'It was like a miracle. I was forty-two. It was absolutely the last chance.'

Candida had retreated a short way from Nicola. 'This is really all my fault,' she whispered. 'I wasn't satisfied with what they told me. I wanted the whole truth, the whole story. I ferreted out all the certificates and worked out who everybody was, and then I wanted to *meet* them all. I never had a grandmother. I liked the idea of Granny Joseph, so I sent her some flowers.'

Moxon finally stepped forward. He stood stiffly in front of Nicola and told her she would be taken in for questioning with regard to the unlawful killing of Miss Nancy Clark. Then he recited the caution. His colleagues escorted her out of the room. She made no resistance. Gwen watched her go with a ghastly grimace, lips pulled back to show her teeth, eyes bulging.

Then Moxon turned to Simmy. 'You need a doctor to check you over,' he said. 'I'll take you to one.'

'I'm all right, I think. Except for my ribs. I hurt them when I tried to push the door open.'

'Your crutches are still in the car, I suppose?'

'I suppose they are. Will they go rusty?'

He was tired, drained, overloaded. The scene he had permitted to unfold without interruption, probably against all regular procedure, had been gruellingly emotional. Which perhaps explained why he laughed so outrageously at her innocent question.

Chapter Twenty-four

RUSSELL WAS OUTSIDE the hotel with a small group of people Simmy didn't recognise. Across the road there was a vehicle with a flashing yellow light, and men issuing loud orders to each other. The car, she realised, was being extracted from the lake. She was in a wheelchair, somehow provided by the hotel upon request. It had never occurred to her before that hotels might stock such things, but she was glad of it. She had been quietly worrying about her crutches for several minutes before Moxon mentioned them, and wondering how she was going to get home without them. The soaking skirt had been pulled off, and a large white towel wrapped around her lower half, giving rise to further embarrassment and worry.

'I presume she is mad,' she said to Moxon, who was personally pushing her chair. 'She didn't seem at all repentant.'

'Not for me to say.'

'Why didn't you interrupt? It was so weird, the way you just stood there listening.'

'I couldn't see any reason to. Her partner needed to hear it and understand as much as possible. After this, there might not be another chance. And I thought *you* might be feeling the same need.'

'Good God! Don't tell me you were doing it for me.' She smiled up at her father, who was listening attentively but uncomprehendingly to this exchange. 'Dad – this man is a real Sir Galahad.'

'I don't doubt it,' said Russell, his face a picture of doubt.

'I was going to take her to a doctor,' Moxon told him. 'But she might be better off just going home and to bed. It's up to you.'

Decisions did not come easily to Russell Straw. 'What d'you think, Sim?' he asked.

'Home,' she said. 'I don't need a doctor. They can send someone tomorrow to look at my wounds and put some new dressings on.'

'Have they come off, then?'

'I'm afraid so, but don't worry. I don't think any harm's been done.' She shivered. 'Well, not physically, anyway.'

'Get her warm,' urged Moxon. 'I'm needed somewhere.' He leant over Simmy. 'Somehow I feel I have you to thank for quite a lot of what's happened.'

She shook her head. 'No you haven't. I didn't do anything. I didn't do anything at all, right from the start. I was just *there* like a dummy.' When she tried to think of somebody who *had* done something, the only name she could find was that of Nicola Joseph. And a quote from somewhere about evil prevailing when good people do nothing.

RUSSELL AND ANGIE got her into the house with some difficulty, the wheelchair's mechanisms a mystery to all three of them. At last they were all in the warm kitchen, the heating turned recklessly high and mugs of hot, thick chocolate grasped in all three pairs of hands. 'I need this as much as you do,' said Angie. 'After all that hassle getting you from the car.'

'Sorry,' said Simmy.

'Tell us what happened,' ordered Angie. 'Every detail.'

'No, I can't.' Images of the dark car filling with water turned the whole world into a terrifying trap that she couldn't bear to confront. 'It was too horrible. I'll have nightmares for years over it, I expect.'

'But who *did* it? Was it deliberate?'

'It was all Nicola Joseph. She killed Nancy Clark and tried to kill me last weekend. And again just now, along with Candida and Jane. It was all her,' she repeated.

'But *why*?' came the familiar cry. And then, 'Who's Nicola Joseph, anyway?'

Simmy did her best to provide a coherent narrative, much of it gleaned from Nicola's distraught confession. There were gaps and confusions. Some of it seemed purely incredible.

'The poor woman,' said Angie, more than once. 'You know – I considered that egg donation thing, years ago. When it first started. But the whole procedure is terribly invasive and I got put off more or less from the outset. It's not a simple business at all.'

Russell looked at her in total blankness. 'I don't remember that,' he said.

'I don't expect I told you. It was just an idea, really. Here I was, with a fine specimen of a child, and no intention of having any more. It seemed a waste, somehow.'

'Candida seems to be a reasonable specimen as well,' said Simmy. 'So it worked out well for the Hawkinses. Even so, it makes you wonder whether it's a good idea, don't you think?'

'Going against nature always has its risks,' said Russell. 'But I still don't understand …' he tailed off helplessly. 'Most of it, actually. Why would the other woman – what's her name? – care one way or the other?'

'Gwen. We can't be sure that she would – but Nicola must have been certain there'd be a catastrophe if she did find out. Apparently Gwen said she'd leave if it turned out that Nicola had lied about having a baby. It sounded as if she's threatened to leave a few times over the years. And Nicola does seem very dependent.'

'Even so,' Angie protested. '*Murder.*'

'I know. Not just once, either. And not on the spur of the moment. She had to get hold of a big syringe, and a sharp needle, and learn how to find a blood vessel. For all we know, she practised for weeks beforehand.' Then she paused. 'And I think she deliberately tried to implicate Malcolm Kitchener, somehow.'

Both parents were fixing her with blank stares, and she realised that there were even more holes in the story she'd told them than she first thought. 'Oh, never mind,' she said. 'I can't talk about it any more this evening.'

'So that's an end to it, is it?' asked Angie. 'The police have got her, and there's nothing more to worry about?'

'It ought to be,' Simmy agreed. 'But somehow that isn't how it feels. There must be something else somewhere. But I won't think about it until tomorrow.' She yawned, but was careful not to stretch, mindful of her bruised and battered ribs. 'I think I might need a bit of help getting to bed, if that's okay.'

SATURDAY DAWNED MILD and dry, without wind or rain or snow. Simmy's emotional state was much the same. She knew in theory that she should contact Ben and Melanie and bring them up to date with events. She should feel desperate sadness for Mrs Joseph, as well as Davy, her innocent daughter. The shame descending on their family would be annihilating, once the details were aired publicly. But instead, all Simmy knew was a powerful desire to remain very quietly in the cosy nest that was her mother's old camp bed. Her body ached persistently, but her mind had closed down. When her mother hesitantly knocked on the door and came in with a mug of tea, Simmy told her she would not be available to visitors.

'What about the district nurse? They're sure to send someone to see you, after what happened.'

'A nurse would be all right,' Simmy mumbled. 'Especially if she gives me something to send me back to sleep.'

'What about that police detective?'

'No, I don't want to see him. He doesn't need me. He never did. I've been nothing more than a pawn from the start.'

'Pawns can be useful.' Her father's voice came from behind Angie's shoulder.

'Not this one. He won't come, anyway.' As she spoke, she knew she was right about this. Moxon would understand how she was feeling and have the good sense to stay away. 'He'll probably phone you to see how I am, that's all.'

'Ben? Melanie?'

'Tell them they can come this afternoon, if they must. I might be ready for them then. For now, I just want to lie quietly and not have to think.'

BY HALF PAST eleven, her parents having conscientiously obeyed her wishes, she was starting to emerge from her hibernation. The house was silent and she began to wonder what they were doing. She had heard one phone call, but no ringing doorbell. She had twisted over enough times for the duvet to be a rumpled, lumpy nuisance. She needed the loo and was hungry. It all reminded her of far-off student days when she had come home for the vacations and stayed in bed till lunchtime, simply because that was what students did. After a few hours it had seemed foolishly wasteful, the bedclothes too heavy and hot for daytime. Even the dog, which habitually burrowed down by her legs to keep her company, would get bored with it after a while.

And then the doorbell did ring and there were voices coming closer and Angie tapped at the door before opening it and saying, 'The nurse person's here. Apparently they're not called district nurses any more.' This irrelevance had evidently elicited deep irritation. 'But it's probably the same general idea,' she added with a melodramatic sigh.

The nurse was in her fifties and appeared harassed. But she behaved with brisk efficiency, examining every one of Simmy's injuries and telling her how lucky she was. She also mentioned, in a whisper, that they really were still known as district nurses, but were trying to change it to *community* nurses, which was more accurate, surely anybody would agree.

'Take no notice of my mother,' said Simmy.

Afterwards she felt much better, with a professional new dressing on her head and an assurance that she had suffered no lasting ill effects from getting wet the previous day. 'I'll get up for lunch,' she said. 'If you can find me something to wear.' The long skirt had been bundled into the washing basket by Angie, worrying that it would have to be dry-cleaned.

'What about your crutches?' Angie asked. 'Can't you get them back?'

'We should have asked that nurse,' Simmy groaned. 'She might have had some in her car. How stupid of us.'

It had been unbelievably stupid, she reproached herself. 'We could phone the police and ask if they've got them,' Russell suggested. Both her parents were in the doorway of her temporary bedroom, the phone a few feet away in the hall.

Simmy sighed. 'I suppose we'll have to,' she said.

Russell dithered about which phone number to use, and who he should ask to speak to, but did eventually manage a conversation with someone who sounded reasonably cooperative. 'If we go down there, they'll let us have them,' he said. 'Isn't that a surprise!'

It was, Simmy agreed, waiting for her father to offer to go right away. 'You could walk,' she said. 'It's barely five minutes from here.'

When he made no reply, she looked at him more closely. 'Dad? What's the matter?'

'Nothing's the matter. I'm perfectly all right.' Which confirmed that he very much wasn't.

Even Angie took notice. 'Russ? You're not ill, are you?'

'Not *ill*,' he said. 'Just a bit … off. Tired. Emotional.'

'Oh, God,' said Simmy. 'I know what this is. He's in shock, just like I was a few days ago. Look at him – he's shaking.'

'You could have been killed – *again*,' he blurted, tears in his eyes. 'I can't bear it, Sim. How …? *Why?* It's all wrong.'

'Get him warm,' Simmy ordered her mother. 'Put him in the kitchen with a hot, sweet drink. He'll be all right in a few minutes.'

With no very good grace, Angie did as she was told. Simmy then demanded the wheelchair be brought to her and she hoisted herself into it with no help from her mother. Manoeuvring it through the doorway was difficult, and she scraped her knuckles on the doorpost, but she needed to be mobile. She positioned herself by the phone and made a call to a number she had taken the trouble to memorise the day before.

'Mel? Listen – are you busy? … Good. Can you pop down to the police station and get my crutches? I got separated from them last night. It's a long story. Come over here and I'll tell you every-thing. Bring Ben, if you want.'

Half an hour later, the youngsters were on the doorstep. Simmy was inordinately pleased to see them; however much she tried to explain things to her parents, they never fully grasped the finer points.

The crutches felt like old friends. Simmy celebrated their return with a swift journey all the way through the house and back again to the living room. Angie brought mugs of coffee and a plate of sandwiches. She had a distant look in her eyes, and a tightness around her mouth. 'What's with your ma?' whispered Ben, when she'd left them alone again.

'She's being a martyr,' said Simmy. 'She does that sometimes when things get out of control. My dad's having a panic attack, which hasn't helped.'

'Sounds like my house,' said Mel. 'But they do have good reason to freak, in your case.'

'Did something happen?' asked Ben, with unusual delicacy.

'Surely it's been on the news?' Simmy asked, thinking she should have stirred herself to at least listen to the radio before this.

'An arrest has been made – that's all they said. And something about a car driving into the lake, which has some mysterious con-nection to the case.'

'I was in it.' She waited for the reaction with interest.

'Told you,' said Melanie to Ben. She turned to Simmy. 'The bloke who gave me the crutches hinted that was it. I know him a bit, but he wouldn't say anything for definite.'

'You were *in* it?' Ben echoed. 'Really? You escaped drowning twice, then? You must have been born with a caul.'

'What?'

'You know. The membrane thingy. Sometimes it's still on a baby's head when it's born. It's lucky. Sailors used to buy them as charms against drowning.'

'Oh. Well, we were never likely to drown – but it was dark and cold and extremely horrible.'

'We?' repeated Melanie.

'Me, Candida and Candida's mother.'

'Explain,' Melanie ordered, which Simmy duly did. It took more than twenty minutes.

'So it's all over?' Ben summarised at the end.

'I suppose it is,' Simmy agreed. 'But it doesn't exactly feel like that.'

'Too right,' he agreed glumly. 'It feels more like a virtual case, where there's nothing real to experience.'

'Excuse me!' Simmy at first could not identify the hot surge of emotion that seized her. '*What* did you just say?'

'Ben, you idiot,' Melanie said. 'Simmy's experienced more than enough, don't you think?'

The word *rage* came to her. Such rage that she couldn't speak for a full minute. Not so much against Ben, but against her attacker and everything in that woman's life which had brought her to do what she did. And then a déjà vu moment gripped her, and she paused. She'd been here before, placing the blame on a complex system of accidents and mistakes and human imper-fections. This time it was different. She was enraged directly at Nicola Joseph. She wished she'd managed to strike her or curse her the previous evening. Creative curses now came to her, along with sincere hopes that they would still operate. 'I hope she never knows another moment of peace,' she snarled. 'I hope she loses everything she loves and lives into a long and miserable old age.'

'That's the spirit!' Melanie applauded.

'I'm really sorry, Sim,' grovelled Ben. 'You're not going to curse me as well, are you?' His worry seemed genuine, and Simmy relaxed into a reassuring laugh.

'Not if you promise to mind what you say in future.'

Melanie took them back to the main point. 'Nicola Joseph really did confess, then? Just like that?'

Simmy did her best to fill in the gaps calmly. 'Sort of. She was explaining it to Gwen. And Candida, in a way. Isn't that *weird*, though? Your biological child that you didn't carry for nine months or deliver or ever see or hold.' As she spoke, she relived the minutes she had had with her stillborn daughter and almost counted herself fortunate. 'It must feel so strange.'

'Did they ever tell her there was a child?' Melanie wondered.

'They must have done, or she'd have had no reason to kill Nancy Clark. I suppose Nancy herself told her, actually. Then blackmailed her, because she'd found out how Gwen would react.' She thought for a minute. 'You can sort of see how that could have gone, can't you? Nicola probably blurted it all out from the start. Something like, "Oh, God! If Gwen ever finds out, she'll leave me" kind of thing. Gave Nancy her chance, there and then.'

'Candida kept saying Nicola must be mad. She said, "I'm the daughter of a madwoman." Not just mad, though. She could easily have killed five people – no, four. I'm counting myself twice.' She laughed. 'But what an awful business. Candida's own mother seems really nice. Sensible, affluent, open-minded.'

'The sort of woman who'd tell the kid the whole story from the start, you think?' asked Ben.

Simmy thought for a moment. 'No, Candida said she wasn't told until quite recently. How *would* you explain it, anyway?

You'd have to wait until the child understood the mechanics of reproduction.'

'That'd be when it was about four,' said Melanie, 'if my sisters are anything to go by.'

Ben returned to the central issue of motive. 'But she said she did it to stop Gwen finding out? And that meant killing everyone who knew about it – including the girl herself *and* her mother? That's worse than mad, surely? That's totally ludicrous.'

'I'm not totally sure she seriously meant to kill us last night. She just wanted to stop the story spreading. She wanted the Hawkins women to go back home and never speak to her again. It was a sort of extreme warning.'

'But she did want you dead, because she pushed you off that bridge. It *was* her, wasn't it?' The boy narrowed his eyes, thinking hard. 'Is that for definite?'

'Who else could it have been?' Simmy shivered at the idea of a second would-be killer. 'Of course it was her. When you think about it, it's exactly what a woman like her would do. No blood, no getting her hands dirty. She could just walk away as if nothing had happened.' The rage threatened to return. 'What a foul person she must be. Look what she's done to me.'

'You'll be fine in a few more days,' Melanie assured her. 'You'll be bored stiff and wanting to get back to work.'

Simmy looked around the room and felt the walls closing in on her. The stack of DVDs by the telly looked painfully small. She wasn't sure she could lose herself in a book for more than a couple of hours each day. 'You could be right,' she said.

In the calm that followed, she wondered about her father and his panic attack. 'I ought to find out if Dad's all right,' she said. 'He lost it a bit this morning.'

'It must have been awful for them,' Melanie sympathised. 'You being their only one. All those *what ifs* must have got through to them by now. That's what my gran said, when she heard. Says it would have been like killing three people, not one.'

'At least nobody seems to be missing Nancy Clark much,' said Ben, obviously striving to show appropriate feeling.

He got no reply, because the doorbell rang for the third time that morning.

Chapter Twenty-five

'WHERE IS SHE? I must speak to her,' came a strangled desperate voice from the front doorstep. When Simmy's mother tried to prevaricate, having no idea who this new visitor might be, he simply swept her aside and limped into the living room. His face was twisted, his hair spiky, his shoulders jerking with tension. When he saw Simmy, he rushed at her. She cringed back in terror, but instead of striking her he flung his arms round her. It took some moments to understand that his intentions were anything but malign.

'Hey!' Ben protested. 'Put her down. She's hurt.'

Simmy pushed him away, more or less gently. 'What's all this?' she asked, feeling weirdly maternal towards him.

'I owe everything to you,' wept Malcolm Kitchener. 'I can never thank you enough.'

For the fiftieth time, Simmy wanted to argue this point, to repeat yet again *But I didn't do anything*. 'Sit down and tell us what you mean,' she ordered.

He was kneeling on the floor, all dignity abandoned. Not that he'd ever had much dignity, Simmy reflected. Poor man – he had been every bit as passive and victimised as she had herself, from the very start. 'Here – sit here,' Melanie suggested, shifting along the sofa to make space for him. With a scramble, he did as invited. 'Now – talk,' said Melanie.

'It's Brenda,' he began. 'My sister. She wants to see you as well, when the police have finished with her.'

Astonishment rendered Simmy, Ben and Melanie speechless. Mr Kitchener went on, 'She had an email from the police, last week, and flew over right away. She's been here since Wednesday.'

'So it wasn't her who pushed Simmy in the beck,' said Ben. Everybody looked at him.

'Of course not,' said Mr Kitchener. He was slowly getting himself together, speaking more clearly, although it was plainly an effort.

'Why didn't you tell us she was here when we saw you yesterday?' Melanie demanded. 'We had all that talk in the car and you never said a word.'

'She asked me not to. She wanted to do a bit of detective work of her own. She had an idea there was something about Nicola Joseph, you see. Some secret that only the two of them knew. It goes back to the time when she emigrated. She went all of a sudden, just vanished overnight, very nearly. My mother was terribly upset.'

'Did they ever meet again?' asked Melanie.

'Oh, yes. Every year, actually. Mum went out there five or six times, and Brenda came here a lot. But she never stayed long, and never looked up old friends. Especially not Nicola.'

'Is she married?' Simmy asked.

'Of course not. She's a lesbian. She's got a partner, Ellie. They live in Darwin. It's very hot.'

'So – Brenda knew about the egg donation. Did she know there was a child as a result of it?'

He stared at her. 'Pardon?'

'Didn't you know about it, then?'

'I don't know anything about that time. Except I knew Nicola quite well, because I was working for her dad. She used to come in and do a bit of casual work when we were busy. And she always wanted the offcuts from the printworks, for some reason.'

'It'll all come out now, anyway,' said Ben.

'What will?'

'The whole story,' said the boy with some exasperation. 'Haven't you come to tell it to us yourself?'

'Egg donation,' the man muttered. 'What's that, anyway?'

'That girl, Candida Hawkins – she's Nicola's biological daughter. She came from Nicola's egg,' said Simmy, hearing how peculiar it sounded, as she spoke.

'Right.' He was obviously having trouble grasping the concept. 'Do I know Candida Hawkins?' He blinked in confusion.

'Let's get back to Brenda,' urged Ben.

Mr Kitchener complied with relief. 'She went to the police yesterday afternoon, and demanded they exhume our mother's body. She's convinced there was foul play. They fobbed her off, but she went back again first thing today, and they told her there was no need to do an exhumation, because Nicola had already confessed to killing her. After everything else she's done, I'm quite surprised they even remembered my poor old mum. She used the same method as with Nancy. She must have been so happy when the police thought I did it.' He gave Simmy a dog-like smile of devotion. 'And thanks to you, that was never a serious proposition.'

'But it does bring the total back to five,' Simmy realised. 'She's practically a serial killer.'

Mr Kitchener was intent on a complete debriefing. 'Brenda came and talked to me about a whole lot of things, last night. We had a bottle of wine and cried together. She's always been a good sister to me. We've got a lot of history, with the way our dad was. She did her best to keep him off me. No wonder she never wanted any truck with men. And now our dear old mum gets herself killed by a madwoman.' He sniffed ominously.

'But *why*?' Ben demanded.

'Bren thinks it must have been that Mum knew something about Nicola that had to be kept from that partner of hers. Now I realise it was because of this egg thing.'

'Hang on,' said Ben. 'This was ages before Simmy delivered the flowers, wasn't it? So the whole thing goes a lot further back than we thought.'

'Makes you wonder whether there were others, years ago, who might have gone the same way,' said Melanie. 'How could anybody live like that – always terrified of a secret coming out and killing anyone who might give it away?'

'So Brenda never said anything about the egg donation?' asked Simmy. 'Doesn't she realise that that's what this whole business is about?'

'I expect she does, but she wouldn't talk about that sort of thing with me.' He smiled weakly. 'Bit of a prude is our Brenda, funnily enough.'

'If she killed Mrs Kitchener with an air embolism, there'll be no way they can find evidence of it now,' Ben asserted. 'So no sense in doing an exhumation. Lucky she confessed. They'd never prove it otherwise.'

'So how did they know Nancy Clark had been murdered, then?' For the first time this detail occurred to Simmy.

Melanie and Ben grinned at her like clever twins. 'A fluke,' said Ben. 'Miss Clark was diabetic, so she'd had countless insulin injections in the past few years. It was all rather obvious – especially because Moxo himself is diabetic, so he knew the procedure.'

'Explain,' ordered Simmy.

'Okay. In a nutshell, you inject insulin into fatty tissue, in your stomach, hips – places where there's some meat. Definitely not into a vein. But the air embolism thing obviously has to go directly into a vein. Moxo saw the site of the fatal injection and made an instant deduction. Plus she was lying on the floor with bruises in all the wrong places. *Plus* she'd been to the doctor the day before, as fit as a flea. He'd done some routine checks on her and swore there was no way she'd die of heart failure or a coronary the very next day.'

'You got all that from your friend Scott?' Simmy accused him. 'And never told us.'

'I told you it was a lethal injection, and it was.'

'So that's it,' said Melanie. 'It really is this time.' She sighed. 'Doesn't seem worth killing anybody for, does it?'

'Just what I was thinking,' said Simmy.

'I blame that Gwen,' said Melanie. 'She must be a real control freak.'

'It does sound like that, but I really liked her,' gloomed Simmy. 'She gave me some bedsocks.'

Ben's laugh lifted her spirits in seconds. Mr Kitchener added his own contribution, with a reassuring smile. 'She's perfectly decent,' he confirmed. 'Brenda went to see her today. Said she should have done it years ago and settled old jealousies. Turns out they've always been jealous of each other.'

'All over the worthless Nicola,' sneered Ben.

'Nobody's worthless,' the man reproached him. 'You have to learn that, lad. It matters more than anything.'

'So, what *was* the motive?' pressed Melanie.

'Fear,' said Mr Kitchener. 'She was terrified that one of them would betray her secret. She'd spent nineteen years keeping it hidden, brushing it out of sight. And almost as bad as Gwen finding out, was her mother knowing about it as well. She simply couldn't deal with the implications of a daughter showing up.'

'And she thought I might betray her as well,' said Simmy.

'She *was* very angry with you,' he nodded. 'Must have been, we think. But perhaps it wasn't planned like the others. She saw you at her mother's front door on Sunday night and saw red, thinking you'd gone to drop her even further into the doodah. It would appear she was panicking by then, and just firefighting, trying to keep the lid on the whole business.'

'That's exactly what she said last night,' Simmy confirmed. 'So we've got it straight at last.'

'You know a lot about it,' Ben accused Mr Kitchener, a trifle sullenly.

'I've spent the past twenty-four hours and more making it my business to uncover the whole story. I saw these two ladies yesterday' – he smiled at Simmy and Melanie – 'and talked things through with them. It helped a lot. You told me about the girl, remember? That got me thinking along different lines. Then I popped into the Elleray for some lunch and the chap behind the bar started gossiping about two women he'd got staying there, and pennies began to drop.' He shook his head in self-reproach. 'It did occur to me to follow them, last night, but I didn't know how to go about it, not having a car. I might have pulled you out of the lake a bit sooner, if I'd been there. As it was, it was far too late when I turned up. By then they were winching the car back onto dry land.'

'How did you know where she was? Candida, I mean?'

'They told the Elleray guy that they were dining at the Belsfield. He was not a little miffed about it, actually. Thought it meant his food wasn't good enough for them.'

'His food's excellent,' said Simmy absently. 'And probably barely half the price.'

'We'll never know the finer details,' Ben announced. 'How A met B and what they said about C. It'd only drive us mad trying to guess. We know everything we need to, now.' He looked at his watch. 'And I've got to go.'

'Hey!' Simmy remembered. 'How did the play go last night?'

'Pretty well. Even better tonight, obviously.' He drooped. 'Shame you won't see it.'

Simmy did a rapid inventory of her bones and bruises. 'I wouldn't give up hope just yet,' she said.

NOT MANY HOURS later, Melanie escorted her into the large school hall, assisted by Wilf, who was hovering near the door as they went in. 'I've saved some seats at the front,' he said.

The play was a revelation to Simmy. The antics of the lion gave rise to agonising laughter that set her broken rib back several days. Ben, the scrawny adolescent boy, was transformed into a gruff warrior wrestling with insuperable moral difficulties. The acting made Simmy's head spin, until she forgot entirely that it was Ben Harkness she was watching. The message of the play seemed to come and go, until she gave up trying to grasp it. None of the characters seemed to be able to put their ideals into practice – that much she understood. It had unmissable implications for modern times, in the reaction of authority to unpopular sentiments and the power of the masses to demonise certain individuals. It raised questions of martyrdom and persecution and the lure of warfare with a light touch that turned uncomfortable moments quickly to comedy.

It bothered her not at all that Christianity came out of it so badly in the first act, because the direction of the play made it plain that the real Christian was Androcles, who made the audience laugh and clap with almost every line. What bothered her more was that Ben had not been given the starring role. The Androcles boy was good, but Ben was light years better.

'Wow!' she gasped, when the final curtain came down. 'That was amazing.'

She looked at the youngsters on either side of her, eager to debate the themes of the play. But they had no eyes for her. Wilf was leaning back in his chair, his gaze running past her to Melanie, who was equally canted backwards. Simmy sat forward, fumbling for her crutches. 'You should have said you wanted to sit together,' she complained.

'Yes, we should,' Melanie said. 'Next time, we will.'

ON THE WAY out, they almost collided with Ninian Tripp, and Simmy automatically looked round for Julie, associating the two in her mind. But her friend was nowhere in sight. 'Hello!' she greeted him. 'On your own?'

He pushed long hair from his face. 'I am, yes.'

'Do you know any of them? The people in the play?'

'Oh, no. It's just that I'm mad keen on Shaw, and when I saw they were doing it, I had to get a ticket. Wasn't it wonderful? Didn't they make a brilliant job of it!' He was pink with enthusiasm.

Simmy wanted very much to stay and talk to him about it, but Melanie was clucking round her and insisting she be driven home immediately. 'You're dreadfully pale,' she said.

'Sorry,' she told him, helplessly.

HER MOTHER HELPED her to bed, listening to an account of the play. 'It puts things into perspective,' Simmy said haltingly. 'Made me see Nicola Joseph as a martyr, in her own way. Nobody likes major changes in their lives, do they? Look at you, and the way having me here has been so difficult.'

'Oh dear,' said Angie. 'Have I been that awful?'

'Not at all. It's just human nature. But, Mum – can we make another change to the plan for Christmas Day?'

Angie looked wary. 'What is it?'

'Can we invite Ninian Tripp to join us for Christmas dinner?'

Read on for a sneak peek at the first book in the
Lake District Mystery series

An Excerpt from

The Windermere Witness

Chapter One

WHAT A DAY for a wedding! Sheets of rain sluiced across the windscreen, giving the wipers a harder task than they were equal to. The road ran with water, so it resembled the lake that lay a few yards to the right. The turning into the hotel was ahead, somewhere, on a pimple of land jutting into the lake. On a bright day, it would be a stunning venue for a wedding; the photos spectacular. Today it would be madness for a bride to venture outside in silk and lace and expensively wrought hair. The many thousands of pounds that must have been spent on the event would do nothing to mitigate the disappointment, if Simmy was any judge. There would be huge umbrellas on standby, of course, and other tricks with which to defy the weather, but rain on this scale would defeat every attempt to save the day.

Behind her, the back of the van was filled with scent and colour, conveying all the layers of meaning that went along with flowers. She was confident that her work would meet all expectations. She had laboured over it for a week, selecting and matching for colour, shape and size. The scheme was a rosy peach ('Definitely not peachy rose,' said the bride with a grin, when she and her mother had come to talk it over) with scatterings of rust and tangerine to echo the autumnal colours outside. Colours that were muted to grey by the rain, as it had turned out.

The hotel's facade was a pale yellowy-cream on a good day. There was a confident elegance to it, despite the lack of symmetry. The older part boasted a columned entrance that Simmy suspected might be a loggia, officially. She had been profoundly impressed by the whole edifice, on a previous visit two months before. The chief element in its reputation, however, lay in the setting. The lake itself was the real star, and the various architects who had created the Hall had had the good sense to realise that. All the ostentation lay indoors, where no expense had been spared in grand ornamentation.

She parked the van as close as she could get to the humbler entrance where deliveries were customarily made. A team of hotel staff was on hand to assist, and within the hour, the centrepieces, swags and two monumental arrangements had been set into position. During that hour, Simmy lost herself in the creative process, immersed in colour and form that were intended to enhance the romantic significance of the event. She gave brisk instructions to the people detailed to work with her, their tasks restricted to pinning and tying, fetching and carrying. The florist herself attended to everything else. Everything fell perfectly into place, exactly as she had envisaged. Clusters of red berries to suggest fruitfulness; luscious blooms for sensuality; some dried seed heads for permanence – she loved the understated implications that few, if any, wedding guests would consciously grasp, and yet subliminally they might appreciate.

'Just the bouquets and buttonholes now,' she told her helpers. 'Where do they want them?'

The bride's mother was telephoned, and Simmy was asked to take the flowers to the suite upstairs. In the lift she balanced the large box on one hand and thought briefly about weddings. Just as births and funerals conjured a kaleidoscope of personal memories and associations, a wedding always called up comparisons with others one had experienced. In her case, it was her own, nine years earlier.

She was on the third floor before she could get far in her rueful reminiscences. Room 301 was awaiting her, the door already open. Inside was a flurry of female activity, half-naked girls with hair in rollers, a heavy atmosphere of near hysteria. 'Flowers,' she said, superfluously, looking for a familiar face. She saw herself reflected in a gold-bordered full-length mirror – a misfitting figure amongst all the froth of silk and lace, dressed in a blue sweatshirt and jeans. Her hair was untidy, her hands not entirely clean. She had given no thought to her own appearance, which made her a complete alien in this room where appearance was everything.

'Oh! Let's see!' And there was Miss Bridget Baxter, soon to be Mrs Bridget Harrison-West, fumbling at the lid of the box in her eagerness.

Simmy carefully set it down on a marble table beneath the window and lifted the lid. 'I hope they're what you wanted,' she said.

The bride met her eyes with a direct blue gaze that would instantly endear her to the greatest misanthrope alive. 'They're fabulous!' she said. 'Look, everybody! Aren't these gorgeous!'

'Keep them cool, if you can,' Simmy advised. 'Probably the bathroom would be best.'

The enormous room swirled with bridesmaids and long dresses hanging on a wheeled rail. There were two big sofas, on one of which sat a young girl, intently fiddling with her fingers and apparently muttering to herself. It could only be the smallest bridesmaid, traditionally referred to as the 'flower girl', and as such, Simmy felt herself justified in making an approach. She sat down on the edge of the chintzy sofa.

'There's a special bouquet for you to carry,' she said. 'Do you want to see it?'

The child shrugged, but flashed a quick smile that seemed friendly enough. 'If you like,' she said.

'This is all a bit … *daunting*, isn't it?' Simmy sympathised, with a glance around the room.

'"Daunting"?' the little girl repeated with a puzzled frown.

'Overwhelming. Stressful.'

'It's a wedding. This is what they're like. I went to one before.'

'Did you? Were you a bridesmaid then, as well?'

'No. They were all grown-ups that time. Thank you for the flowers.'

Simmy felt subtly dismissed, by a child who was probably accustomed to being attended to by people paid to do it. She smiled briefly, understanding that there was no further role for her.

There was a smell of lavender soap and warm ironing. Ms Eleanor Baxter, mother of the bride, was nowhere to be seen. Simmy was not sorry to miss her. When choosing the flowers, she had been a disconcerting mixture of autocratic boredom and penetrating exigency. The flowers had to be right, because this was a wedding, but weddings were actually a tedious necessity that she very much wished she didn't have to bother with: that had been the general message that Simmy picked up.

'Look at that rain!' cried one of the girls, standing by the window. 'The lake will overflow if it goes on like this, and we'll all be washed away.'

'It's a disaster,' said Bridget cheerfully. 'I knew this would happen.'

'But last weekend was so *lovely*!' moaned the girl. 'Warm and sunny, and lovely. How can it change so quickly?'

'That's England for you,' said Bridget. 'It's all Peter's fault, of course. He wouldn't miss his sailing, even to get married.' Everyone within earshot laughed, causing Simmy to suspect that the reality was something rather different.

She made her departure, with a murmured good-luck wish. Not that it was needed. Miss Baxter, spinster of the parish of Windermere, was so comprehensively blessed that a rainy wedding day would hardly dent her faith in her husband, or in the world. Although the florist had been given no special confidences, she did happen to be acquainted with the bride's hairdresser, who had. 'She loves him, Sim. They've known each other for years, and he always said he'd marry her the moment she was old enough.'

'Don't you find it the weeniest bit creepy?'

'Why? Because he's twenty-five years old than her? No, not at all. It's lovely that he's waited all this time for her. It's like a fairy tale.' Julie was a romantic creature, and Sim saw no cause to undermine her illusions. Besides, from the glimpses she had gained of Bridget, it seemed she would wholeheartedly agree with her hairdresser.

The wedding was scheduled for eleven, which left an hour and a half for Julie to work her magic. 'She wants the whole works, with tendrils and pearls,' she'd gloated. 'I can't tell you how much she's paying me. It's embarrassing.'

Simmy had felt no envy. The proceeds from the wedding flowers would keep her in business for some time, and do her reputation no harm at all. There was every chance that the hotel would recommend her more often, now she had been selected for the Wedding of the Year. The pictures in the gossip columns would cement her position, with any luck.

Outside, the van was about to be joined by others. Two vehicles were making a stately approach down the lesser driveway, and Simmy realised they would want her out of the way. She would do best to leave by the main entrance. As she drew level with the loggia, she saw that a knot of men had gathered, under huge umbrellas. Somebody amongst them was smoking. They looked like a clump of bullrushes growing beside the lake, their seed heads exploding in black arcs, silhouetted against the water behind them. They were laughing together as if the weather meant nothing to them. Too soon for wedding guests, surely? Family and close friends would be staying at the hotel; others would arrive in relays – some for the ceremony, some for the wedding breakfast, and another batch for the obligatory evening disco. Getting married at eleven meant a marathon fifteen hours or more, these days, albeit with lengthy interludes during which nothing happened. Simmy remembered it well.

The jocular group eyed her van as she drove slowly past them. One individual detached himself and flapped a hand to stop her. She opened the window on the passenger side and heard one of the others call out in puzzlement – 'Hey, Markie, what're you doing?'

'You're the florist,' he said, with a glance at the stencilled logo on the side of the van before peering in through the window. 'You live in my house, in Troutbeck.'

She stared uncomprehendingly at him. 'Pardon?'

'I was born there. We moved away three years ago. The new man didn't stay long, then.'

'Mr Huggins? He lost his job, apparently, and had to go to Newcastle to find another one.'

The boy shrugged. 'It's a nice house. I hope you're happy there?'

'It's lovely,' she said.

He smiled, and changed the subject. 'Did you bring the buttonholes?'

'I did,' she nodded. 'Why?'

He was very young, perhaps not even eighteen. Simmy suspected she was more than twice his age – not that this detail seemed to deter him from flirting with her. 'I hope mine's the nicest one,' he grinned.

'You're not the best man, are you? It's my guess you'll be one of the ushers.'

'The *most important* usher,' he corrected her. 'I'm the bride's brother.'

Aha! thought Simmy, remembering the gossip she'd heard about the family. The coincidence of the Troutbeck house gave her a sense of fellowship with him, and she tilted her head teasingly.

'Well, I'm sorry to tell you the buttonholes are all the same. Won't you get wet, standing about out here?'

'We're waiting for my pa. He'll need an escort to give him the courage to go in. We can't just let him turn up without a welcoming committee. He's due at any minute.'

'I see.' *Pa*, she concluded, was father of the bride, the very much divorced one-time husband of Eleanor, Bridget's mother. George Baxter had been married twice since leaving Eleanor, and was assumed to be not finished yet. And that made the effervescent Markie, even if he was brother of the bride, deserving of no special treatment where buttonholes were concerned. 'Is that the groom?' She peered through the rain at a moderately handsome figure with broad shoulders and full lips.

'Peter – yes. He's a good bloke. Known him all my life.'

'So I gather,' she said recklessly.

'Talk of the town, right?'

'Wedding of the year,' she agreed. 'I've heard the whole story.'

'No, you haven't,' he corrected her, with a sudden change of expression. 'You haven't heard a word that's true, I can promise you.' The word *dread* flashed through Simmy's mind, only to be dismissed as far too dramatic. Even so, the boy plainly wasn't looking forward to the arrival of his pa.

'Stressful business, weddings,' she offered.

'Too right,' he agreed. 'I'm never going to forgive Briddy for this.'

'Well ...' she put both hands on the steering wheel, 'I should get out of the way. My part is finished.'

He seemed reluctant to let her go, glancing back at the cluster of men. Only one of them was watching him – a tall man in his early forties, with brutally short hair and a green waterproof jacket. His egg-shaped head looked all wrong without a decent covering of hair. 'That's Glenn,' whispered Markie. 'Peter's best friend.'

'The best man,' Simmy nodded. 'Is he worrying about his speech?'

'Not so's you'd notice. He was drinking till four this morning, apparently, but you'd never guess. I was legless by midnight. The other chap is Pablo. He's Spanish.'

'And under the loggia?' She had only just noticed another man, sitting in a wheelchair out of the rain. Once glimpsed, she could not take her eyes off him. He was also watching Mark with lowered brows.

'Oh, that's Felix. Peter's cousin.'

'Really? I don't think he was in the stories I heard about you all.'

'He ought to have been. Broke his back falling off Castle Crag, a year ago. Dreadful business. But he's being totally heroic about it. They all say so. Peter wanted him for the best man, obviously, but he flatly refused. He's getting married in the summer himself.'

Simmy dragged her attention away from the damaged man and smiled a vague acknowledgement of Markie's innate politeness in keeping her abreast of the personnel. 'Shame about the rain,' she said. 'It's not slacking off at all, is it?'

'It'll stop at eleven-fifteen, that's official. Nothing to worry about.'

'Really?'

'Yup. Glenn's got a hotline to the Met Office, or something.'

She revved the engine. 'Have fun, then,' she said and drove away.

THE TWO-MILE DRIVE to her shop involved negotiating crowds of disconsolate visitors in Bowness. Despite Saturday being 'changeover day' for self-catering as well as most of the guest houses, there were plenty of exceptions to this rule. They came in caravans; they stayed in hotels costing anything between £50 and £250 per night; they thronged the B&Bs, such as the one her mother ran in a quiet backstreet in Windermere. The lake cruisers still plied up and down from Lakeside to Ambleside, doing even better business than usual, in the rain. Stuck in a traffic hold-up close to the jetty, Simmy watched a large ship approach. Even after nine months, she still found them incongruous on a freshwater lake, albeit ten miles long. Like an overlarge toy in a bath, it struck her as wasted when it should be taking people across the open waters of the Adriatic. But there was seldom any difficulty in filling the hundreds of places aboard, and nobody else appeared to share her slight sense of absurdity.

'Persimmon Petals' was in the main street of Windermere. While Simmy was at the hotel, her teenaged assistant Melanie was holding the fort. Melanie lived on the eastern edge of Bowness and attended college at Troutbeck Bridge, taking Advanced Level Management for a year, aspiring eventually to become a hotel manager. The time-table contained enough gaps for students to find paid employment around the town, and Melanie worked at the flower shop for fifteen hours a week. She talked a lot about 'the hospitality industry' and its innumerable ramifications. Simmy could often not understand her.

'Everything okay?' she asked, having located Melanie in the back of the shop. Her large figure was generally easy to spot. As tall as Simmy, she had a generous covering on her bones, and a big round head. She also had no sight in one eye, thanks to a fight with her brother when she was four.

'Fine. How's the bride doing?'

'She's disgustingly relaxed and cheerful. Doesn't care about the weather. Loves the bouquets. Julie's going to be in her element. I was a bit surprised that she hadn't got there yet, but nobody seemed worried.'

'You haven't heard, then?'

'What?'

'Julie won't be doing it. She's broken two fingers.'

'*What?* But none of the wedding people seemed to have heard – they'd have been in far more of a flap if they had. How do *you* know? What happened to her? I only saw her on Thursday.'

It was a daft question. Everybody knew everything in Win-dermere. Behind the throngs of tourists, there was a small core of residents, both dreading and yearning for the few quiet weeks after Christmas when they could breathe more easily and com-pare notes as to how the year's business had been.

'Graham Forrest came in for some roses, five minutes after you left. He's lodging with Doreen Mills now, in case you didn't know. And she's Julie's aunt. It happened yesterday. She trapped her hand in a hairdryer, somehow. It "jackknifed backwards", that's what Graham said. Lucky it wasn't a customer. She'd have been sued. You'd think—'

'Yes,' said Simmy hurriedly, hoping to avert a short lecture on health and safety. 'Right. So who's going to do the hair? Will they still *pay* her? My God! This is going to wipe the smile off young Bridget's face.'

'Yeah,' said Melanie, her expression mirroring Simmy's own mixture of concern and thrill at this unexpected setback in the life of the local golden girl. Except, even this might not seriously upset her. She could get married with her hair in a simple chignon, and the sky would not fall. 'They've sorted out somebody else, I suppose. The hotel will have a list. They always have a contingency plan.' She spoke proudly of her chosen profession. To Melanie, floristry was a poor lightweight line of work. She made no secret of the fact that she was only there because there'd been no other choice with the right number of hours.

'But it won't be the same. And the *photos*,' Simmy said. 'She's got to have proper hair for the photos.'

'They're sure to find somebody else,' Melanie insisted. 'Julie's not the only hairdresser in town.'

A fussy customer occupied the next ten minutes, but Simmy's mind was not on the job. Poor Julie – she must be feeling wretched, not only because of the wedding, but because fingers were painful when broken, and extremely necessary for any sort of work. 'Which hand was it?' she asked.

'Oh, the right. First two fingers on the right. She won't be able to do anything for weeks.'

Outside it was still raining. The deep grey-brown of the local stone had turned black from the soaking. The big building at the top of the street looked like a looming battleship. 'Shirley C's got a great big puddle outside,' she observed. The biggest shop in town was another incongruity that Simmy still had to wrestle with. It sold lingerie, with the long street window full of plastic torsos modelling knickers and corsets for every passing visitor to admire. How it managed to survive, nobody knew. *Thriving mail order business*, some know-all suggested. The sheer brazen take-it-or-leave-it attitude was what struck Simmy most power-fully, seeming typical of the whole approach to life in the region. Nothing was done for ostentatious show – the stone walls were simply there to keep the sheep in; the houses were made of the same material as a matter of course, but if someone wished to add stucco nobody objected. It all worked out quite peaceably, because the fells and the lakes were of so much greater interest and signifi-cance than any human activity.

The wedding remained at the front of her mind for the rest of the morning. At eleven-fifteen, she gave up all attempts to concen-trate on the work in front of her, and went back to the street door to examine the sky. Markie Baxter's predictions came back to her – that it would stop raining at exactly this time, which would be more or less exactly the moment when Bridget and Peter became man and wife. Assuming everybody presented themselves punc-tually, of course. That, in Simmy's experience, seldom happened.

The puddles and rivulets in the street were deterring most would-be shoppers. The beck alongside her mother's house would be frothing and scrambling in full spate after so many hours of downpour. The lake would be lapping at the jetties and piers along its shores, and creeping closer to the hotel that had been built so hazardously close to the water. Had it ever flooded, she wondered? It was hard to see how it could have avoided it, in the two centuries since it had been built, and yet she had heard no local stories of inundation.

As she watched the little town centre, she realised that there were faint shadows being thrown by the few shoppers as they walked along the shining wet pavements. Umbrellas were being closed, and chins released from enveloping collars. 'Mel – it's stopped!' she called back into the shop. It was like a tap being turned off, and she marvelled at it.

'What did you expect?' came Mel's voice behind her. 'The Baxters and the Harrison-Wests between them are more than a match for the weather gods. Nobody would dare rain on their special day.'

'The boy, Mark, said it would stop at eleven-fifteen. It's like magic.' Simmy still couldn't credit it.

'What boy would that be?'

'Mark. Markie – whatever they call him. Her brother, isn't he? He stopped me for a chat as I was leaving.'

'Half-brother, Sim. He's her half-brother. Don't you know the story?'

It was a question she must have heard a hundred times since relocating from Worcestershire. Everywhere there was a story, a piece of local history that she was expected to have absorbed within weeks of arriving. 'Different mothers?' she ventured. 'But they can't be more than a year or two different in age.'

'Less than a year, actually,' grinned Melanie. 'There was never any secret about it. Poor old Eleanor just had to put up with it.'

'But I thought she divorced him?'

'Not until the children – that's Markie as well as Bridget – were old enough to cope with it.'

'Why would it affect Markie? What difference did it make to him?'

'I'm not sure, exactly, but everyone says there were major changes to both their lives. Once George had gone, both Eleanor and Markie's mother would have been on the same footing. The balance of power would shift.'

Simmy did her best to imagine how it would have been. 'So how old were they, then?' she asked.

'I don't know exactly, but they weren't babies. And then it was *George* who divorced *Eleanor*. He'd fallen for the Plumpton woman by then, and wanted to marry her.'

'Lordy, Mel – it's like something out of Noel Coward.' Except it wasn't really, she acknowledged. It was all quite commonplace in the present day. Mixed-up families, with no two children sharing the same two parents, and everybody more or less amicable about it. It was she, Persimmon Brown, who was out of step. She was the one who could not find it in herself to forgive or forget or cease to wish every sort of hell onto her one-time husband, Tony.

About the Author

REBECCA TOPE lives on a smallholding in Herefordshire, UK, where she plants trees and watches wild birds, but manages to travel the world and enjoy civilization from time to time as well. Most of her varied experiences and activities find their way into her books, sooner or later.

www.rebeccatope.com
www.witnessimpulse.com

Discover great authors, exclusive offers, and more at hc.com.